What I'm
Trying to Say is
Goodbye

What I'm
Trying to Say is
Goodbye

Lois Simmie

COTEAU BOOKS
WWW.COTEAUBOOKS.COM

Edited by Edna Alford.
Cover and book design by Duncan Campbell.
Cover image, *Businessman Standing in Sea* by Stephen H. Sheffield/Photonica.
Printed and bound in Canada at Marc Veillieux Imprimeur Inc.

National Library of Canada Cataloguing in Publication

Simmie, Lois, 1932-
What I'm trying to say is goodbye / Lois Simmie.

ISBN 1-55050-264-6

I. Title.
PS8587.I314W43 2003   C813'.54   C2003-
911242-X

1   2   3   4   5   6   7   8   9   10

401-2206 Dewdney Ave.
Regina, Saskatchewan
Canada   S4R 1H3

Available in the US and Canada from:
Fitzhenry & Whiteside
195 Allstate Parkway
Markham, Ontario
Canada   L3R 4T8

The publisher gratefully acknowledges the financial assistance of the Saskatchewan Arts Board, the Canada Council for the Arts, the Government of Canada through the Book Publishing Industry Development Program (BPIDP), the Government of Saskatchewan, through the Cultural Industries Development Fund, and the City of Regina Arts Commission, for its publishing program.

To all my friends and Bill's friends.

Chapter One

Matthew lies listening to the muffled roar of rain on the roof two floors above, the steady trickling, dripping, splashing through the downspout just beyond his window, and the intermittent gush of water onto the paved parking lot below. Wind-driven gusts rattle his bedroom window. The rainy season on Vancouver Island.

A sodden Virginia creeper brushes and bumps the building by the head of Matthew's bed – bony fingers tapping Morse code messages through the wall. Memento mori. In fact, he would not be all that upset at the idea of dying; thinks, in fact, it would be a definite improvement on his present state of consciousness. For a depressed insomniac, there is no more desolate sound than the steady pounding of rain in the dark. Old Glory, on General Schwarzkopf's balcony above, snaps wetly in the wind. Something light, a plastic pop bottle maybe, bumps and rolls around on the parking lot.

He swings his legs out of bed, lights a cigarette in the dark, and gets up to look out the window. Rain bounces on the roof of his old green Volvo parked just below.

Across the parking lot a figure is bending down, peering into a new white Toyota Camry. Suite 325, Joyce Fowler, checking to see if she rolled up the windows, if she locked the doors, if she's parked too close to the next car – if, if, if.

Come on, Matthew urges under his breath, as she takes a few hesitant steps toward the building, then stops, her hands over her ears like the Edvard Munch figure on the bridge, and just as desperate, he suspects. Her dark raincoat, sodden with rain, clings to her spindly legs.

Poor Joyce. Poor tormented woman.

See, that dimwitted Edwin in his group would say, you could be a lot worse off. Edwin was always running into people whose lives were so shitty they filled him with joy. And "gratefulness," mustn't forget that. Edwin is the most grateful idiot Matthew has ever had the misfortune to meet. Watching Joyce Fowler standing out in the pouring rain only makes him feel worse. He watches to make sure she gets safely in, then turns on his light and picks up the book he abandoned a couple of hours ago, a biography of Nelson Mandela that both awes and horrifies him.

But it's not for a dark, mournful night, and throwing back the covers he gets up and pulls on wrinkled khakis and a faded green sweatshirt, and with Adidas on his bare feet sets off on his nocturnal march through the halls of Kensington Manor.

Kensington Manor, for God's sake. All he needs is a black cape. Well, it is Halloween night. November first, 1998 actually, The Day of the Dead.

Delia knew how he hated November, it's likely why she left when she did. He can't recall much of last November, and not a lot about December except for trying to think what he did in November.

He feels somewhat better as soon as he starts to move. As far as he knows his tenants – charges might be a better word – are not aware that their caretaker roams the halls at night like the unquiet spirit he is. Until last night, when Tessie Thatcher opened her door on the chain and Matthew turned to see a small, baleful eye watching him through the aperture. Not by the hair on her chinny chin chin.

"Just checking the building, Mrs. Thatcher," he called over his shoulder. She grunted and shut the door, just forcefully enough to let him know what she thought of the caretaker prowling around the place at night. Caretaker, ha, he can't even take care of himself and Tessie probably knows it, with the nasty person's radar for other people's weaknesses. He wondered what malevolence Tessie, built like a Sumo wrestler, was plotting at three a.m.

He passes Suite 229. Bo Peep, a sweet old soul always hugging a hot water bottle in a sheep's wool case with black feet and ears. For the pain in her ribs, Delia told him. She used to do the caretaking when he was still gainfully employed drinking with the guys in the back of the composing room, or the lawyers at the courthouse, or nipping from his flask on the way to the scene of an accident.

When he still didn't know he was an accident himself.

He passes the Major's door. He moved up from California with a van full of bloated leather furniture, and the moment he raised Old Glory over their heads he became General Schwarzkopf to Matthew and Delia. Stormin' Basil. He marches everywhere, making smart right-angled turns, star-

3

tling Edna Burton, his English professor neighbour – "I'm always colliding with the silly man." Her habit of reading while walking might have something to do with it.

Ouch. That Dewers pain in his liver again. It was worse when he drank, but then the damn thing could fall out on the street for all he cared. Too bad it's not a Glenfiddich pain, if he was going to kill himself drinking he'd have liked to do it in style. He came close last time. Almost crossed the Styx, but dog-paddled back somehow. *The grave's a fine and private place, but none, I think, do there embrace.* Oh lovely. In what forgotten chamber of his addled brain was that cheery little couplet stored? And a fine and private place was it? Private, anyway.

An ancient glass case on the wall with a tangle of firehose inside reminds him of his irritable bowel. When the mutant waters are on the move he stays close to home, thinking dark thoughts about bowel cancer and wondering if the tremor in his hands will ever leave. He's like an old car that's hit the 200,000-mile mark.

"Get off the pity pot," Edwin would say. Jesus, you've got Edwin on the brain tonight, you'll be talking like him soon, clichés falling like rain, "God never gives you more than you can handle," is one of Edwin's favourites. Oh, really, thinks Matthew, who sees His Almightyship giving people more than *he* could handle every day, though he doesn't believe God gets out a list and says, Oh, I guess I'll give that boring Edwin whatshisname a bit of bad luck today (even God doesn't know the last names of people in A.A.). Let's see, I'll let him run out of coffee. But that Matthew whatshisname, I'd sure like to give that whiny little prick more than he can handle. It wouldn't have to be much, but what can I do, My hands are

4

tied. And God sighs, causing a typhoon or tidal wave on the other side of the planet where people don't know that God won't give them more than they can handle.

Really, Matthew thinks, you shouldn't have to suffer fools gladly unless they're buying you drinks.

Halfway down the south wing the door of 212 suddenly opens and Patrick Donogh backs out dragging a large green garbage bag and, turning quickly, almost collides with Matthew.

"Aha! Disposing of the body, I see," Matthew says.

"Oh, Lord, you startled me! I didn't think anyone else would be up."

Patrick, a good six foot two, bends his head when he talks, giving his most casual conversation a conspiratorial air. His sandy hair is combed and he's neatly dressed in khakis and a sport shirt, even a belt. His long, pleasant face shows no sticky eyes, no pillow creases or other new wrinkles, all of which decorate Matthew's physiognomy, he knows.

"Insomnia," Matthew stage-whispers in his horrible morning breath.

"Me too." Patrick's voice drops, "Actually, I've buried the body and am just destroying the evidence. Do you think any-one will hear the washer?"

"No," says Matthew, who hasn't a clue if it's true or not. Maybe the whole damn building can hear it. "But if I were you I'd go down the other way. Mrs. Thatcher saw me mak-ing the rounds last night."

"Ooooh." Patrick shudders. "Wouldn't want to meet up with that in a dark alley."

Matthew cackles, and Patrick laughs, bending over and raising one knee, like some large water bird watching for something tasty to swim past. Shouldering the bag, he falls into step beside Matthew.

"I'm going up to third," Matthew says. "See if anyone there is up and about the ward."

Patrick smiles. Almost all the Kensington's residents are seniors and have been for some time. Patrick and Matthew are the teenagers of the block.

"Come up for a drink sometime, Matthew."

"Thanks but I'm off the stuff." And, at Patrick's inquiring glance, "I tend to get drunk and disorderly."

"God, I wish somebody would around this mausoleum. Make it coffee, then."

Matthew finds it torture to sit and talk longer than fifteen minutes without a drink. Knock off ten if the other person is having one. "Sure, thanks," he says.

He plods up to third. Just two flights make him puff. Three, call 911. He should quit smoking but can't imagine life without cigarettes. Delia hated his smoking.

Is she sleeping with Nick tonight, her abundant middle-aged breasts warming his back? He wishes he could blame her for Nick, but like the man who jaywalked in front of a truck, he doesn't have a leg to stand on.

He counts the mostly silent grey doors − from behind some the murmur of television, 311, 313, 315, like Count Count; Kate loved the Count when she was little. Thinking of his daughter, he frowns. That bloody Michael, with a beard as long as Methusalah's, is getting weirder all the time, and now he's got religion of the fundamentalist stripe, Matthew hates to think. He's got to get up-island to that sixties time warp and check things out.

He plods up one silent hall and down the other. Under the weak light from the recessed ceiling fixtures, those doors, some with dusty, dispirited decorations, depress him.

He scowls at a lacy twiggy flowery thing. These people all live in a pretty how town. e. e. cummings must have lived in Victoria. God's waiting room, and he's never seen a cemetery except the old Ross Bay one, where he likes to walk. No room for the quick and the dead on this tight little island. And speaking for himself, the quick are not all that quick.

Downstairs again, in the dim lobby – Mister Funk's timed lights have gone out while it's still dark, of course, cheap old bastard – Matthew smokes and peers out the window at the deserted street. Some half-hearted reveller has heaved a single egg at the heavy plate glass and it's slid down, the shell and yolk, almost intact, nestled in the grass. You needed to be on the prairies for that, where it froze solid and had everyone out cursing and scraping the next day. He hopes Sam had fun trick-or-treating last night. His only grandchild is on his mind a lot lately.

In the fuzzy light from the window the bowl of Halloween treats he set out is still full, a somehow melancholy sight. He unwraps a hard black sucker and sticks it in his cheek, remembering the long chewy black ones he and Blair used to fight over. He can still see the waxed orange wrappers with black witches zooming in all directions. He should phone Blair, tell him he's sober, but doesn't want to hear Blair's patient sigh.

He peers up and down the empty street. Wind is driving the rain into the covered entryway, wetting the facing iron and oak benches where people wait for taxis or grey-haired children to pick them up. Or just sit. A sheer curtain of rain becomes visible against the dark cypress trees lining the side-walk; stiff, ugly damned things, grown so often in cemeteries because they're no more trouble than the tenants. Don't blow in the wind, don't fling their leaves around, don't do anything.

A bright yellow sports car splashes its way past on Foul Bay Road and suddenly he feels tired. It's after four, he'll be able to sleep now.

That thought makes him happy. These days it's the only one that does.

In the pre-dawn light the battered tan pickup bounces and rattles over the old logging road bordered by an almost solid wall of dense, dripping trees. The windshield wipers barely cope with the heavy rain, but the driver seems oblivious, his pale blue eyes fixed somewhere beyond the road ahead.

The boy, sitting as far away from the man as he can, stares bleakly out the passenger window, his narrow hands fiddling with a buckle on his blue backpack. The man's tuneless whistling sets his teeth on edge. It's raining so hard he can barely see the occasional houses and barns cut out of the woods. No sign of the horses either, they must have all taken shelter. He likes seeing the horses. They pass a bunch of sheep all huddled in a circle with their black faces together. Like a big woolly flower with a black centre. Like a daisy. He wishes his mother was there, she would like that. They used to have fun driving to school.

He gets a bad feeling whenever he thinks of her lately. It seems like she's always sleeping. It's like she's stoned or some-thing. He smells pot on Michael a lot, but not on her. The only sounds in the truck cab are the squeaking wipers and rain drumming the roof, which almost drowns out the man's monotonous whistling. It suits the boy, who doesn't want to talk, especially doesn't want to listen.

"Do you know this song, Sam?"

He leans his forehead against the window and closes his eyes. Of course it was too good to last. It always was.

He sighs. "No." It was a hymn, of course, something about the Lord coming and trampling the grapes of wrath or something, whatever that meant. Like Godzilla. He likes the marching tune.

"What did you say? I can't hear you."

"No! I said no!" He shouldn't have said it like that. Michael is the only one who's allowed to talk like that.

"Still mad, are we?"

The pale blue eyes narrow as the boy, trying not to be obvious about it, shifts his body a bit closer to the window.

"Who's we?" he says, trying for a neutral tone, "I don't see anybody else here."

A large hand clamps his shoulder, yanks him away from the window, and the truck swerves.

"Don't get smartass with me. And don't sit with your back to me."

"Sorry," the boy mumbles.

The hand lets go and he wants to rub his shoulder, which feels numb, then tingly, but he refuses to show that it hurts. When he was younger, Michael used to yank his head back by the hair. It's too short now and he hopes that bugs him.

"I've had just about enough of that sullen behaviour of yours, Sam. Just because you couldn't go Halloweening. You're getting too old for that anyway."

"So how old were you when you stopped?"

"That's got fuck all to do with it! It was before I knew a lot of things I know now."

"All I wanted was to have fun with my friends."

"I told you before that kind of fun is dangerous. It's Satan's opportunity. You've got to be on guard every minute."

Sam closes his eyes. Michael gears down to drive through a low spot in the road that's filled with water. The rain is falling now like it's being poured from a giant pitcher in the sky, or like maybe they're driving under a waterfall. Sam has never seen it rain so hard.

"See that rain? That's just another sign that The Day is coming." He always says The Day with capital letters in his voice. "And if you're lucky you'll be leaving all those friends behind so it doesn't matter anyway."

Sam sighs and rolls his eyes. On the back of the truck there's a sign that reads, If the Rapture Occurs, This Car Will Be Driverless. And another that says Beam Me Up, Lord. If only, Sam thinks. Maybe he'd better learn to drive for the day Michael sprouts wings and flies off with all the good people.

Yah, right.

"That's just La Niña," he says. "Causing the rain."

"Pffft! That's what everybody thinks, but they've got another think coming. That's no more La Niña than I am, and one of these days the shit's gonna hit the fan!" Michael cackles and smacks the steering wheel and the truck heads for the ditch, then swerves wildly back again, "Yessireebob, The Day's getting closer all the time when the shit's gonna hit the old faneroo. And I for one can't wait to see it. The Day when all those people who think…"

Sam tunes him out. In a way it's a relief. Once he got going on that subject Michael didn't expect an answer, didn't even want one, he just wanted to hear his own voice. Sam concentrates on the windshield wipers, which also hold a low opinion of the man raving away behind the wheel — shut up, you jerk, shut up, you fool, shut up, you shit. Sam smiles, careful to turn his head away when he does.

Why can't Mom drive him to school instead of Michael, who's always spouting horrible stuff about the end of the world like it was some big party he could hardly wait for? Emerald, too. No wonder Mom's depressed, with Emerald living right in their yard now. The weekend was deadly. The only person he had to hang out with was Joey and he's only three.

They reach Oceanside Middle School and pull up in front where Sam opens the door and is out before the truck completely stops. When he reaches in for his backpack, Michael shoves it across the seat so hard it drops on the ground, spilling some pencils from an open pocket. As Sam bends to retrieve them the truck jumps ahead and he leaps backwards. He hears Michael laugh.

At the top of the steps, Sam hears the truck tires squeal and the engine backfire as it speeds up. He surreptitiously gives it the finger and hears a familiar laugh.

"Hey Sam!" It was Jeff, heading for the door from the parking lot. Oceanside Middle School is in the country, so most everyone comes by bus or car.

"Hey Jeff." Sam stops and waits for him.

"Too bad you couldn't come with us last night," Jeff says as they shove their way through the door and head for their lockers.

"Yah. That sucked."

"I guess Jesus never went trick-or-treating, huh?" Jeff grins, shrugging out of his backpack. His red hair is sticking up everywhere. Jeff has natural spikes.

"Nope. Only Satan."

"Hey, I think I saw that guy last night. He had more candy than I did."

And Sam tries to smile as he dials his locker combination but his insides feel all jangly, like a pinball machine, the way they usually do now after riding to school with Michael.

"Never mind." Jeff is cramming stuff into his messy locker. "I'll give you half my candy. I got tons."

"Thanks." But it isn't about the candy. They both know that.

"Hey Sam! Hey Jeff!"

Chad, coming through the door in a knot of other kids, waves, his long black face lit up in a grin, and the three of them start down the hallway together, laughing and talking as if they hadn't been together just yesterday.

"Good morning, boys." Mrs. McCormack looks up and smiles as they pass the principal's office.

"Good morning, Mrs. McCormack." They like her.

Sam takes a deep breath and feels his insides start to slow down.

Chapter Two

Matthew and the Beast are vacuuming. He's finished the main floor hallway, hauling the beast along by its twenty feet of hose that feels like it's lined with lead. Matthew calculates the Beast weighs a hundred pounds, give or take an ounce. It's ancient, and as soon as he figures out how to sabotage it without being found out, he will. Once, while cleaning the laundry washroom, he accidentally vacuumed up the water in the toilet, but as soon as the Beast dried out it was raring to go again. A high decibel snarl emits from its innards, which changes to an outraged scream when Matthew scoops up something indigestible.

Matthew does not have a good rapport with vacuum cleaners. Delia took the diabolical old Filthy Queen with her and good riddance. In a weak moment at home with a wicked hangover he once let in a Filter Queen salesman who scattered elephant bullets all over the living room, zapping them up with such a clang and clatter he bought the damn thing just to get rid of him. And because they were always shooting elephants in the living room and missing, of course.

The Filthy Queen clamped onto attachments with a death grip, worse after he beat it on the back steps in a fit of temper. He's thought of spraypainting FILTER QUEEN SUCKS on their depot some dark night and, lest that be misunderstood, the word OCCASIONALLY under it.

He wrestles off the carpet attachment, clamps on the brush, then turns the corner into the laundry room and the motor dies. He goes back and pushes the Beast along with his foot until the hose straightens out and it roars into life again, snarling and snuffling like a lion at the kill.

Outside the laundry room's large double window the rain sluices down from a low, leaden sky. Still, it's a cheerful room with sunny yellow walls Delia painted and a row of red geraniums blooming on the windowsill. She also papered the small washroom – she had no trouble extracting money from the old tightwad – and the women all love the laundry room now. Compared to some of the laundry rooms in Matthew's past, it was dazzling to begin with.

He'd better get a move on. Mister Funk has taken to "dropping in to see how you're doing dear boy" a couple of times a week since Delia left – and his gimlet glances don't miss a thing. He's a skinny, spry eighty-year-old who reminds Matthew of Homer Simpson's boss. He has owned the building for forty-odd years, "one of the best investments I ever made," and he has made many, judging by his Lincoln – a new one every year. That way you don't have any nasty surprises, he told Matthew. But when Matthew, whose life has been full of nasty surprises, the Beast being one, suggested that the Kensington needed a new vacuum cleaner, Mr. Funk bridled. Oh, no, dear boy, they don't make them like that any more. And he was right about that, the Beast could suck up Desmond Funk from ten feet away.

Matthew cautiously vacuums the edges of the bookshelf where residents exchange books and magazines, and the Beast attempts to inhale a hefty Janet Dailey, perhaps accidentally, perhaps not. Since she is the highest-paid writer in the world, and he is the lowest, he once perused a Ms. Dailey and found the experience extremely depressing. The Beast gives an outraged shriek as *Beware of the Stranger* momentarily sticks in its maw before he wrestles it out. Sorry old boy, says Matthew, who didn't know the Beast had literary leanings.

Shutting off the motor, he scans the shelf for something to read. General Schwarzkopf once left a darkly fascinating book about the Third Reich there. Matthew's subscriptions to *Macleans* and *Time* and *Harpers* have run out and he waits for them to appear here or peruses them at the library reading room. He's joined the disparate mix of people who like to read with strangers. Some of them quite strange.

He shuts off the motor and checks each dryer for forgotten garments. In the last one a pair of peach bikinis slither into his hand and he pins them up on the bulletin board. Nice. Very nice. What woman in the building would wear them? Maybe the good-looking one in 306. Elizabeth Wright, he thinks her name is.

Tessie Thatcher sways her titanic body through the doorway.

"Good morning, Mrs. Thatcher."

"Hmmph!" A snort is Tessie's greeting of choice. "Admiring the laundry, Mister Kelly?" she says, as if she's caught him in some nefarious activity.

"I don't know," he says. "I think they need some lace, don't you?"

Tessie ignores this, rifling through the magazines Matthew just straightened. Then catching sight of a Danielle Steele, she snaps up *A Perfect Stranger* along with several magazines. There are a lot of strangers in those books.

She suddenly glares at him.

"What are you doing about that cat?" she says, suddenly.

"Cat? What cat?"

"Don't tell me you haven't heard a cat in the building?"

"No, I haven't." Though now he thinks about it, he did hear something once that sounded like a cat. He'd forgotten about it.

"I'm sure you're mistaken, Mrs. Thatcher." If he saw a lion looking in the doorway behind her he'd have said the same thing. "There's a no pet rule in this building, you know," he says. "It's against the rules to even let in a fly."

Tessie's small eyes blink and her forehead scrunches down. This man might be worse than dissipated. He might be crazy. What was he talking about flies for?

"I'm glad you think it's funny. You're supposed to be the caretaker." And having set him straight on that, she turns and sways out the door.

Gone to warn the ladies about his underwear fetish, no doubt. And to get on with a vicarious romance courtesy Ms. Steele. The thought of Tessie feeling romantic is too much for Matthew. He wonders if her husband bolted long ago or if he's dead, and if so, if Tessie killed him.

"Top of the morning to you, Matthew."

A small, round, ruddy-faced man with a crooked ebony

wig beams from the doorway. In his yellow slicker and matching hat he could be heading out for a day's fishing on the high seas. Or to kindergarten.

"Ah, Mister Reilly. Braving the elements, are we?" God, did he really say we?

"Call me Roland." Mister Reilly catches sight of the bulletin board and his face lights up.

"Oh, lovely. Wonder whose those are?"

"Such a thought never entered my head," Matthew says, and Mr. Reilly giggles.

"So," says Matthew, "what are you up to today? Just living the life of Reilly?"

The little man laughs obligingly. "Going for my constitutional. You've got to be fit to live the life of Reilly, you know."

"Actually, I wouldn't know," Matthew says.

Though he meant it as a feeble joke, it came out sounding gloomy, or worse, self-pitying. A weak, watery sun has broken out and the rain in the parking lot thins to sparkling silver threads, then stops. He nods his head toward the window. "Better hurry before you miss it."

Alone again, Matthew empties the lint traps, wipes the washers and dryers down and empties the waste barrel into a large garbage sack. He whistles under his breath as he delivers the Beast to its lair, emerging to see the explorers, Mrs. Thompson and Mrs. Erickson, one tall and thin, one short and stout, both excited looking, just leaving the building on another expedition. Life begins at your husband's funeral, he thinks, as the door closes behind them.

He forgot to water the laundry-room plants. Waiting for the watering can to fill, he glances in the mirror at his slack, lined face and pouchy eyes, wondering idly if he stays off the booze if he'll lose his dissipated look. Sam says he looks like Patrick Stewart, aka Jean Luc Picard, captain of the USS Enterprise. Well, he's bald, anyway.

Patrick, carrying a large file folder, sticks his head in the door. He glances at the bulletin board and his face flushes.

"Hi Matthew. Didn't happen to find a black sock, did you?"

"No. Sucked into the Black Sock Hole, I'm afraid."

"Oh, well. See you." And his face still red, he hurries out.

Patrick was blushing. Maybe the bikinis belong to a girl-friend who left them behind. He can't imagine a woman forgetting her underwear but what does he know, he's never been deafened by the sound of falling knickers.

The sky is darkening again, and with it his short-lived buoyant mood. Another dingy goddamn day. A good day to get drunk. He envies everybody thus pleasantly employed.

He flicks off the light and a nebulous gloom settles over the room. A large black spider races out from under a washer. He steps on it and kicks the remains back where it came from.

Ha! Make it rain you little bastard.

In Suite 206 Maurice rolls away from her and lies panting as if he's just run a marathon. But sex with Maurice is no marathon, Liz knows. More like the fifty-yard dash. He breathes deeply a few more times, then yawns widely, displaying his many capped teeth. "Oh, that was good," he says.

Liz looks at the ceiling. Her mother, in the suite directly

above, would be wondering why she didn't drop in after work today.

Maurice is propped up on his elbow now, running his fingers through his thick, wavy grey hair. He was once described in the *Vancouver Sun* as "leonine" and he loved it. "Was that good for you, Liz?" he asks.

"Well, it was –"

"My God!" Maurice has caught sight of his Rolex. "It's almost six o'clock."

He sits up on the edge of the bed and reaches for his valentine boxers, tossed on the chair in the heat of passion. Maurice's, that is. "Eileen's invited guests for dinner," he says.

His wide back and buttocks are slick with sweat. Maurice has all sorts of plastic plumbing running around inside him, and Liz worries someday he might die in the act. With her. She has visions of trying to dress Maurice and drag him somewhere. Her back would never take it.

Maurice pulls on his underwear and shirt, then loses his balance pulling on his pants and sits down hard on the bed. He yawns as he buttons his snowy white shirt.

"Oh Lord. My phone will be ringing off the hook." As he ties his red, paisley tie he turns to look at Liz. The shirt and tie set off his dark skin. Maurice is a good-looking man. Liz sits up with the sheet held in front of her and reaches her plum-coloured robe from the foot of the bed, pulling it hastily on under the sheet. In her limited experience she has noticed that men don't give a fig about what they look like naked, they think themselves irresistible in their pelts, while she is painfully aware of the shortcomings of her more-than-middle-aged body.

She clambers awkwardly out past him and heads for the

bathroom, where she drags a hair pick through her thick, dark hair, pausing to pull out a new white strand.

"Liz, I can't find my socks," Maurice calls through the door.

"Oh? They must be there somewhere, wherever you left them." The man is helpless without his secretary or his wife. "Look under the bed."

The phone in the living room rings. Liz sighs, knowing full well who is calling.

"Hello, Elizabeth, it's Mother."

"Yes, Mother, I recognize your voice."

"There's no call to be sarcastic, I only phoned to see if you were all right, since you didn't come by after work today."

"Yes, of course I'm all right. Why wouldn't I —" Liz covers the mouthpiece. Maurice is standing in front of her in his pin-stripe suit mouthing something and pointing at his naked white feet while Liz's mother natters excitedly in her ear about needing to talk to her about something right away.

"My socks!" Maurice hisses.

"I'll have to call you back, Mother. Someone is just leaving."

"Oh, you didn't say you had company." Liz's mother makes company sound like a sexually transmitted disease. Well, sometimes it was.

"Be sure you do, Elizabeth. It's very important."

Liz, who has never yet forgotten to call her mother back, resists the urge to hang up in her ear.

"Yes Mother, I will."

She sighs. What was that about? Is she planning a trip? A nice thought, but not too likely. She hears Maurice pawing around in the bedroom and goes to check.

He's down on his knees peering under the bed. His

exposed pink soles look defenceless and kind of innocent. His mother probably kissed them when he was a baby. They're not calloused, but then he doesn't walk around on them much.

"Don't you ever vacuum under here?" he asks. He's pulled out *Macleans* and *Saturday Night,* her sneakers and a navy pump she couldn't find to wear to work this morning.

"Apparently not. I'm glad I hid the *Playgirl* before you came." Trying to cover her embarrassment.

Maurice ignores this and stands up, brushing at his dark suit. He sneezes violently, pulls out a snowy white handkerchief and blows his nose.

"Oh, Lord. I'm allergic to dust." He looks accusingly at Liz. "Try to find my socks, will you?" he says, in an it's-the-least-you-can-do tone of voice. And having delegated the problem, like any overworked executive, he goes off to make his phone call.

He looks rather rakish in his suit and bare white ankles, Liz thinks, peering under the couch moments later. She knows damn well his socks aren't there but doesn't want him looking under there, too. She's just spotted an earring she thought was lost, winking faintly through a dust bunny.

"...yes, Eileen," Maurice is saying, "I was unavoidably delayed. What? Two cartons of whipping cream." He motions to Liz for pen and paper. "Fresh strawberries, how many? Really, Eileen, you knew we were having guests. Oh, that's too bad, you should have cancelled. I've told you this kind of thing is too – what? Blueberries, too?" He raises his eyebrows at Liz and waggles one bare foot.

She pads obediently off to look for his socks, behind the

bathroom door again, behind the bed, under the dresser, and down behind the cushion on the bedroom chair. Really, it was most peculiar, Maurice's socks disappearing like that. Both of them. Where the hell could they go?

"Liz, if this is a joke, it's not funny." Maurice, having placated his wife, frowns at her from the bedroom doorway.

"I didn't think it was." But laughter bubbles up in her throat — it's partly nerves. She feels intimidated by Maurice. Sometimes she wonders if that's why she's sleeping with him.

Silly euphemism, she's doesn't sleep with Maurice and never will. It's a mystery to her why she even goes to bed with him. It's sure not his lovemaking, he's like a man who thinks he can play the piano because he can find middle C. She's probably flattered that he wants her and not some younger woman. And he's important. She hates to think that might attract her. She reaches around under the bedclothes in case Maurice removed his socks between the sheets as she sometimes does after her feet warm up.

"I haven't got a clue where your socks are, Maurice," she says, knowing she looks guilty as she always has when something is missing anywhere in her vicinity. Maurice is giving her the same low-browed suspicious squint her grade four teacher did when someone stole Jackie Saunders's pencil case. She wonders fleetingly where Jackie Saunders is now. She had a crush on him till he laid her scalp open with a tin-edged ruler.

"I'll check the bathroom again," she says, and flees.

In the bathroom, she leans against the door and nervously bites a bath towel that needs washing to keep from laughing.

"Liz, I've got to get home," Maurice says sternly through the door. "Eileen's got another migraine."

"Oh, that's too bad." Liz thinks of the tentative-looking Englishwoman on Maurice's Christmas card to his constituents, flanked with Maurice and their two loutish-looking sons beside their Christmas tree. Both football players, a matter of great pride for their father. "I'll be right out," she calls, splashing her face with cold water in an effort to compose herself.

A few frantic minutes later, Maurice takes his bare ankles, or they take him, down the stairs, into his car and (eventually) home to Mrs. Maurice Dickson, wife of the honorable MLA for greater Victoria, who is concocting a story as he drives through the rain to the Safeway store.

He was attacked by a dog on the grounds of the Parliament buildings this morning. No. Morning was no good, Eileen would ask why he didn't send his secretary out for a new pair. After work, then, the vicious brute tore his black Bruno Mali and sock right off his foot. Maurice could see the ugly thing now, a pit bull owned by one of the hippy protestors who were always lolling around in front of the House, smoking and drinking from thermoses and littering the grass with placards against clear-cutting trees.

Yes, he could see the slavering beast, now upgraded to a Rottweiller, growling and tearing his sock to shreds in its ugly cavernous mouth. Actually, those hippie protesters usually had puppies with bandanas around their necks. Maurice shakes his head at all that good government money going for Puppy Chow. They've got to do something about all those people lazing around downtown, scribbling on the sides of buildings. It's bad for the tourists.

Maurice is honing his story into a fascinating dinner-table anecdote when he sees the men's socks hanging on a rack in Safeways. Happy Feet, for God's sake, or something that looked a lot like them. His father swore by Happy Feet, they let Maurice's father's feet breathe. Maurice throws the offending brown socks – there were no black – in the cart with the strawberries. When he tells her what a close call he had, Eileen won't worry about such a small thing as his tardiness. Not when he could have lost his foot.

It was damn strange, that, Liz hiding his socks. She must have, she looked so guilty. Or had she? He didn't really know her that well. He must have imagined he heard her laughing when he started down the stairs.

She wanted to keep something of his, he thinks, rattling out to the parking lot and stowing the groceries in the trunk, it's the only explanation that makes any sense. He smooths his leonine hair in the rear-view mirror, checking for lipstick – "Daddy's wearing lickstick," Sean had told his mother when he was four.

Liz is falling in love with him, he decides, buckling up his seat belt and sighing a deep martyr-like sigh.

He missed Sylvia. He really did. You knew exactly where you stood with old Syl. The first time they'd gone to bed he told her virtuously he'd never leave his wife and she said she sure as hell hoped not, and if he did, not to turn up on her doorstep. He was fonder of old Syl than he realized; he must have been, he could feel his eyes misting over.

How long had it been since the accident? Two months? Two and a half? No, almost three, he remembers now. He missed her funeral because he was on holidays with the family and that was just as well, a man in his position couldn't be too careful. He shakes his head. Over three months, and he's still grieving for old Syl. Imagine. What did they say? You never knew what you had till it was gone?

Poor Syl.

As Maurice awkwardly wrestles his feet into the one-size-fits-all-midgets socks in his car in the Safeway parking lot, Liz, who had put her head back and her feet up in the old La-Z-Boy for a bit, opens her eyes and frowns. Damn it, why couldn't whatever it was wait till tomorrow? She'd like to just stick a Stouffer's something in the oven, have a long soak in the tub with her new Ruth Rendell, and maybe watch a little TV. *Frasier* is on tonight.

Now she has to get dressed, put her face together, and go upstairs. Her mother said it couldn't wait. She wrestles with the recliner's failing mechanism and it suddenly shoots her upright. She's developed a Goldilocks complex shopping for a new chair, they're too hard, too soft, too small, too big, too smooth, too furry.

At the bedroom door, she stops. Side by side, neat as you please in the doorway lie Maurice's socks. Long, black executive socks still faintly holding the shape of Maurice's calves, the feet pointing the same way on the mushroom-coloured broadloom. Toward the entrance. Or exit, depending on how you looked at it. They are unmistakably there, Maurice's socks, looking as if they'd been pressed. Not quite believing her eyes, she stoops down and touches the toe of the right sock with the tip of her finger. They're real, all right.

She steps over them and sits down on the bed. How could it be? They'd each been in the room several times, looking, it wasn't possible they both stepped over them and hadn't seen them. But there they were.

He'd never believe this. He suspects her, she knows, of hiding his socks away like some lovesick teenager with a strand of Ricky Martin's hair. Well, what else could he think?

Finally, shaking her head, she gets up, pulls on a pair of cords and a T-shirt and, reluctant to touch them again, steps over the socks and heads for the door.

Matthew's desk is cluttered with rental envelopes tenants have stuffed into the wooden box outside his door. CBC 2 plays quietly in the kitchen, or what passes for a kitchen, as he works.

343 will be vacant the end of the month – Mrs. Salisbury moving to a nursing home – and he must remember to check the paint supply. So far no one has even looked at the suite but better to paint it right away. The thought still intimidates him but he surely can't go too far wrong covering pale peach with pale peach.

Three apartments haven't paid yet and it's the fourth of the month. He's going to have to evict the two young guys in 303, this is the third time they're late, and last time they didn't pay till the 15th and Desmond Funk needs his money on time so he can add it to the piles already in the bank. And they're noisy, the tenant below them complains about them practising karate or something. Worse yet, they have a party occasionally, God forbid anyone in the building should be having fun.

The Findlays always forget and he has to go around and collect. They sit side by side on the sofa holding hands like small, guilty children, their feet not quite touching the floor. And Mister Reilly, the merry widower, who answers the door with his mouldy black wig slapped on any old way – once it was back to front. Sometimes Matthew feels he's in charge of an old folks' home. The blind leading the halt, if they only knew it.

He hates asking the young guys to leave, they added some life to the place. But it isn't winter in Saskatchewan, after all, they're all living in Lotus Land, as Mister Reilly is fond of pointing out. Matthew thinks Mister R must have a secret cache of lotuses himself, he's so full of simple-minded good cheer. And so he should be and so should they all on such a beautiful day in such a beautiful place, Mister Reilly would say and does say as he sallies forth each day. It's a wonder they didn't name the place Shangri-La instead of Victoria.

Matthew misses the prairies a lot lately.

A knock on the door makes him jump. What now? Nothing he needs to fix, he hopes. He opens the door to two women, one old and determined looking, the other, the fifty-ish, good-looking one from the second floor.

"Yes, what can I do for you?" he says, none too graciously. It's odd, but just two people standing outside your door can look like a delegation, and delegations seldom mean anything good. The expression on the younger one's face seems to confirm that. He doesn't remember the older woman's name, has only seen her a couple of times, but the younger one is Elizabeth Wright.

As they're standing there the elevator door opens and Tessie Thatcher, looking like a fire engine in her shiny red raincoat steps out, with Mister Reilly close behind, like a tugboat on the wrong end of a steamer.

"May we come in?" the older woman says, looking pointedly at Tessie.

"Oh, certainly. I'm sorry." He opens the door wider, closing it after them, but doesn't ask them to sit down.

"I'm Mrs. Wright. 343," the older one says, full of business.

"And I'm Liz Wright from the second floor. I don't think we've actually met." She holds out her hand and gives him a firm handshake.

"Mother and daughter?" Matthew asks.

"Yes," the elder Wright says.

Matthew glances at the daughter. A slim, dark woman who looks about to scream. What's going on here?

"I understand Mrs. Salisbury is moving at the end of the month," the old lady begins.

"Yes, that's right." Oh, on the second floor. Across from the daughter's. So that was it.

"I'd like to move into her suite when she goes, and we've come to give you notice on my suite."

Matthew looks at Liz Wright, whose fine dark eyes are fixed on his with the desperate look of a hostage trying to telepath a message in front of her captor.

"I'm sorry, that suite has been rented," he hears himself saying, and the daughter closes her eyes.

"Oh?" the old lady says suspiciously. "Mrs. Salisbury told me just this morning that it wasn't rented yet."

"Well, it is now. And it doesn't have a balcony, you know. Your suite is the better one, in my opinion."

"That's what I told you, Mother," the daughter says, enthusiastic with relief. "And yours is sunnier, too."

"I *know* it doesn't have a balcony. I never *sit* on the balcony. And I don't care about the sun, it just makes it hot in the summer." Her set little mouth is turned down at the corners. A woman used to getting her way, if Matthew ever saw one.

As she shepherds her mother out, Liz Wright turns and smiles at him over her shoulder. "Thank you," she says. She has a wonderful smile. Good bones. Nice mouth. What the Irish called a handsome crayther. They called Delia that the year they went to Ireland. His Irish aunts, who looked like truck drivers in drag, had said it often. A handsome creature. Much better than a pretty one, for his money. The kind of looks that last.

He pours himself a cup of coffee, about the tenth today, and sits down at the desk again.

What the hell is he going to do now? The suite isn't rented. Well, he'll have to think of something. He knew a desperate person when he saw one. Bad enough to have the old woman in the same building, let alone on her doorstep. God. Had the daughter ever been married, he wondered. Sometimes they took their maiden names back. She looked nice.

Matthew reaches for the phone and waits as the phone in the homey apartment on Cook Street rings and rings. Hey Ma, where are you? I want to play Scrabble. Eighty-two-year-old women are supposed to be at home nodding off in a rocking chair, or making their adult children miserable.

As usual, she's out somewhere; the library for her week's supply of books, aquacizes or swimming at the Oak Bay Rec Centre, playing bridge. Or beachcombing at Willows Beach maybe, the rain never stopped her from doing anything. She loves the ocean because it's flat, she always says, like where she grew up south of Regina.

He hangs up the phone and sits. His mother plays a mean game of Scrabble. Delia hated it. When he told her the man who invented Scrabble had died, she said Oh good, now I won't have to kill him.

Now the evening looms.

Someone in the building has a cat, Tessie is sure of it now. She heard one meowing in the night again. Telling that useless caretaker did no good. His wife was all right, but she left, who could blame her, and now they're stuck with him. Prowling around the halls at night. What was to stop him from coming right into your place while you slept with God knows what on his mind? Or that silly old goat in the black wig, flirting with all the women. She keeps the door chain on all the time.

As usual, she's in her large brown recliner with its view of the parking lot so she can see the comings and goings and keep an eye on that crazy woman who's always peering into her car. In a large aquarium against the wall an anxious-looking Oscar fish hangs halfway in the water, his eye fixed on Tessie. As she reaches for another chocolate turtle, he wriggles excitedly for a moment, then lapses into suspended animation once again, his underslung jaw forlornly ajar.

That car is parked in her spot again, and just thinking about it steams her and she reaches for another chocolate. It's the handsome grey-haired man again. He's somebody important, she's seen his picture in the paper, somebody in the government, but that doesn't give him the right. Who does he come to see here, that's what she'd like to know. He always hurries away from the car with his head down like he doesn't want to be recognized. When she complained to that dissipated caretaker he just said she didn't have a car, did she, and when she said she wanted it for her visitors he looked about to say something nasty but changed his mind. She has a good mind to report him.

Rain or not she'll have to go out tomorrow for Oscar's food. She heaves her bulk out of the chair and sways across the room, joints snapping and crackling like a bonfire. At her approach Oscar speeds excitedly back and forth.

"And what does Tessie's bad boy want? Hmmm?"

Oscar bumps his head on the bag of minnows that floats on top of the water. The minnows dart frantically in the bag of water as Oscar whizzes around in circles, almost meeting himself as Tessie reaches for the bag. She removes the clamp that holds it to the tank and empties it in the water. Oscar snaps up the fleeing minnows, churning the water as he speeds this way and that, two of them wriggling from his mouth at once, then three, bits of fins and flesh and heads flying out behind him, like bodies from a bombed airplane. One minnow hides down under the greenery in the bottom of the tank. Never mind, Oscar will get him sooner or later.

She flops back into her chair, reaches for the TV remote, then changes her mind. That crazy woman who keeps peering into her car will soon be home from work. Every time she parks she looks and looks in her car, then all around it, even under it. What in the world is she looking for? Watching her is better than a soap opera.

Chapter Three

Sam is dreaming he's in a treehouse. A big treehouse like the Swiss Family Robinsons', and it's awesome. It's in a humungous tree that probably only grows in the tropics somewhere and the roof is blue canvas like a little kid's treehouse with leaf shadows dancing on it. The sides are open and a big red parrot perched in the tree keeps squawking "fucking brilliant" which has Sam and Jeff and Chad rolling on the floor laughing and the parrot laughs, too. Smashing Pumpkins are singing the song about being full of rage like a rat in a cage on Sam's portable – Michael took it away last week but somehow he has it back and that's cool.

Jeff is hanging upside down by his knees from a tree branch with a can of Pringles in one hand and is conducting the music with a Pringle in his other hand, reaching up now and then to give a bite to the parrot who eats it and says "fucking salty." Sam is playing bongos along with the Pumpkins song, palm swiping and fingers flying like he saw on TV.

Chad is hammering – making a bookcase with six shelves, two each for their comics and stuff, and he starts hammering in time to the music and Jeff starts to laugh, nearly choking on a Pringle and he pulls himself up like a gymnast to get a drink from a wooden tap that Sam didn't know was growing out of the tree. And he's thinking, oh cool, this is so cool, the whole thing, even how the tree-house tips when you walk too close to the edge on account of it's an environmental treehouse. Chad wouldn't let them nail it on in case it killed the tree, and even if it didn't, trees have feelings and feel pain, and how would you like some-body nailing a treehouse onto you? Chad usually knows what he's talking about because he reads all the time, and so the treehouse is just sort of slung up there on ropes. Sam is thinking it's going to be so sweet sleeping there, rocking in the wind with the parrot asleep, too, and the stars twinkling through the branches.

Their sleeping bags are neatly rolled and Felix, his big black and white cat, is curled up on his. The guys agreed Felix could stay because he wouldn't go telling people where they were, which wasn't likely anyhow seeing as they don't know themselves – on a desert island somewhere. Felix, who hates water, must have floated on a piece of wreckage like those people in *Titanic*.

The Pumpkins are finished and Chad starts pounding ordinary like, nailing on the top shelf, and the hammering keeps getting louder and louder....

Sam opens his eyes, or tries to open them, they're stuck almost shut and his head hurts. He covers his ears and tries to get back into the dream, to will it back, but it's no use. The dream is gone but the hammering isn't, it's real and it's loud, right outside his wall, and he covers his head with the pillow, wondering why he's got such a bad feeling in his chest when the dream was so great.

And then he remembers.

It's Saturday. Jeff's thirteenth birthday party. A wall-climbing party for six guys, and then they're going to see the new *Star Trek* movie. He's been looking forward to it for weeks. Until last night at the supper table. Jim, the old guy who's camped in their woods, was having supper with them for the first time and Sam was pleased. He visits Jim sometimes in his tent.

"I need you to help me tomorrow, Sam." The crumbs from Michael's bun were falling in his beard. "I want to start tiling Emerald's floors tomorrow."

Sam looked at his mother, who was mechanically dipping hot and sour soup into Emerald's bowl like her mind was a zillion miles away. Emerald was always there lately.

"I can't. It's Jeff's party tomorrow, remember? I told Mom about it a long time ago." He tried to say it in a normal voice – it never paid to let Michael know how much you wanted something – but it came out kind of whiny. Joey, in the chair beside him, started to slide off his pillows and Sam propped him up again.

"I can help you, Michael," Jim said. Michael gave him a dirty look.

"Kate, did you say Sam could go to a party tomorrow?"

His mom looked like somebody just woke her up. Her wavy black hair shone under the fringed light that hung over the table and she frowned like she was trying to remember. "What party?" she said.

"Mom! You did so know about the party. Jeff's wall-climbing party, remember, I told you a long time ago and you said it sounded like fun."

She nodded slowly – everything she did lately seemed like slow motion – blowing on her soup to cool it.

"Yeah, I guess maybe you did, Sam. I'm sorry I forgot. I seem to forget a lot of things lately."

"You got that right," Michael said sarcastically, and Emerald smiled at him and Mom with that sappy, loving, understanding look she wore a lot. When she wasn't smacking Joey around, she didn't look like that then. Her no-colour hair was skinned back from her long, pale face. She didn't like Sam any more than he liked her and he knew it.

Felix, who was sleeping in a big mixing bowl on the counter, got up and stretched his back up, meowing hello like he always did.

"Felix remembers, don't you Felix?" Sam, whose insides were getting shaky, trying for a light note. Felix turned around twice in the bowl and curled up again with one large black and white paw draped over the rim.

"Felix!" Joey called, waving his spoon in the air. "Felix merembers! What does Felix merember, Mum?" But Emerald was too interested in what was happening to be distracted; she had her still, hooded-eyed look, like an eagle that's just spotted a mouse.

"Well, this is the first I've heard about a party tomorrow," Michael said. "I can't drive you to town, I've got too much to do. And anyway I need your help."

"Okay, sure, I can help you in the morning." Sam was thinking fast. "I'll get up as early as you want, just call me, and Jeff's party doesn't start till two."

"Two, did you say? Well, that's just not good enough, Sonny." Sam hates it when Michael calls him that.

"I'll do it, Michael," Jim said, looking like he wished he was anywhere but there. "I can tile that floor myself."

"And I can help Jim. I could meet the guys later, at Vic's." I'll get up at –"

"Who's Vic?" Michael asked, his tone implying it must be another one of Sam's depraved friends.

"The guy who has Vic's Vertical Walls, where the party is."

"Kate! Wake up for God's sake and listen to your son. I'll be the one climbing the walls around here if this keeps up." He smirked at his brilliant joke, and Emerald laughed.

Kate jumped and smiled at Sam. "That rock climbing isn't dangerous, is it honey?"

"No. You've got a rope all the –"

But Emerald gave Michael a significant look which revved him up even more.

"I don't give a flying fuck if it's dangerous or not! He's not going. Somebody around here has to take charge. There's a hell of a lot to do around here and not much time to do it."

Sam shoved his soup away and it tipped, spilling tofu and peppers and mushrooms they had picked and dried, all kinds of stuff, on the pine table.

"Oh, oh, Sam made a mess," Joey said quietly and began to slide sideways again on his pillows. Jim straightened them up.

Sam clamped his jaw so he wouldn't say what he wanted to. Then he'd miss the party for sure. His stomach had that shrinking feeling again.

"Sorry. I'll clean it up, Mom."

"That's okay, honey. It was an accident."

"You aren't going and that's final," Michael said. "I need more help if we're going to get this house done before winter."

And Sam lost it, yelling "Well, it wasn't my idea to have a bunch of..." he looked at Emerald... "*people* move to our place. Why can't they help you?"

The old border collie asleep by the door lifted his head.

Michael jumped up from the table, his hand raised menacingly, and Joey started to cry, a high, screaming cry. The dog scrambled up and over to Sam, who reached down to touch his head. "It's all right, Buddy."

The dog whimpered, looking anxiously around the table.

"You apologize to Emerald." Michael's hand trembled.

Sam's mom never hit him before she married Michael and she wouldn't let him either. Now, he doesn't know. "Sorry," he mumbled, without looking at Emerald.

Michael glared at Kate, then sat down hard, yanked in his chair and started shovelling in the soup as Sam mopped at the spill with some paper towels, wanting more than anything to grind the whole slimy mess in Michael's face. He had that pinball feeling inside him again. He managed to pick up most of the vegetables and then wiped the rest with the dishrag. Buddy sat down, nervously lifting one paw, then the other, his toenails clicking on the wood floor.

"Mom, I'm going out with Buddy for awhile." Buddy's ears went up and he looked at Sam.

"All right, Sam."

He grabbed his jacket from the peg, almost tripping over Buddy, as anxious to get out as he was. Michael would take down the Bible after supper and start to read out loud and he got mad if you left once he started. Jim looked like he wished he could leave too.

Sam stood on the deck and breathed deeply several times till his heartbeat slowed down. Buddy pushed against his leg, licking his hand, and he reached down to pat him. "Good boy," leaning down to rest his cheek on the top of Buddy's warm head, "good dog."

A light was on in Michael's workshop behind the trees where he made furniture, awesome stuff people paid lots of money for. Sam never went there any more. The misty air had the fresh lumber smell Sam used to like, but now it meant everything was changing. Some more of Michael's Jesus friends were moving out cabins soon. And once the addition to the house was done their nice place was going to be awful, like a motel, with cabins and weird people everywhere. Except for Jim. He was okay. He said he'd help tomorrow, but Michael just wanted to spoil Sam's fun.

Their whole life changed when Michael got born again, as he calls it. If anything wasn't about Jesus it was supposed to be bad. And if you didn't think like those people, you were going to Hell and they were quite pleased about it, too, it seemed like. Sam didn't know a lot about Jesus, but didn't he hang out with all kinds of people? And forgive them no matter what they did. Like prostitutes and stuff? He heard that somewhere.

He could hear Michael starting to read and it would go on and on. He was reading from the book of Daniel, which was about a guy who had nightmares he should have kept to himself, in Sam's opinion. But Michael's favourite is the Book of Revelations, which gave Sam nightmares. He wished he knew more about the Bible so he could argue with Michael. When he asked Michael questions like why God would turn Lot's wife into a pillar of salt instead of stone, Michael couldn't answer. That was the weirdest thing. A salt statue would melt in the rain, or be a salt lick for cows, wouldn't it?

Buddy woofed and nudged his hand, looking up expectantly.

"Okay boy, come on," and he clattered down the steps and headed out in the direction of the road. It wasn't raining and it felt good being out there in the dark with Buddy padding and panting along beside him and the cool, cedar-scented air on his face. And pretty soon he was running.

He'd have kept on running, too, all the way to the highway where he could hitch a ride to town, but he couldn't make Buddy go back and was afraid he'd try to follow and get hit by a car in the dark. So he came back.

Emerald's light was on but the workshop was dark. Away back in the trees he saw the soft glow of Jim's tent. Skinny old Jim with his funny beard, who looked like he just crawled out of a cave or a gold mine. He wasn't like Emerald, he just helped out and didn't bother anybody. He called Sam Samuel and referred to himself as Jim. "Jim is very pleased to have a visit from Samuel, yes." Like that, he talked. Kinda like Yoda in *Star Wars*.

When he went in, Michael wasn't there. Praise the Lord, as they all said. All the time. He smiled at that, hanging up his jacket, feeling better from the run. His mom was watching TV, just staring at it, really, her arms hugging her chest like she was cold.

"Do you want some hot chocolate, Mom? I'm going to make some." They used to make it a lot at night while they talked or watched TV.

"Oh, no thanks, sweetheart. I'm not having chocolate for awhile."

He didn't ask why, afraid it might be one more thing she wasn't supposed to do any more. And then he didn't want any either. He wanted to kiss her good night and tell her he loved her like he did when he was younger but tears jumped into his eyes at the thought, so he didn't. He turned around halfway up the stairs and she was just staring at the black window, her hands open in her lap. He saw how thin she was, the shadows under her eyes almost black in her pale face. And suddenly he felt scared.

"Night, Mom," he said, but she didn't answer.

In bed he thought about how great it was before, with all that space to fool around in, and his friends would come out and make huts and play survival games and sleep in the barn. Now he never saw them except at school and he was afraid after awhile it wouldn't be the same. Mom and him used to sit on the deck a lot just talking, Michael too, sometimes. And she was always excited about a painting she was doing for somebody's new kids' book. Not any more.

He cried a long time, trying to not make any noise. Until finally he fell asleep.

But now he's awake. It's pouring buckets again and there is bloody Michael hammering away like a madman, and now Sam is mad instead of sad, and that feels a whole lot better. No way is he going to miss Jeff's party to help Michael. No matter how mad he gets.

He pulls on clean jeans, t-shirt and his Captain Spock sweatshirt. He takes ten bucks for Jeff from his Borg bank, then takes another five for himself and tiptoes downstairs carrying his Nikes as if Michael could hear him with all that pounding. Buddy is snoring on the living-room rug. That's good, he won't follow. Sometimes Michael makes him sleep outside. In the deserted kitchen he sticks three banana muffins in a paper bag, leaves the message GONE TO JEFF'S PARTY. STAYING AT JEFF'S TONIGHT on the bulletin board, then pulls on his rain jacket and slips out the side door.

Jeff's party is awesome. Wall climbing is so cool and it isn't scary at all with the rope on your waist going up to the ceiling and from you to the guy on the floor, but you're still climbing alone, imagining how great it would be to climb a mountain sometime. The guy holding the rope is called the belayer and is anchored to the opposite wall by his harness. You work in pairs and they have six guys. Vic explained all the equipment and the signals and what to do if the climber starts to fall. It's so much fun when Jeff's mom comes to pick them up they don't want to stop, so she goes away and comes back later.

And now it's almost midnight at Jeff's house, Chad is staying over too, and Sam is telling them about the dream. He's in his T-shirt and Jeff's long flannel boxers and feels all over comfortable. The three of them are kicked back on the couch in the den waiting to watch *South Park* which doesn't come on till midnight and is hysterical even if it is gross. They like Sam's dream, especially the parrot.

"Yah, *Swiss Family Robinson* was cool," Jeff says.

"Yah, but sort of phony too, though," Chad says. "I always wondered how come all that heavy stuff they needed just happened to float ashore, like hammers and kegs of nails, I mean you dump a keg of nails overboard and it's gonna sink like a boulder."

"Well, only the dad had a real hammer, didn't he?"

"What's a boulder?" says Jeff, who can be clueless sometimes, but he's funny and that makes up for it.

"A humungous rock," says Chad, "and you think even one hammer's gonna float? You drop it in the water and the only thing it's gonna nail is maybe a fish on the way down."

Jeff chokes on a nacho, laughing, and reaches for his can of Sprite. "Fucking salty" he says and they crack up again. The parrot's got a name now. Homer.

"Well, I don't care. I loved *Swiss Family Robinson*. I wanted to be wrecked on a desert island, just like them," Sam says.

"Me, too. I wanted to be Jack."

"Yah. Same."

"Yah. Jack was cool."

"He was.

"Yah. Cool."

"Yah."

Jeff's brother, Justin, wanders in wearing his karate gi and brown belt. He's seventeen and way cool. "The three musketeers, eh?" he says, and finding his karate magazine on the coffee table, wanders out again.

Jeff's wiry, yellow dog, Floyd, comes in and sits down, looking at them with his little close-together eyes. Floyd is not the brightest light in the canine world. Chad remembers an IQ test for dogs he read about where you can test IQ by how fast your dog gets out from under a blanket. Jeff gets a blanket and throws it over Floyd, who just sits there, breathing the blanket in and out, sending them into fits of laughter. The longer the blanket sits there breathing the harder they laugh, and finally Floyd just lies down under the blanket and goes to sleep.

And then *South Park* comes on, and sitting there between his friends with their feet up, laughing at the singing chef and the dancing poo and Kenny dying again, Sam is happy. If they wouldn't think he was weird he'd have liked to put an arm around both of them.

In the morning Sam tries to make a collect call to his grandpa. The answering machine comes on and he finds out you can't make a collect call to an answering machine. And what would he say in a message anyway? Hi Grandpa, my life sucks big time? Mom's turned into a zombie? I'm scared?

Beam me up. Sam smiles. Grandpa would understand that.

But now that he thinks of it, he shouldn't leave a message anyway. Grandpa might phone back before he gets home and Michael would answer.

"Did you get your grandpa on the phone, Sam?" Jeff's mom asks.

"Uh, no, he wasn't home. It's okay, I'll talk to him later."

And when they drive him home, he says he'll walk in from the gate. He doesn't want them to run into Michael.

Or see the place.

Chapter Four

Matthew hears it as soon as he opens the church's side door, and he pauses a moment at the top of the basement stairs to listen. The sounds of a party; the buzz of talk and laughter, the smell of cigarette smoke – the only things missing are the tinkle of glasses and ice, the smell of booze. Instead, there is the aroma of coffee that always smells better than it tastes.

Suddenly he's glad he managed to drag himself away from the idiot box, though it's Inspector Frost tonight on *Mystery*. Frost, that homely, irascible, oh-so-human little man, is special. He'd've taped it but Delia took the VCR.

When he opens the meeting-room door the noise level jumps. A good turnout tonight for sure, there won't be time for everyone to talk in the meeting, so he'll pass. He's still not comfortable talking, and Edwin isn't the only one to drone on too long.

Jeannie, one of his favourite people here, beams him a big smile. She's obviously got somebody new in tow, a girl who can't be more than seventeen, who looks sick and sorry and like she wants to bolt. Her head hangs, her lank, dispirited hair skinned behind her ears. Poor kid. All those dry, dreary years ahead of her.

He waves at Jeannie and threads his way past knots of people, young, old, in-between, is greeted warmly by name several times. Big Dave smiles at Matthew and mouths "good to see you" over the heads of two people Matthew doesn't recognize, a middle-aged man and a woman. If he didn't know better he'd think the members were out beating the bushes this week. But he knows it doesn't work that way, when they're ready they'll come and not before.

He's still not sure he's ready. He came to keep Delia from leaving and she left anyway, but here he is again down a church basement with a roomful of drunks who look, surprise surprise, just like ordinary people. If you don't look too close.

There's Edwin, smiling away in a brown and white sport shirt with horses galloping madly up the front and around the collar. Edwin's thinning brown hair is combed neatly across the top of his head, his unfortunate gold earring glinting under the light. He's talking to a plain, worried-looking woman about his own age.

"Good to see you, Matthew. Howzit goin' buddy?" Edwin calls everybody buddy.

"It's going," Matthew replies.

Edwin is immediately sympathetic. "Had a bad week, Matt?"

"No. Just a long one." He doesn't like being called Matt. "Nice shirt," he says, heading toward the back of the room, where the literature table is neatly covered with pamphlets and books, and the pass-through counter of the church kitchen is set up with the A.A. bar. He takes a thick coffee mug that reminds him of the Chinese cafés of his youth, fills it with hot water and vacillates in front of several brands of tea, herbal and otherwise.

A dark, curly-haired woman, filling her cup from the coffee machine, laughs.

"Got a problem making decisions?"

"Just wondering whether to throw caution to the winds and have the Red Zinger. It sounds dangerous."

"Go for it." She sticks out her hand. "My name's Amy."

She's got a good firm handshake, the second woman to shake his hand that way lately. He likes that.

"Hi. My name is Matthew and I'm an alcoholic." They both laugh.

"Me too. Ain't it great?"

"You're kidding. Right?"

"No, I'm not. Really." She smiles at his expression. "Stick around, it takes awhile."

"Yeah, I guess." And the pope's handing out condoms on a Vatican street corner. Sometimes he thinks these people are brainwashed.

His hands tremble as he rips open the envelope and dunks the teabag up and down while making small talk. He glances down and yanks out the teabag. Lord, what will he be drinking next?

There's a sudden run on the coffee and tea as people top up for the meeting, and then drift over to the long tables, set out in a T formation tonight. Folded cardboard slogans in black and red script march down the centre of the tables like little pup tents: One Day at a Time. First Things First. What You Hear Here Stays Here. Let Go and Let God.

He sits down beside the young girl, and Jeannie, on her other side, introduces him to Tina. The name suits her, all skin and bone, pulled in on herself trying to disappear. She vibrates all through the meeting, fear or withdrawal or both, her head down, hair hiding her face. Poor little kid. Jeannie pats her quivering hand.

Dave and Susan, a pretty young woman with a hayload of bleached hair and a western-style vest and boots, are chairing tonight. She should have Edwin's shirt. Or he should have her vest. They all rise and say the serenity prayer, and another A.A. meeting begins.

"'Rarely have we seen a person fail who has thoroughly followed our path...'" Dave begins reading the preamble and Matthew tries to listen but his mind wanders. His hand shakes as he lifts his cup and he spills a magenta puddle on the plywood table top. Better than on his crotch, like last time.

He looks around the tables, about thirty-five here tonight. He's starting to know who some of them are. There's Trudy, the meek little housewife who can't stay sober longer than a few weeks, looking sick and sorry again, but who has the guts to keep coming back. He has to admire that.

"'If you want what we have and are willing to go to any lengths to get it...'" Dave stresses "any lengths" – they don't make it sound easy, do they, like maybe you should go train for an astronaut instead. But there's Trudy listening as if her life depends on it, and maybe it does. A young blond guy across the table grins and waggles his fingers at Matthew – Clark, a likeable idiot who went down a hotel waterslide in a tuxedo on his wedding night; and next to him, Bobbie, a good-looking redhead, who got chased around the rectory table by a man of the cloth when she did her fifth step. Matthew doesn't want to think about that step, poking around in the past and telling some stranger all about it.

He's still struggling with the first step. Sometimes he thinks he was just a heavy drinker. Yes, his life had become unmanageable, but so were lots of other people's, and they weren't all alcoholic.

A few more faces around the tables are becoming familiar. He associates them with their stories, which, so far, he finds interesting, but keeps expecting that to pall. He's heard some of them more than once already. Sometimes he finds the quiet ones who didn't get drunk in public and make four-star idiots of themselves in public the most arresting.

They're already passing the basket for rent and coffee and he's missed most of the preamble again. He likes what's read while the basket goes around, though with the rustling of purses and wallets and money clinking into the basket it's always a challenge to hear it:

> Alcoholics Anonymous is a fellowship of men and women who share their experience, strength and hope with each other that they may solve their common problem and help others to recover from alcoholism. The only requirement for membership is a desire to stop drinking.

Very elegantly put. *Alcoholics Anonymous,* the Big Book, as A.A.s affectionately refer to it, is exceptionally well-written, or what he's read of it is. He didn't know what to expect and was relieved by that. The snobbery of the somewhat well-read.

He's still surprised by the laughter around the tables. Many of these people are very funny and he's charmed by them in spite of himself. He never could resist people who made him laugh, drunk or sober. It's one reason he keeps coming back.

Gillian, who lost her job to downsizing, is telling about her interview with a social services worker who said, "Do you think it was wise to write 'F All' in this space for income?" And Gillian said "Well, there wasn't enough room to write 'family allowance.'" That breaks them all up, and Matthew thinks how different Trudy looks when she laughs. Even Tina lifts her head a bit and smiles.

It's a good meeting, he thinks, though his mind keeps wandering. When he's asked to speak he passes. He doesn't want to say he's not sure he's alcoholic and is only staying sober to get his wife back.

Still he likes being here. There's a relief in knowing you weren't the only one who hid your booze in ever more creative places, had an ego as big as the world when you drank, lost chunks of time when you're sure you did reprehensible, maybe even iniquitous, things.

They all laugh as Judy talks about taping tiny booze bottles to her body under her clothes when going out, and driving the car into the side of the house one night and saying "Honey, I'm home" when her husband came running out.

The new, older woman starts to cry when Trudy speaks and she soaks one Kleenex after another, dabbing hopelessly at the tears that keep sliding down her plump, middle-aged cheeks. She tries to speak when asked, but gets no further than "My name is Kathy and I'm..."

Read scared to death, thinks Matthew. Read guilty, humiliated, thirsty. Lonely.

With some surprise he's discovered he felt lonelier when he drank, even with Delia near, than he does now; an existential loneliness just this side of despair that had nothing to do with being alone. Words fail him when he tries to describe that feeling, but people nod when he flounders trying. They know.

Matthew declines an invitation to go for coffee after the meeting, though he usually goes. His mother still hadn't answered the phone when he left home and there was no light in her apartment when he drove by, so he'll feel better if he checks on her. It's a wild, wet, windy night, what else is new, and he wouldn't want to think of her being out in it.

Driving to her apartment, he reflects on the meeting. He liked the discussion meetings better at first, they were more entertaining, less committed, but those words *If you want what we have and are willing to go to any lengths to get it...*keep reverberating in his head. And that means doing the twelve steps, one by one, no matter how difficult, and some look damn difficult indeed.

And what do they have that he doesn't? Many have also lost spouses, jobs, homes, but he has to admit there's something in those rooms he doesn't feel anywhere else. The honesty, yes, that, but also a brand of non-pious spirituality that appeals to him more than he ever would have suspected. He wonders if a lot of people were looking for that in the bottom of a bottle. If he was himself. He smiles, thinking how they always called the bottle opener the church key.

His mother's third-floor apartment is lit now, the warm light from her Tiffany lamp cozy on this stormy night. The building is not far from the water and it's always windier there, the large weeping birch lashing its wet fronds madly around in front of her window, like a frenetic modern dancer pretending to be a tree. Matthew knows his mother likes this kind of night. He's just wondering if he should go up when she appears in front of the window and stands looking out, a lean, angular woman, her hair up. She reaches up to loosen her hair before closing the venetian blinds. She'll be getting ready for bed now.

He pulls away and heads down to the waterfront. He especially likes that drive on nights like this, might even go for a walk. He's developed a paunch, and it's only the luck of the genes that it isn't worse. Also he's getting desperate for a good night's sleep, and a walk on the wild side might help.

He turns down Dallas Road and onto the promontory where the kite flyers congregate on fine breezy days, and where you don't even have to get out of your car to feel close to nature. The waves are crashing on the rocky beach just below and splashing up over the bank and onto the cars as high as the windshields. He parks between two cars whose occupants, two in each, haven't come for the view. Lucky them.

He smokes and rolls the window down enough to hear the big waves crashing in, then rattling out over the shingle to make way for the next. He loves the sound. The suspiration of the sea.

He thinks about the meeting again. About the first step. He hates to admit his life was unmanageable, but drinking cost him his job, didn't it? A job he loved and could once do almost effortlessly. Cover a news story and write it up in minutes in succinct, graceful prose. Cut to the heart of it. Took pride in it and was valued for it. Editors overlooked his drinking as long as it didn't interfere with that.

But it finally did.

"You've gotten sloppy, Matthew, and one thing a newspaperman can't be is sloppy," Jack Connelly said. "Quit drinking and come see me in six months." That was in September. Delia left in October.

Ah, what the hell, deep down he knows it, has known it for a long time. He has measured out his life in whisky glasses. Right from the first drink, he loved it. Was an alcoholic waiting to happen. And watching the dark sea he admits it to himself for the first time. He's not just a heavy drinker, who can quit if there's a reason. He's an alcoholic, like his father. A drunk. He takes a deep breath, filling his lungs like he's just found fresh air after a long time in a stuffy room.

The island of grass circled by the road is covered with gulls, hundreds of them, all hunched down facing away from the wind, their rump feathers ruffled, looking supremely pissed off. Every single one of them. Like an audience of homeowners who've just been told their taxes are going up. He didn't realize a bird could actually look like that, and laughs as he reaches into the glove compartment for a pair of earmuffs and gloves.

He steps out of the car and gasps. The wind yanks his breath away and drills through his rain jacket and the wool sweater beneath. He pulls up his collar and sets out, determinedly marching back on the empty promontory road and turning left onto Dallas Road. His head is freezing already and the earmuffs won't stay on. He sticks them in his pocket and the tumultuous roar of wind and surf assaults his senses, fills his ears. He covers them with his gloved hands and pushes headfirst into the wind. He'll walk as fast as he can to that first bluff, then he's turning back. If this is a taste of La Niña, he hates to think.

He meets only one person on the walk, a little old man being briskly blown along with his English bulldog. The man's clothes and white hair claw madly at him as if they're trying to escape.

"Nasty night," Matthew says.

"Oh no!" the man laughs. "It's luvly! We luv it, don't we Winston?"

Winston glowers up at Matthew like maybe *he* had something to do with his being dragged out on such a night, and maybe Winston should register his displeasure by helping himself to a chunk of Matthew's leg.

To each his own. Back in the car, he's chilled to the marrow, his bald head numb, then tingly and clearheaded as if the wind had blown right through it. He turns on the motor and cranks up the heater, rubs his hands to warm them, and lights a smoke.

His neighbours on either side pull out one after the other, but he stays on, smoking and watching the foaming waves, the dark sea beyond, and the discombobulated gulls.

He feels – okay. Peaceful, almost.

The moulded, orange plastic chair is cold and hard. The stained, brown plastic, paper-matted tray in front of Matthew holds a tipped-over cardboard container of fries leaking ketchup and vinegar, a hamburger discharging runny mayo and mustard, and a cardboard cup of scalding coffee too hot to hold that tastes like it was made last week. The onion rings that look so good leave a peculiar aftertaste after just a few bites. The placemat is a soggy mess, the hamburger impossible to eat without dripping condiments on his chin, shirt, and pants. He balls up yet another messy paper napkin. The table looks like the inside of a dumpster.

He throws down the napkin in disgust, removes the coffee from the tray and gets up to tip the whole sodden mess into the trash container. He asks the zitful young guy at the counter if they happen to have any coffee made today and with a look that says don't hassle me man, the boy takes his time producing a fresh cup.

Back at the table, still hungry, he lights a cigarette and gives some serious thought to his dining habits. This place is convenient but there's a limit. Trying to eat with no plates and cardboard coffee is more depressing than staying home.

Surely there are places where you can get something decent to eat for not much more. He still has debts from his profligate drinking days and his salary as a caretaker on probation, though the word has never been used, doesn't stretch much beyond payments, eating out, and cigarettes, which he can't give up. An old man at a meeting said he stopped drinking and smoking the same day and six weeks later his wife ended up on the psych ward. Matthew knows it would be him.

He hates eating at home alone. Breakfast is okay, he often made his own anyway, and doesn't want much. And lunch is not a problem, slapping together a ham sandwich, a can of soup, something from the deli on Oak Bay Avenue where he sometimes goes for lunch. But it depresses him as evening closes in to sit down alone to eggs and beans, or maybe weiners and Kraft dinner, with a grocery store pie, and so he goes out where there are people and feels better for it. Most of the time.

The place is only about a quarter full, the steady lineup at the counter mostly takeouts. Those with young families seem to be enjoying the experience; some others, like him, look like it's their last meal before the execution chamber.

There are two children in the plexiglass room partly filled with coloured balls. The girl keeps pushing her little brother down under the balls, and he comes up terrified and shrieking, till she tires of it and leaves to sit with her mother, who says "Behave yourself, Billy."

The boy stays on in the little room, lifting handfuls of coloured balls and letting them tumble down over his tear-stained face. His eyes are closed and he is smiling. Was it Flannery O'Connor who said if you survive childhood you have enough to write about for the rest of your life?

An immensely fat man in an *X Files* T-shirt, and with a portable oxygen tank and tubes in his nose, has been trying to talk to everyone within hearing distance. Poor wretch probably doesn't get out much, but when he smiles in Matthew's direction, he nods and looks quickly out the window beside his table. He's just realized there are a lot of fat people in this room, one at almost every table. He's got to stop eating fast food.

It's long ago dark outside, a heavy fog condensing on the window and trickling slowly down the glass. Under the parking-lot lights a lone boy is skateboarding. Over and over he jumps the sidewalk that runs alongside the building, glides past Matthew's table in his big pants and backward cap, and leaps off farther down to slalom around the lampposts and back again. He leaps, he spins, he floats, his body compact, graceful. Each light illuminates a cone of fog so the almost empty parking lot looks like a nomad encampment of ghostly tents, empty except for the solitary figure weaving among them.

Pulling on his quilted vest, Matthew sees a huge ketchup stain on the middle of his shirt. He looks like he's been shot in the chest, for God's sake, and crankily zips his jacket over it.

The car radio jingles, "You deserve a —" He stabs it off.

She'll have a Big Mac, fries, onion rings, and a chocolate shake after her errand, Tessie thinks, waiting for the elevator. When the door pings open the old fool is standing inside. If she didn't need to get to the pet store before closing she'd wait for a later one. Tightening her hold on her handbag she steps in and presses *M*.

The door closes and starts downward.

"Lovely weather," says Mister Reilly. And when Tessie doesn't reply, adds, "for ducks."

Tessie's lips tighten. If he thinks he's going to get a word out of her he's got another think coming.

"You're a widow, aren't you?" he says, out of the blue, surprising her into looking at him. The little runt is smiling at her. "I just thought maybe you might like..." he waggles his eyebrows suggestively.

The elevator door opens and Tessie barges out, knocking Mister Reilly into a corner and his wig offside.

"That woman has a very nasty disposition," he says out loud as he straightens his hair in the empty lobby.

Chapter Five

"**N**o, Michael! Stop! Mom!" Sam screams as Michael drags him, kicking and squirming, toward the workshop. He lunges with all his strength over and over against the iron-strong arm hammerlocked around his neck and upper arms, tries to pry the arm away. Michael pants as they struggle down the brick path.

"It's time you learned who's...boss around here. And I'm going to...ouch, you little shit...I'm going to show you!"

"Mom! Mom!"

In the house, Buddy starts barking.

"Never mind your mother, she can't hear you."

"Why? Why can't she?" He's terrified now. "Where is she?"

Buddy barks frantically, scratching the door. What does he mean, she can't hear him? He kicks Michael's shin, raking his heel down hard and twisting free when Michael swears and grabs his leg. Sam sprints for the house amd almost falls over Buddy who bolts outside when he yanks the door open and shut. She's not downstairs, and he takes the steps two at a time.

"Mom! Mom!"

"What? What's happening? What's wrong with Buddy?"

She's sitting up in bed fully dressed, her face flushed and creased from the pillow. Sam leaps onto the bed as the front door slams, and as Michael bounds up the stairs he rolls off and under the bed in one movement.

Michael stops in the bedroom door.

"Where's Sam?" Now Buddy is outside hysterically barking to get in.

"I don't know. Michael, what's all the yelling about? What's the matter with Buddy?"

"Sam needs to be disciplined, that's what's going on."

"What do you mean, disciplined? What for?"

Sam, on his stomach, heart pounding, can see Michael's dirty sneakers and the frayed bottom of his jeans. He's rubbing his shin.

"Where is that little bugger? He thinks he can do whatever he wants and not suffer the consequences. That's your doing, Kate." He pulls up his pantleg and Sam smiles to see a long scrape seeping blood. "See what he did to me? Where the hell is he?"

"I said I don't know, and you're not going to hit him. What's he done?"

"He went to that party when I said he couldn't. He's got to know who's boss around here or we're in for lots of trouble."

"Michael, I gave him permission to go. He hardly sees his friends any more since you sold my car."

Yah. Sold it and then made sure the truck was gone when they needed it for soccer or anything he wanted to do in town. He lies perfectly still, scarcely breathing.

"You promised not to hit him, Michael."

"I know I did, but I'm following Higher Orders from now on, Kate."

Michael's standing by the bed now, his muddy shoe on a corner of the nice blue quilt Mom made. The faint sour smell of Michael's feet wafts under the bed.

"Kate, you've got to understand. We are supposed to discipline our children when they need it. 'Withhold not correction from the child: for if thou beatest him with a rod he will not die.'"

"*What?* That's horrible."

Jeez, is that why Emerald hits Joey? Michael probably made it up. Outside, Buddy is yelping.

"Proverbs 23. We believe the child should not associate your hand with punishment."

"Oh, we do, do we? And what holds the rod? What's happened to you, Michael? I don't know you any more."

"Kate, you've got to decide and there isn't much time. Are you going to hand that child over to God or to Satan?"

Sam rolls his eyes.

"Oh, Michael! Shut the hell up about Satan."

Yay, Mom! Sam smiles.

"You and Emerald are driving me crazy. First it was books, then movies, then art. Everything I love is against God's will according to you."

God swill, it sounded like and Sam smiles.

"It's because Emerald cares about you and Sam. She's worried because you aren't saved."

Yah, right. Something about Emerald is trying to push its way into Sam's mind.

"...can't stand it, Michael. All that talk about 'the end times,' hinting if not saying it outright, and what's so wonderful about it if you believe most of the people you know are going to...."

Sam has heard it all before. He squeezes his eyes shut hard. What is it about Emerald? Something he just saw, it seems like, and then he remembers. When he was trying to get away from Michael he saw her in the workshop window. She was watching with that weird intent stare, stepping aside when he saw her.

"I'm not a bad person. I believe in God. We had such a good life before." His mother's voice wavers.

No! Damn it, don't cry! Sam breathes in some dust and has to press both fists under his nose to hold in a sneeze. A mean-looking black spider is carefully making its way down the leg of the bed. He hates spiders and this one is big. Not wolf spider big, but big.

"I just want my life to be the way it was."

The springs creak as Michael sits down on the bed. The spider falls the last few inches, maybe from fright, and turns in his direction. His heart lurches.

"But Kate, we lived that way because we didn't know any better."

Damn, it's heading straight for him. He looks frantically around, spies a used Kleenex partly under Michael's shoe and cautiously reaches for it. It's stuck under the shoe and he doesn't dare pull it.

"Well, you're not hitting Sam."

Michael leans over and Sam yanks the Kleenex free and smashes the spider, just inches from his face.

"I'll let it go this time," Michael says. "But, Katie, a good father has to do what God says is right for the child."

"You're not my father," he mouths. "Praise the Lord." He feels a giggling fit coming on, like he used to get when he was little and hiding on somebody, he'd get that tickling feeling in his stomach first and then he'd giggle, that's how they always found him. And when he starts to laugh he still can't stop sometimes. He squeezes the spider hard inside the Kleenex and that helps.

"It's all right, Katie." Michael stands up, both dirty feet on the trailing quilt now. "You're still a baby spiritually but you'll learn."

Sam makes a face.

At the door, Michael stops and Sam sees blood on his pantleg. "You don't have to get up. Emerald will fix dinner."

"No, she's not. I'm making dinner," Kate says firmly, swinging her legs out of bed.

"Suit yourself. I'd think you'd appreciate it the way you're feeling." Michael's I-can't-do-anything-to-please-you voice. "I'm going back to work now. Where's the methiolate?"

"In the bathroom cupboard. Where it always is."

As Michael turns to leave, Sam makes a gun with his hand and points it at his leg. Kerpow!

When the outside door slams, Buddy scrabbles, yipping up the stairs. Sam wriggles out on his back as Buddy skids into the room and starts licking him all over his face.

"Whoa! Yuck!" He covers his face with his hands, rolling over on his stomach as Buddy's cold nose snuffles and snorts in his bare neck, tickling like crazy. He rolls around on the floor, laughing. His mom laughs too.

He pulls himself up and sits beside her, pulling the quilt up off the floor and brushing at the dirt from Michael's shoe. He loves the colour of it, indigo, Mom said. He likes the word, too. Buddy presses himself between them, his chin on the bed and they take turns stroking his head.

"Geez. Thanks, Mom. That was scary."

She presses her lips together. "Michael's being such a jerk. He's not himself anymore."

Sam's not sure about that. Thinks maybe Michael is more himself than ever.

She's feeling around under the bed for her shoes, and he reaches them and hands them to her. She stands up and tucks in her faded black T-shirt, then goes to the dresser and pulls a purple hair thing through her crackling, fly-away hair.

Down in the yard, Emerald's car starts up and Sam looks out the window. Joey is standing up crying in the front seat, his pale, despairing face and open mouth pressed against the window, his eyes squeezed shut, and Emerald's gunning the motor like she's mad. Joey doesn't want to go, Sam thinks. He's scared.

"She should make him wear a seat belt," he says. But he turns away from the window, feeling lighter. Maybe they're going to town to eat.

"Can we have chili for supper, Mom?" She looks better now. Not so pale.

"That's a good idea," she says, bending her head sideways to put on a silver earring with dangly purple beads. "Get some hamburger out of the freezer, okay? I'll stick it in the microwave."

"Okay. Want me to chop the onions?" She always cries but he doesn't.

"Yes, please. I'll be right down."

"Come on, Bud. Let's go!"

Supper isn't too bad, Michael doesn't say anything and that's a relief, and Sam talks his mother into going for a walk after supper.

"I think I will, Michael. It's stopped raining and I haven't had a walk for ages."

Michael just shrugs and takes the Bible down, his expression saying you'll be sorry when The Day comes.

"Pray for us sinners," Sam says when they're outside, and his mom laughs. And it's almost like old times, out walking with her, throwing sticks for Buddy to chase. Talking nonsense. Making her laugh. That night he sleeps better than he has for quite awhile.

When he gets up in the morning, he sees the TV is gone. He sighs. Michael's got one in his shop so it's just more of his meanness. He's already taken his radio/cassette player away. What else is he going to take?

But in a way it's kind of exciting, too, trying to figure out what the enemy will do next. And what you'll do if he does this or that. Like a war.

When Michael drives him to school the next morning Sam expects a lecture but it doesn't come. In fact, Michael starts asking him stuff about school, science particularly, and if they study evolution. Something about the way he asks makes Sam uneasy, but he can't think why.

"Yeah, of course. It's the best part."

"Except it's just humanist propaganda."

Sam has no idea what he's talking about. "Oh?" he says. Whatever.

"W-E-A-L-T-H-Y. There," Claire Kelly says. "Double letter *W*, twenty points." She smiles gleefully as she enters her new score. "Admit it," she says. "I'm very good at this game."

"Modest, too." Matthew laughs, looking at the new configuration on the board. "All right, W-A-T-E-R-Y. Triple letter *Y*. Take that."

He sits back with his arms crossed, smiling at her. His mother is neat in a grey skirt and rose cardigan. Still dressing like a schoolteacher. The wallpapered dining room, with its rosy drapes and old Tiffany fringed lamp on the sideboard casting a warm glow, is Matthew's favourite room.

"I bet that lamp would bring you a couple of thousand now," he says.

"Maybe. Your name is on the bottom of it."

"Thanks, Ma."

And sitting there, an old man himself, he has a glimpse of the loss he will feel when she dies. Beside the lamp are university graduation photos of himself and Blair and a framed enlarged snapshot of his father laughing, that young himself.

"Y-O-K-E-L. Double word 24." She hasn't let a sentimental moment slow down her game.

"L-I-M-P-I-D," he shoots back

"I suppose you think you're smart," she says.

He laughs. It's what she would say when he'd bring home an A grade.

"Mom, have you heard anything from Kate lately?" He sits back, reaching in his shirt pocket for his cigarettes.

"She called me on my birthday. I thought she sounded kind of down."

Oh, damn, he forgot again. It was Delia who always

remembered. "I'm sorry, Ma. I'll take you out someplace nice for Sunday dinner."

"Oh, good," she says, waving her hand to dismiss another birthday, as if she has innumerable left.

"I hope she's not depressed. She gets that way sometimes." He gets up to put the match in the ashtray on the sideboard. Then picks it up and walks around a bit. Damn rain. His hip pains like a toothache.

"I know. She feels bad about you and her mother, of course."

"She's not the only one," he says, stopping to look out the rain-wet window.

"And you're not the only two," says his mother, then quickly goes on, "Blair called and said to say hello."

"Oh? What's new in Saskatoon? How's the judge?"

"Sitting at a trial in Regina this week. He'd just come in from shovelling snow. They're having a mild spell," she said.

Matthew feels a sudden stab of envy. Of his brother who always does things right. Who has a happy marriage. Who lives where the sun shines. He thinks of Blair shovelling snow, sees it sparkling in the sunlight off the end of the shovel. "Do you miss the snow, Ma?" he asks, stretching and sitting down again.

"No. It's the sun I miss." She arranges and rearranges the tiles on her board.

He sighs. "Yeah, that, too. I might have to move back sometime."

"You might," she says noncommittally.

He ponders things for a bit. "Maybe they're not getting along," he says.

His mother looks up, puzzled. "Blair and Jan?"

"No. Kate and Michael."

"I don't know, but Michael worries me with this funda-mentalist thing. You know how he goes overboard about everything."

"He's a goddamn fanatic, you mean. That's scary stuff for a kid." The window rattles in a sudden gust of rain.

"I know. And did you know Michael has built a cabin on their property? For some friend who's moved there with her child. Or children."

He turns quickly to look at her. "No. I didn't. That's damned odd if you ask me. What does Kate think about it?"

"She didn't say. She said the woman — I think her name was —" she raises her eyebrows *"Emerald,* she said her little boy was sweet."

"Emerald? God, why does the word 'commune' spring to mind?" He gets up again and goes into the kitchen for coffee, taking the cigarette and ashtray with him.

"People aren't living in communes any more, are they?" his mother calls over the sounds of him rattling around in the kitchen.

"I don't know. But you know up there where they live is a mecca for back-to-the-land types."

He comes back with two cups of coffee and sets them down, stubbing out his cigarette as he slides into the chair and reaches for another. His mother looks about to say something, then changes her mind.

"It worries the hell out of me lately, Ma, them living so far from anywhere. What if Sam had an accident? Or if Kate needed help for herself?"

Why she would need that he doesn't know, but the idea

occurs to him a lot lately. As if to underscore his thoughts, an ambulance howls its way down Cook Street. A hard gust of wind whips the sodden birch fronds into feverish motion, wetly brushing the window like the chamois strips in a car wash, before dropping out of sight. He can't concentrate on the game and, apologizing for his restlessness, gets up to pace the living room. He'll have to leave soon. It comes on him suddenly, even here where he's most comfortable.

Matthew prowls around the living room, cup in hand. His mother doesn't comment, she always knew when to be quiet, a lesson he wishes he'd learned from her. Over the haunting notes of Charlie Parker's "Past Midnight" on the radio he can still hear the distant roar of the rain.

He sighs. "I have to get up there soon and see what's going on. Delia and I should go, really."

"Yes, you should," his mother says. "Now, will you please sit down and stay down so we can finish this game? I've finally got a word that starts with Z." She places three tiles on the board.

"Z-E-B-U." she says.

"Some sort of animal, right?" He sits down and hikes his chair forward, glad of the distraction of the game.

She reads aloud from the Scrabble dictionary: "'Zebu. A domesticated bovine mammal of Asia and Africa, having a prominent hump on the shoulders and a large dewlap.'" She laughs, waggling the loose skin under her chin. "Actually, it sounds a lot like me."

Matthew looks at his mother. She still has the bright, intelligent blue eyes he remembered as a child. He can't remember her ever getting angry with him about anything except his drinking. And the way he treated Delia, which often came down to the same thing.

"Why are you looking at me like that? Is my face dirty?"

"You don't have a prominent hump."

"Oh, I suppose that passes for flattery at my age."

Looking down at his letters, consonants, every one, he blinks away the tears that have suddenly filled his eyes. They ambush him a lot lately: the sweet excitement in a child's face, a whiff of Delia's perfume on a passing woman, the memory of his young father and mother whirling around to some lively music on the record player. He's turning into a touchy-feely Iron John man, for God's sake, he'll be out waving his dick around over a bonfire next thing he knows, bonding with the boys.

He's just *feeling* again, as they say at A.A., without the booze to stifle it. All he knows is he's up and down like a yo-yo – well, mostly down – and he doesn't like it one damn bit. But it's like it or lump it when you're sober, isn't it?

Driving home through the dark, wet streets he thinks of his father, a dear Irishman with a raging thirst, who lost the battle with booze on Vancouver's skid row when Matthew was sixteen. He was going to go there that summer and find his father – rescue him for his mother, but his father didn't wait.

The rain has stopped and thick fog rolls in, shrouding his windshield, the streetlights, everything. At an interminable red light he's stopped beside a lighted shop window bristling with angels blowing golden trumpets.

Oh Christ. Christmas.

Back home he checks his messages.

Hi Matt, it's Edwin. Just called to say I hope you're having a good week. Mine is going great. Call me any time. Goodbye and have a great day.

Hey Matthew. Marty. Haven't seen you around. Come by and have one on the house. Coffee, that is. Hey, I'll even make it a cappuccino.

He smiles at Marty's message, remembering how surprised he was to see the voluble, witty proprieter of the local fish and chip shop at an A.A. meeting. They're everywhere, he's beginning to realize, and he likes bumping into them unexpectedly: clerking at the Bay, lending money at the bank, roofing a house, behind the dentist's drill. Likes the instant rapport that, though sometimes it's just a wave and a friendly greeting, leaves you feeling less alone.

He smokes a cigarette before pushing himself up and out the door, taking the steps to the third floor. He does that every night now, and notices it's getting infinitesimally easier. He only has to pull himself up the last few steps by the railing now. He sure as hell doesn't feel like it tonight but trudging around the boring halls is better than staring at the ceiling in the dark.

Being with his mother has him turning over old bones in his head again. His mother and his sixteen-year-old self riding the bus from Saskatoon to Vancouver, to the small, fly-specked room at the top of a long flight of narrow, graffiti-enclosed stairs where Patrick Kelly died with eleven cents in his pocket. Matthew wondered how his father ever made it up or down those stairs drunk.

He sees the room in his mind as clearly as he saw it when they opened the door forty-four years ago. A neatly made bed covered with an afghan crocheted by some colour-blind person. On a small oak table a tidy stack of dog-eared paperbacks – John D. MacDonalds mostly, a large "25" scribbled in black felt pen on their covers – and a book of Dylan Thomas poems. Also a huge jar, like the ones holding pickled eggs in bars, inexplicably full of amber water with used tea bags suspended in it.

The window over the bed looked out on the asphalt roof of the Chinese café next door and the air coming in past the ragged blind smelled of rancid oil and ancient chop suey, but at least it let in some light. In the closet his father's pitifully few clothes, a plaid wool jacket, too warm for summer, not warm enough for winter, and certainly not the garment for that sodden part of the world.

As they stood there his mother took Matthew's cold hand in her strong, warm one.

"I want you to take a good look at this room, Matthew," she said. "Your father was a good man. He didn't need to die alone in a place like this. Think of this room if you're ever tempted to drink."

She didn't know she was already too late.

The halls are empty, all the doors shut, the faint sound of a TV behind several of them. Old people and insomnia are synonymous, he's learned. Frost was not the only one acquainted with the night. He finishes the third floor and takes the stairs down to the second.

Going home on that bus he read the John D. McDonalds, wanting some connection, however tenuous, to his father, and the Dylan Thomas poems, encountering for the first time the father poem. Did his father rage against the dying of the light? At sixteen he was sure he would have. Now he thinks not.

And it feels a lot like grieving, all this thinking. For Delia, the love of his life. For his father, gone so long. And for his old friend, Booze, who could always be counted on to make it all go away.

Sometimes that room at the top of the stairs beckoned.

"Mmmm, nice wine, Liz," Maurice says.

"Good. I'm glad you like it."

"What is it? No, let me guess. One of the new American wines?"

"I think so. I just asked somebody in the liquor store since I don't buy it much." She does, but she's not telling him that.

"You might try the Portuguese next time. It has a bit more bouquet...hmmm, more everything, really."

"Oh."

"Of course the good stuff is quite expensive."

"Oh."

"You're not offended? I only thought you'd like to know, if you're entertaining."

"No, no, of course I'm not offended, Maurice. Why should I be offended? Left to my own devices, I go for the porch climber every time."

"You are offended."

"I'll learn to live with it."

"Oh, come here, you silly girl. I'm sorry. This is quite good wine, really."

"Yes, it is. And I'm going to have another glass of it."

"Oh? Well, go ahead. I can't stay that long today."

"Less than your usual hour, you mean?"

"Well, I know it's Saturday, but we're going out for dinner to celebrate Sean's touchdown this afternoon. That'll cost me an arm and a leg the way those big lugs eat."

Oh, God, did he really say big lugs?

Maurice gets up and goes into the kitchen where Liz is pouring herself another glass of wine, coming up behind her and nuzzling her neck.

"Oh, come on, honey, don't be mad at Maurice. You know I think about you all the time."

"Don't say things like that, Maurice. It insults my intelligence."

But he's running his hands up and down her front and, hating herself for it, she turns around.

Not more than twenty minutes later, Maurice is frantically looking for his plaid flannel boxers.

"Oh, no," Liz thinks. His underwear. Now he'll really think she's a pervert.

"Maurice, you might not believe this, but" – she goes to the closet and reaches his socks from where she threw them – "I found these lying on the floor in the doorway right after you left last time."

He's sitting on the edge of the bed with his hair standing on end and the sheet draped around his portly midsection, like some modest Roman senator at a bacchanal.

"You what?"

"I found them. Like this." And she lays them out in the doorway, smoothing them down, then sits back on her haunches in her black satin slip and looks at him. "I think I have a poltergeist."

His expression is unreadable. "You surely don't believe that."

"As a matter of fact, I do. I know it sounds crazy to someone like you. But that's where they were. You can believe or not. Right there, only flatter, as if they'd been ironed." She laughs. She feels a bit giddy, the way she often feels after sex with Maurice. "Think about it, Maurice. Neither of us has left the room. If you don't believe me, look around. Maybe they're under the bed. In the dust." It feels liberating to talk to Maurice this way.

"I never leave my shorts under the bed." He crosses his arms across his chest.

"Well, no doubt they'll appear after you're gone. Hanging from the lampshade, maybe." She sits down on the bedroom chair.

Maurice looks hopeful when she suddenly gets up and leaves the room as if she's just thought of where they might be. But she returns with a new package of Matinee cigarettes and matches and sits down in the chair to rip the cellophane off, open the pack and light up.

"I didn't know you smoked," he says disapprovingly.

"Well, you don't know much about me, do you, Maurice. Actually, I don't smoke. These have been in the freezer since I quit."

"Why didn't you tell me before?" He reaches for his shirt on the chair and she hands it to him.

"Well, I haven't seen you till today, and the 'cocktail hour' wasn't long enough to go into it. If I'd known your shorts

were going to disappear I'd have told you the minute you
walked in the door, since I'm sure you think I'm spiriting
away your undies for lascivious purposes."

Maurice sighs. "No, of course I don't," he says unconvinc-
ingly, as if he's not quite sure what the word means. He
reaches for his pants and pulls them on, wincing as wool
seams instead of flannelette greet his privates. "I don't know
what to think."

"I don't either. It's something to do with this place, and
I'm not afraid of ghosts but don't really want one for a
roommate." She drags on the cigarette, which is making her
dizzy. "Did Sylvia ever tell you about odd things happening
here?"

Maurice's expression changes suddenly, becomes – what?
Momentarily alarmed?

"Did she say anything to you about things disappearing?
About sensing some kind of presence?"

"Who? You mean Sylvia McCracken? No! Of course not.
I hardly knew her." And he shakes his head as if to dislodge
something and gets dressed with the speed of someone who's
just heard the fire alarm. Then gives Liz a hasty peck on the
cheek and is gone. Jiggling down the stairs thinking, oh my
God, I can't go back there. I thought she was so sensible.
Where can I get some shorts before dinner. *Poltergeist!* What
bloody nonsense.

Liz goes into the kitchen and knocks back the glass of
wine she poured earlier, then picks up the bottle to pour
another. And lights a dry, evil-tasting Matinee.

In spite of the wine she feels a sudden chill, and looks to
see if the kitchen window is open. It isn't. Of course she's

wearing only her slip, but it's as if suddenly someone opened a freezer door. She wraps her arms around herself.

She should go and put on her chenille bathrobe, or better yet, warm pants and sweater, but she doesn't want to go back into the bedroom. She curls up in the armchair, wrapping herself in the rose mohair throw and gazes out the window, sipping. Odd that it only happens when Maurice is here.

She shivers and pulls the throw closer.

Poor baby. He had a moment there, didn't he? A moment when he wondered if I had something to do with his disappearing lingerie. But it passed quickly, of course. Everything passes quickly with Maurice, and I knew that all along, not being a woman given to illusions. Deep down, Maurice is shallow. How bloody like him to take up with someone in my old apartment. Saves him having to learn a new address when he has so little time.

Except for the day I left, euphemistically speaking, though leaving was the last thing on my mind. Maurice's wife was away and he had magnanimously consented to letting me prepare a dinner for us at my place. And I, foolish woman that I was, was happily planning a romantic dinner for two. I had never had more than two consecutive hours with Maurice, usually less; he was almost as bad as the one before him, a gynecologist who would have preferred me draped and in stirrups, I'm sure. The trouble was, and I'd have had my fingernails pulled out rather than let him know, I fell in love with Maurice. God knows he didn't deserve it, but when did that have anything to do with it?

So this dinner was important to me, and I hurried off to the liquor store just a few blocks away for a bottle of the Portuguese wine he liked and a nip into Safeway's for sour cream and mushrooms — he'd requested steak and baked potatoes with sour cream, how original, and he fifty pounds overweight and just recovering from heart surgery. Well, let his wife put him on a diet, I thought, it wasn't up to me. So off I went.

I bought the wine first, then detoured through Safeway for fresh mushrooms and was tripping back home as happy as if I was in my right mind, and was crossing Foul Bay Road at a walk light when a car speeding around the corner knocked me into kingdom come. Literally. Just like that I left without a murmur. Well, maybe a polite, surprised oh!

The man was drunk, I saw that from a vantage point just above the trees somewhere, looking down on the whole frantic scene. There I was, propped inelegantly against an oak tree where I landed with my head leaning over at a very peculiar angle with my skirt rucked up and my legs every which way in knee-high pantyhose, ghastly, unflattering things, still holding the bottle of wine, unbroken, though oddly missing its paper bag. One black patent shoe was still on my foot, the other lay in the middle of the road marinating in sour cream with a sprinkling of mushrooms. More mushrooms dotted the road.

My favourite shoes. How many times in my life had I seen just one shoe somewhere and puzzled over how someone could lose just one shoe. Surely all those people weren't hurled into eternity by a rogue car.

Such a lot of commotion: the drunk man crying and pleading with me to speak to him — I felt sorry for him, actually, I've driven with a few under my belt myself on occasion; the woman who ran into her house to phone 911 and then came back out to pull down my skirt, bless her heart, it was such a kind gesture from one woman to another, and she wept as if it was her sister sitting there. Shock, I suppose.

Then the police, and the handsome young ambulance driver who, thank goodness, knew I was beyond the indignity of resuscitation. From my point of view it looked a bit like a Norman Rockwell illustration if you left me out of it: the student with the backpack peering into the car; people standing and pointing this way and that reconstructing the accident; the woman with pruning shears looking over her fence, the old man in the Tilley hat — apparently a witness — talking to the police; the girl with the bicycle. Of course, Norman wouldn't have a dead woman leaning against a tree, it would be just a fenderbender with a good-natured-looking tow-truck driver scratching his head and, oh yes, a kid and a dog. No jaws of life for Norman.

No revenge in Norman's world either.

I see now that revenge is vastly underrated. A healthy dose of revenge is good for the soul, and I should know. Not anything too nasty, certainly, that's not what I'm talking about, though I'm sure there are lots who would. I don't want Maurice to die because I kicked the bucket making a special trip to the liquor store for his damned Portuguese wine, I just want to puncture his complacency. No, more than that. I want to humiliate him.

It serves him right for taking up with Liz. I introduced them not long before I handed in my notice, metaphorically speaking. I don't blame Liz, she didn't know we were lovers. She's too good for him, too.

If you have to die, I suppose it's a good way to go, but it pissed me off. I'd have liked a little notice. Some time to do things right. Clean out my bathroom cupboard for one thing. Wear pantyhose instead of knee-highs.

Oh well, it could be worse. At least if you aren't ready to leave you get to hang around for awhile and have a little fun. Who would have thought it?

Chapter Six

His mother looks shocked. "Sam. Are you sure?"

"Yes. I saw her through the window. She punched him right in the stomach. That's why he cried so hard last night." He's sitting beside her on the bed. "I bet it was her idea for Michael to beat me up."

"Oh, no. Surely not."

"It's true, Mom. She was watching from the workshop when I was trying to get away from him. She wanted him to, I could tell." He cracks his knuckles, he can't seem to stop doing it and is afraid he's getting weird, too. Hammering starts up somewhere on the other side of the bedroom wall and his mom squeezes her eyes shut as if that will shut it out. "Does he have to do that all the time?" Sam says. "It's making me crazy."

"I know, Sam. Me too." She's sitting on the edge of the bed rubbing at a deep groove in her face with trembling fingers. "I'll have to talk to Michael about Emerald. I've never seen her hit Joey."

"She doesn't want you to, that's why."

He wants her to get up, damn it. He's been home all day hating the way the house feels when she's asleep. It's pouring out and the house is gloomy. It even smells gloomy.

"It's true, Mom. I think she'd do anything. It's like she's trying to take over the place. She's weird and you know it, wearing that long Jesus dress and cross, and those people moving out here after Christmas are gonna be weird, too." Sam hears his voice going up and up and tries to stop but he can't. "I don't want to live with a bunch of people who talk about the end of the world all the time."

He gets up and flops into a wicker chair, banging his head on the sloping ceiling. "Ow! Fuck! I hate this fucking place!" he yells, jumping up and rubbing his head. It really hurts and he's mad at her too. The hammering suddenly gets louder and he grabs a stick off the sill that's for propping up the window and bangs on the wall with it. There is a sudden surprised silence on the other side and then it starts up again, louder than ever. Buddy, snoozing by the bed, gives a belated woof, then sits up and yawns.

"Shhh. Calm down, Sam. That won't help. And I feel the same as you." She doesn't say anything about his language.

"You do? Do you ever wonder if they're right, Mom?" He holds his breath, waiting for her answer. Buddy looks at her too, his head cocked, like he's been wondering about Armageddon himself. Like where do the dogs go?

She pauses. "No. Most of the time I don't."

"You mean you do sometimes?" He cracks his knuckles. He does, more than sometimes, actually, thinks what if it's true, all that stuff? Those horrible beasts and flying devils. The four horsemen; for some reason they're the worst. He had a nightmare one night where they stepped one by one out of the woods and into the clearing around the house. It still makes him shudder.

She sighs. A long, tired sigh. "No. I don't."

Feeling the bump on his head, he remembers when he liked this A-frame house, like living in a hut, or tent, he thought. Now he wants to push the dark sloping walls away. Take an axe to them. His head aches and he's tired. He's tired all the time, it seems like. He paces around the room like something caged.

She's feeling around under the bed for her socks, "Don't worry, Sam, the world isn't coming to an end any time soon." She pulls on the red smiley socks he gave her for her birthday. "People have been talking about that forever. Groups heading for the hills to wait for the world to end. They all had to come back."

He stops pacing. "Jeez. I didn't know that. And you don't think you have to think like them or go to hell?"

"No. They believe that if you haven't asked Jesus to save you, you're doomed. Even if you've never heard of Christianity, some think. Who could believe that? God isn't stupid."

"Yah, I've thought about that, too," he says, "like if you're a Buddhist in China, or somebody living in a jungle somewhere. They believe in something that's just as good for them."

"Yes. It's all one God, Sam, just with different names."

All one God. Yah. As soon as she says it he knows it must be right. It's the only way that makes any sense.

"And I don't believe in Hell, either. Don't crack your

knuckles, Sam." Sam closes his eyes. Buddy is asleep again.

She gets up and starts to straighten the quilt on the bed. She stands a moment deep in thought, hugging a pillow, before putting it on the bed and pulling the quilt over it.

"Let's just see what happens, Sam. Michael goes overboard on things. He always has."

Sam perches on the windowsill, gripping it on either side. "Mom?"

"What?"

"Do you think I could go live with Grandpa?"

She looks shocked. "Oh, no. Grandma's not there. And Grandpa might start drinking again."

"He wouldn't if I was there, and I'm old enough to look after myself anyway. If he did I could go to Grandma's. Or Gran's."

He grips the windowsill hard, trying desperately not to cry. He's thirteen now. A sudden gust of rain hits the window and he jumps. "Shit!" he says, swiping his cheeks with the heels of his hands. "I do, you know. Hate it here." He turns and stares bleakly out the window at the dark sky. It's only four o'clock but it's dark already. Emerald's light is on. He reaches over and switches on the bedside lamp, a dim puddle of light in the dark-walled room. She hasn't answered.

"You could go, too," he says, not looking at her. "You don't like it either." He gets up. He has to get out of this dark, smothery room. He doesn't feel like that about his room, even though it's smaller. There's more light and the fish tank and all the posters help.

She comes over and leans her forehead against his, he's as tall as she is now. Her wild curly hair tickles his cheek. "No. I can't do that. I'm married to Michael, honey, this is our home."

"Yah, so why did you let him spoil it?"

"I know. I tried. But he wouldn't listen."

She goes back to the dresser, turns on the beaded antique lamp and picks up her lipstick. Swiping it on her bottom lip, she turns to look at him. "Sam, if it makes you feel any better, I don't like Michael now either," she says. "And I hate what's going on as much as you do. If things don't get better, we'll leave."

"Mom! They're going to get worse. When can we go?"

She caps the lipstick, pressing her lips together. Then, after a moment, "We'll leave when I'm feeling better. I can't face it right now. This has been our home."

"Well, it isn't any more. It's just his." And Emerald's, he wants to say, but he doesn't.

She sighs. "I promise. Now why don't you go do your homework?" She pushes her feet purposefully into her old green clogs. "I'll be down soon."

But after Sam leaves, Kate sits back down on the bed and stares out the window. Sliding off one shoe, she puts a stockinged foot on the sleeping dog's side and rolls him slowly back and forth, floppy as a rag doll.

She sits there for a long time.

Chapter Seven

Matthew stands in the furnace room with his hands on his hips. It seems they aren't going to postpone Christmas this year in consideration of his delicate feelings. He'll have to get through it somehow. Preferably sober. And now he's got to decorate the bloody place. They always put the tree up early, they say. If he had his way it'd go up Christmas Eve and down Boxing Day.

Where's our Christmas tree? asked Mister Reilly. Can't have Christmas without a tree, huffed General Schwarzkopf. Even brisk, no-nonsense Edna Burton wants a Christmas tree. And when Bo Peep heard them discussing it, her little face lit up and she said, Oh, is it Christmas? I love the smell of a Christmas tree.

So here he is, crashing and fumbling around in the dim furnace room for the artificial tree that won't smell like anything but dust and the decorations Delia told him were on the top shelf in the back when he pocketed his pride and called her. She laughed and said, I'd like to see you decorating that Christmas tree, Matthew. Well, you're welcome to come and watch, he replied sourly. He always liked watching Delia decorate the tree, giving her the benefit of his advice with a glass of rum and eggnog to sharpen his critical eye.

He finally spots a large brown box with the message "8 Foot Christmas Tree" printed on the side. He supposes that might be a clue, but with Delia you never knew. He drags down the heavy box and carts it out to the lobby, depositing it on the ugly marble-topped coffee table, and goes back for the ornaments. Four big boxes of them. He's not decorating the Empress Hotel for God's sake. Or the White House.

Back in the lobby he dusts off his hands. When he opens the box, half its contents spring out like a jack-in-the-box, like maybe it morphed in the dark into a 16-foot tree. Gingerly he feels through the stiff branches, half expecting to encounter the mouse whose droppings decorated the shelf. The tree stand isn't there – nor is the mouse – and it's not in the other boxes.

Back in the furnace room he feels around the shelves in the half-dark with no luck. That sneaky old miser Desmond Funk replaces the single light bulb with a 60 watter every time, turning the large furnace room into a gloomy cave. Matthew finally finds a small metal tree stand, or the parts for one, in a plastic bag hanging on the wall behind the furnace. Trust Delia. She never put anything back in a logical place. He doesn't know how she's been an operating room nurse so long. Head nurse, at that.

In the lobby as he's sorting through enough tree branches for a rain forest he sees Liz Wright fumbling for her keys outside. He opens the door for her.

"Oh, hi," she says. "Thanks, Mister Kelly."

"Matthew, please," he says. She takes off a damp red scarf and shakes out her dark hair, cut shorter than he remembered.

She's wearing handsome silver hoop earrings. He's always liked hoop earrings on a woman.

"All right." She smiles at him. "And I'm Liz." She looks around at the piles of ugly branches molting on the carpet. "You look like you could use some help."

"Are you offering?"

"Sure."

"Well.... But you're just getting home from work, you don't want to get into a mess like this, do you, even though I can't think of anything I'd like better."

She raises her eyebrows. "That bad, eh?"

Shrugging off her navy raincoat, she sits down on the generic lobby couch with her dark-stockinged legs crossed. Very good legs indeed. In a short-skirted grey suit with a red poinsettia pin on the lapel she is a damned attractive woman. "Good Lord, this must be some tree."

"Eight feet, it says, but someone's been watering it in the furnace room. I hate artificial trees, don't you?"

"As a matter of fact, yes."

"But no way is Mister Funk going to spring for a new tree every year."

She laughs. "He hasn't sprung for one for at least thirty years, I'd say. This one's an antique."

"Like its owner. What do Christmas trees cost these days?"

"Depends on the size. Fifty dollars, maybe more for one big enough." She eases off one black pump and massages her foot. "You'd need a pretty large one for here."

"Well, Christmas is depressing enough without this ugly thing. Would you help me pick out a real honest-to-God tree?" He's surprised and a bit alarmed at what he's just said. "No, that's not fair. You offer a hand and I grab for the whole arm."

"No, you haven't. I'd like to. Really. Just let me get changed first."

While she's gone Matthew tries to wrestle the tree back in and close the box, and wrestle with his sudden attack of nervousness. Don't be silly, you haven't proposed to the woman. You're just going to buy a Christmas tree.

They find a tree lot and pick out a nice, bushy, eight-foot tree, and the guy at the lot kindly offers to have his teenaged helper deliver it.

"I'm hungry, and you must be, too," he says. "Let's go and eat somewhere, shall we?"

The evening is mild and misty, the kind of evening that reminds you why you live in Victoria and not wherever you came from. They head off to Marty's Ye Olde Fish & Chip Shoppe where they both order the sole from Don, Marty's bleached-blonde waiter, as gay as a tree full of chickadees. It's not far from the Kensington and Matthew eats there often, joined for coffee when business is slow by Marty, an ex-merchant-navy man and raconteur of the highest order. If Matthew ever gets around to getting an A.A. sponsor, he'll probably ask Marty.

To his relief, Liz doesn't order a drink.

"How long have you lived at the Kensington?" Matthew asks.

"Seven years. I moved there after my divorce."

Seven years. A long time for a woman like her to live alone.

"But I just moved to the corner suite awhile ago. For the light."

"A damn scarce commodity around here, if you ask me."
Don brings their coffee.

"Seven years," he says. "Does it get any easier?"

"It takes time, but yes, it does. You know the old adage, time heals."

"I hope so." He hopes that didn't sound as self-pitying as he thinks it did.

She doesn't comment. Just smiles. "Where are you from, Matthew?" He's attractive, this man, she thinks, in a kind of depressed bloodhound sort of way. He looks a lot like Patrick Stewart, Captain Picard on *Star Trek*, or would if he looked like he ever slept.

"Saskatchewan. Saskatoon. And I miss it a lot lately. I actually envied my brother the other day for shovelling snow. Do you mind if I smoke?"

She shakes her head. The cigarette immediately makes him feel more comfortable. That and the strong coffee. He reaches for the green marble fish-shaped ashtray probably acquired by Marty on a well-oiled shore leave in some exotic country. He served as a cook in the Merchant navy for years. Various fish prints liven up the smoke-darkened wood walls. A couple of tables over, the Explorers wave "yoohoo" at their caretaker and Liz before deciding what to have to drink.

Mrs. Thompson, the little one, is smiling up at Don, "Oh, I think I'll have a seizure," she says.

To his credit, Don doesn't crack a smile but lifts an eyebrow at Matthew. "Right!" he says, writing on his pad and turning to Mrs. Erickson. "And what about you, Ma'am? Would you like a Caesar also?"

They both keep a straight face. "Where do you work, Liz?"

"At the public library downtown. I look after the fine arts department. Or try to."

"Oh? I'm there quite often. I've become a reading room habitué."

She smiles. "Oh? You and the man who knows the royal family, eh?"

He laughs. "Right. And the one who's always grumbling and glaring at everybody and shuffling the newspapers into piles."

"Do you know Annie, the little bag lady?"

"Oh, yes. She says she doesn't think that man knows the royal family, he doesn't look like somebody they'd know. And I agree with her."

Liz laughs. Over her shoulder Matthew sees Marty leaning in the kitchen doorway in his white apron, a large spoon in his hand, waggling his eyebrows at him. Matthew ignores him.

"I'll drop by sometime and see if you're free for coffee."

"I hope you will."

After rhubarb and strawberry pie on the house, and a cup of coffee with Marty, they take their leave.

Back in the Kensington lobby, he takes one look at the tree and the tree stand and knows that never the twain shall meet.

"Damn! Of course it won't work. And where do I even look for one this time of night?" He's already envisioning a total disaster, but before he can get too worked up about it Liz goes down to the storage area and comes back with a large one with a flat round base they fill with water from the laundry-room tub. On the second attempt they get the tree screwed in straight, and Matthew sighs with relief. In his experience, the worst is over.

He tests the ancient lights, which amazingly still work and

are quite beautiful, shaped like moons and stars, while Liz unwraps the ornaments. She takes one look at the bald, tarnished tinsel and drives to the nearest drugstore for new. And Matthew starts to cautiously enjoy himself.

Once the lights and tinsel are on, the tree becomes a magnet, people on their way in or out stopping to watch awhile and maybe hang a ratty old decoration or point out bare spots in need of one. Edna Burton brings a big pot of tea and shortbread cookies. Mister Reilly brings some very good Christmas cake. "Mother made it," he says, which sets everybody thinking how old she must be, and suddenly it feels like a party. Patrick goes and gets a large treetop star.

"I'm going away for Christmas and and it's too big for a small tree anyway. I'll donate it to the place."

"It'll save the Boss making one out of tinfoil," Matthew says.

Patrick laughs. "So it will. So it will."

The Explorers come in, Mrs. Thompson's face flushed like she might have had another seizure after they left. When Liz asks if they enjoyed their dinner they assure her they enjoyed it immensely; they enjoy everything immensely as far as Matthew can tell. He's reminded of something he saw once, a graph based on a huge survey that showed old women to be the happiest people, and old men the most miserable — a direct inversion of where they were in their twenties and thirties. He's beginning to believe it.

As if to put paid to that theory, the elevator stops and discharges a glowering Tessie Thatcher, carrying a laundry basket.

"Isn't this a lovely tree, Mrs. Thatcher?" calls Mrs. Thompson.

"Hmmph!" Tessie replies, without looking, and disappears into the laundry room.

When Tessie barges back out and the elevator door closes behind her a collective breath is drawn and the warmth returns.

"It smells wonderful, doesn't it?" Edna says, jogging Matthew's memory, and he asks if she'd mind going up to see if Mrs. Moore would like to come and watch.

Edna finishes hanging an inebriated-looking Santa in a moth-eaten suit. "Yes, I bet she'd like to." She goes off and comes back in awhile with Bo Peep, in a pink chenille robe, on her arm, and settles her on the sofa, pouring her a cup of tea, and for the next hour she nibbles cookies and watches them decorate, her eyes shining like a happy child waiting for Santa Claus. She reminds Matthew of his grandmother not long before she died, and if he doesn't miss his guess, this little lady doesn't have very long.

She has a touchingly sweet smile, and Matthew, untangling old round red and green garlands, keeps glancing at her. How do you live that long and come to the end of it with such a smile?

Liz glances over at him. This is one sad man, she thinks.

Matthew notes the affectionate camaraderie between Liz and Patrick and wonders if they might be lovers, though it sounds more like friendship. Their suites are almost next door. He likes them both, and needs friends. The last year of his drinking they drifted away, except for the easy camaraderie of the also-addicted; everybody your friend in the bar, even if you couldn't remember them the next day.

When the tree is finished, and the helpers and observers have left, Liz and Matthew clean up, packing away the dregs, throwing out broken ornaments, putting back boxes. Except Mr. Funk's tree.

"Want me to help you put that away? It's got to weigh a ton." Liz's face is flushed and smudged with dust. One earring is caught up in her hair and he wants to reach out and free it. He looks away quickly, his face reddening.

"I think it's *hasta la vista* for this baby, don't you?" he says.

"Oh, good! Let's do it!"

And they carry the heavy box out through the back and heave it into the dumpster. He sees Tessie silhouetted in her balcony door, watching them, her hands on her cascading hips. For the first time he notices the glowing fish tank against her south wall. A very large, glowing fish tank. With one very large fish suspended in it.

"A piranha," Matthew says, and Liz laughs.

Entering the lobby, they stop. The softly lit tree is enchanting; beardless Santas, tailless birds, wingless angels and all. Its warm glow transforms the pine-scented lobby, the diffuse coloured lights shimmering back from the plate glass window.

"Oh. It's splendid, isn't it?" Liz says.

"It is indeed, and I'm ever so grateful to you. I owe you a dinner for sure."

She smiles. "You already bought me dinner."

Stepping into the elevator, she holds the door open a moment. "But drop by my office sometime. I go for coffee around three."

"I will."

The doors close and the elevator hums upward.

Matthew looks around the lobby, which needs vacuuming but it's too late to fire up the Beast. Reluctant to unplug the tree lights, he sits down on the couch with his feet on the coffee table and, lighting an illicit cigarette, leans back and admires the evening's work. He hopes Delia will see it. He's going to make damn sure she sees it.

Through the window the streetlights are haloed with fog, everything wrapped in a benevolent gauzy shawl, all hard edges softened. He massages his tight neck muscles, feels them loosen ever so slightly, just enough to tell him how tense they really are.

Wouldn't it be great to have a drink right now? To prolong the moment. Reward himself for getting through the evening without one. This makes perfect sense to him. He sees the scotch pouring over the ice. Hears the ice cubes clink in his favourite glass. Feels the first swallow going down, the instantaneous warming and loosening inside.

He jumps up and looks out the window, breathing deeply several times, then reaches down to unplug the tree lights and heads for the stairs. He'll be walking long tonight.

He was on TV last night. Maurice Dixon is his name, and he's somebody high up in the government. He was talking about how the city had to crack down on graffiti. We live in one of the most beautiful cities in the world, he said, and people with cans of spray paint are trying to ruin it. Lack of respect for other people's property could not be tolerated, he said, especially in a city so dependent on the tourist trade.

Well, Mister Maurice Important Dixon, that parking spot in front of my apartment is not marked Visitor, is it, so someone is paying for it, namely me, and that means you're invading my private property every time you park there. What kind of respect is that? From you or that alcoholic caretaker who lets you get away with it?

He was there just last week again, pulled up and was out of the car and out of earshot before she could get herself untangled from her chair and get the balcony door open. And he left while the paper boy was ringing her doorbell and she missed him again.

He didn't come to see his family, there's no Dixon mailbox. She checked that out. And he always walked fast with his head down like he didn't want to be recognized. Now why would that be, unless he was doing something he shouldn't be. That's probably why he didn't want to park in a Visitor spot. They get noticed more. Weren't those government men always involved in some kind of sex scandal? Hiring prostitutes or whatever and then just saying they were trying to counsel the poor girl or some such crock of you-know-what. He was married, because he mentioned his wife finding their garage door decorated with graffiti.

Well, Mister Big Man in Government, who thinks you can park anyplace you darn well please, we'll see about that.

Everyone calls it the little park with good reason. An empty corner lot next to the Kensington was transformed almost overnight with grass, flowers, benches, ornamental plum trees and a cedar path. Ecstatic Kensington residents woke up to this little miracle one day, and have made good use of it ever since.

Matthew sits on a park bench, arms spread along its back, enjoying the sun. A beautiful day in Victoria can seduce you into thinking there's no place else to live, the soft air that always smells of growing things – *there lives the dearest freshness deep down things* – another of the lines from a long-ago English class which oddly leap into his head more often as time goes on. Gerard Manley Hopkins, he thinks, who burned his poems when he joined the Jesuits. Did he burn them all, or just ones that would offend? Love poems, maybe. Like burning part of himself away, it must have been.

On a balcony railing across the way, a large orange cat surveys the neighborhood. He likes cats and remembers some great ones from his past. Especially George, a.k.a. the Cat Burglar, who took to raiding the neighbours' clotheslines, dragging home everything from a brassiere to a double bedsheet. Once he scored an entire Mickey Mouse suit; T-shirt and pants one day, jacket the next. The neighbours in their town joked about hanging out dirty things for his mother to return washed.

He loved that town as a kid. Playing in the lumberyard, leaping boxcars on the tracks behind the Pool elevator, playing hockey on frigid nights – their raucous shouts, the sharp scrape and clatter, the puck smacking the boards. Rafting on the pond that appeared every spring down by the elevators, daring each other across it on rubbery ice. Jean Shepherd wrote about boys drifting around town willy-nilly, changing direction like a school of minnows, and it struck him as so right. He envies that gift, has had moments of thinking he could write a book, but years of writing by the inch have left him with the attention span of a grasshopper, and he knows it.

He still thinks of that little town with yearning. Even his father's drinking didn't spoil it, since he didn't have a mean bone in his body, drunk or sober. People always said that about him. Maybe if they'd lived in the city he'd have found A.A. Or not.

When Matthew left for university, his mother wanted him to room with Blair, a couple of years ahead, but he insisted on rooming with his best buddy Bill Stevenson, both of them already alcoholics in training. And they trained hard. They made it through by cramming like crazy, only holding it in their heads till the exam was over and they headed for the bar, where it promptly leaked out, much of it never to return. Except for those literary fragments, some of whose authors and source he remembers, most not. Everything was funny back then, even Bill passing out in a snowbank on the campus after a party, and being picked up in a snowplow bucket, almost giving the operator a heart attack. He'd have frozen to death otherwise, but it didn't even give them pause. You're going to live forever then.

He'd started out for a walk but stopped here, looking at a few faded pink roses clinging for dear life to the ends of their thorny stems. And he'd always thought roses were so fragile, an unfortunate symbol for love, drooping unopened in vases, or dropping their petals behind your back faster than you could say happy anniversary.

"Roses blooming in December," someone says. "The place has its charms, doesn't it?" Edna Burton, coming down the path.

"The park or Victoria?" he asks.

"Victoria."

"Some days. I actually have a love/hate relationship with the place." He moves over and invites her to sit down.

"Thanks, I will for a minute." The breeze lifts Edna's sensibly cut grey hair above her sensibly cut features. She is quite a good-looking woman, really, with the kind of intelligent eyes you notice sometimes, even in strangers. "I have to walk every day or risk having bones like Swiss cheese," she says.

"That's an incentive."

The Explorers are trundling their shopping home in the little light carts that are such a boon to the elderly.

Edna turns to look at him. "Matthew, did you know a stray cat spends the nights in Margaret Moore's suite?"

"No kidding? No. I didn't." He sighs, watching the Explorers stoop to admire an ornmental shrub. "Oh, God, flea-ridden, no doubt." He remembers drinking with someone who had cats and seeing fleas bounding out of the carpet. Like having mini DT's. Like the gnats Lowry called the overture. He's reading *Under the Volcano* again.

"And I suppose she likes the cat?"

"Loves it. It sleeps on her bed. It's a big Tabby and so happy to be in out of the rain. Do you think you could just ignore it, Matthew? At least until someone complains?"

He crosses his arms and thinks for a bit. Why the hell shouldn't they all have a cat if they want one. "I can plead ignorance. I don't think she's got very long to enjoy a cat or anything else."

"Neither do I. But don't get yourself in trouble over a cat."

"What cat?" Matthew says.

Besides, he thinks, if this should come to a battle with Tessie, he acquired a new arrow in his quiver last night.

Mister Reilly is waiting by the second-hand store on the far corner, his wig startlingly wig-like even from this distance. At the walk light he heads off smartly down Foul Bay road, swinging his red umbrella.

"Living the life of Reilly, eh?" Matthew says.

"Trying to, anyway." Edna laughs, and he remembers Delia

saying something about the man propositioning women in the elevator.

"Well, I'm off," Edna says, pulling on wool gloves. "Thanks for the lovely Christmas tree. It brightens the spirit." And she sets off energetically.

He leans back and stretches out his legs, trying to shame himself into going for a brisk walk. In the intermittent sunshine everything looks rinsed, more real than real somehow.

A large, one-eyed seagull is pecking at a hard piece of bun someone dropped. Shaking it vigorously, he bangs it on the ground to no avail before whomping it on the leg of a bench knocking a few dry flakes loose. Then, spying a puddle on the sidewalk, the gull marches over, drops in the bun and stands guard before stepping daintily in and dispatching the softened crust in a few gulps. Matthew is impressed.

He realizes he's noticing things more, has become more aware, somehow. Part and parcel of being sober, he guesses; a kind of consolation prize for having to put up with the hard stuff.

Liz Wright is a nice woman. Maybe she'd like to go for a walk sometime. Or have a game of Scrabble; a book lover like Liz is probably good at it. He likes the company of women, always has. But when Delia wanted him to go for walks he almost never did. Now Nick will be striding over the heather with Delia. He's a good deal younger than Matthew, even younger than Delia. Not a day over fifty, he guesses, which doesn't endear him to Matthew who spends a lot of time on his nocturnal trudges thinking of delightful ways to off the guy. At the moment he favours drawing and quartering since in that scenario the miscreant is first hanged but not long enough to kill him, then his privates are cut off and laid in front of his face before they get on with the rest. Ah, the good old days. His balls shrivel up just thinking about it.

The seagull is stalking around, a tough old survivor by the look of it, and Matthew picks up a crust it missed on its blind side and tosses it in the puddle. He's got to phone Delia about going to Kate's this weekend, but what if she turns him down? And if she goes, what will they talk about on the way up there?

He wants to make amends to Kate when he's there. He's starting to think in A.A. terms, but can't remember which is the making amends step: apologizing for your wrongs, never mind what the other person did; clearing the wreckage of the past. And in the process, letting go of things that might have festered for years.

And maybe helping the other person to let go, too.

Though his worst drinking happened after Kate left home, he embarrassed her plenty in her high school and university days. His sarcastic criticism of her boyfriends. His egotistical harangues. Expounding to her and her friends ad nauseum, scotch in hand, about the evils of drugs. God. No wonder she rebelled. Smoked pot. Ran away with a biker.

Damn it, his serene mood of just five minutes ago has vanished. He can't be alone any time now without getting morose. And suddenly it's pissing down rain again, rudely beating on his bald head. In his eight years here, he hasn't got the habit of carrying an umbrella. He'd rather get wet and bitch about it, Delia always said.

Well, he can't go for a walk in this, can he? He pushes himself up off the bench and hunches down the path toward Oak Bay Avenue. See if Marty has time for coffee.

Chapter Eight

Delia, wearing pants and a deep rose sweater that should-n't suit her red hair but does, is perched on the edge of the lobby sofa like someone in a doctor's office. Someone who doesn't know the prognosis but doubts it will be good. Outside a hard, steady rain is falling.

"Matthew, it's lovely. How on earth did you convince Mr. Funk to buy a real tree?"

"I didn't. But I was damned if I'd put up that mouldering fossil." He sits down on the opposite arm of the couch. "I threw it out."

"You *what?*" She laughs. "And you were sober at the time?"

"For your information, I'm sober all the time." Lord, he sounded like a testy old bugger and she was just joking. Or was she?

"Good. I'm glad to hear it. But you must have had some help with the tree, didn't you?"

"Yes, I did. A bit." Let her wonder about that.

"Yes, well.... We'd better get going. I'll just nip into the laundry washroom while you get your jacket."

Aye aye, sir, he says under his breath.

Delia has a mouse-sized bladder, and he was up at midnight, after he'd finally got up the nerve to call her, scouring the washroom to unblemished perfection. She's always "nipping" into a bathroom somewhere, Delia is a drive-by pee-er, and he knew she'd want to check up on his housekeeping. He gets his keys and jacket and Sam's birthday gift and is back in the lounge when she returns, looking bemused.

"You aren't going to leave those lights on, are you?" she says as they're heading out the door.

"Yes, I am. Maybe it'll cheer somebody up, it's such a gloomy goddamn day."

"Those strings of lights are so old, they're liable to catch fire."

"Well, yes, they're old, but think of how little they've actually been used."

Her shrug as he holds the door for her says let it be on your head.

They are out of town heading north in the rain before she asks.

"Have you got someone helping you clean, Matthew?"

"No." All innocence. "Why?"

"I just wondered. Who's looking after the place today?"

"Edna Burton."

"Oh."

He realizes with a stab of delight that she's jealous. Not of him, or of Edna, but of his apparently managing her old territory well. She's always been the reliable, strong one, the one who held it all together, it should be falling apart now she's not doing it any more. That's something for her to run past her Al-Anon meeting. Lots of heads would be nodding over that one, he bets. He used to resent all those sensible women talking about their dipsomaniac husbands. She always said they had better things to talk about but he didn't believe her.

No way is he going to tell her he doesn't know what the hell he's doing at the Kensington half the time, that all those old people depress the life out of him – like looking in a crystal ball – that he can't sleep and prowls the halls half the night to keep from drinking, that there's a pregnant mouse in the furnace room and he can't make himself kill it. No way is he telling her. He's got a little pride left.

"Edna said she'd look after the place tomorrow too in case we decide to stay over."

"Oh, no, I can't do that. I'm on mornings all week." Her tone of voice tells him she wouldn't have anyway, that she's more than a bit surprised he'd suggest it.

And suddenly he's tired. The day is just starting and he's suffering his usual sleep-deprived hangover, only worse. Anxious about today, he only logged four hours last night and he has the caved-in feeling that just gets worse as the day progresses. At least with a hangover you could look forward to feeling better; a couple to settle you down, something to eat, forty winks in your car on the side of the road, and you realized you'd live to do it another day. Maybe even that day.

He pushes in the lighter and his hand trembles as he lights a cigarette. Damn it, he wanted to feel good today, and he feels irascible as hell. Did it have to be such a dark, sodden, depressing goddamn day, coming down stair rods as the English would say, the wipers on high hardly keeping up? He swerves as a red Fiat roars by on his right side. "Asshole!" he yells, and Delia gives him a look.

Through the downpour he spots a service station restaurant just in time to pull in. "Want a coffee?"

"Yes, I'd like one. I'll get it."

"Right. You need to nip into the washroom."

She laughs. And before he can pull out his wallet, she's out of the car.

He watches her walk toward the restaurant, not scuttling through the rain but with the confident, easy gait he always admired, her hair brightening the dull parking lot. A tall, graceful, attractive woman. A good-looking, dark guy leaving the restaurant gives her an appreciative smile as he holds the door open for her, and she smiles her thanks. Fifty-five and still turning heads. Matthew sighs.

She returns with coffee and doughnuts. "I didn't get chocolate for you since you're driving."

"Why?" He scowls at the pink and green sprinkled concoction she hands him on a paper napkin. "I wouldn't register 08 after just one, would I?"

"I just thought they're messy to handle when you're driving."

"I don't mind messy."

"Then go and get yourself one."

But he starts the car and pulls back onto the highway, spilling sprinkles down his shirt front and over his khakis as he eats. Stains. Since he's been doing the laundry he's discovered that everything stains. He threw his leg over the laundry tub the other day and sprayed a big coffee stain that changed configuration before his eyes into a green plaid stain. His boxers leaking through. His clothes are starting to look like an old bachelor's. Well, that's what he is, isn't he?

As usual, the highway traffic is steady, though not nearly as bad as in the summer when you don't dare take your eyes off the road.

He glances at Delia. "Remember when we first came out here what a pleasure it was to drive this road?"

"Yes. I do. Before it got so built up. It was wonderful then."

Everything was, he just didn't have the sense to know it. "You were right, though," he says, "we should have bought something up here even if we never lived in it. We could have doubled the money."

"Well. Hindsight is better than foresight," she replies.

And he's struck again at what a generous woman she is, really. Always was. Sure, she's miffed that he isn't as helpless as he pretended to be all those years, but she hasn't become mean-spirited with the years like some people. Or self-righteous like some of those Al-Anon women. He once heard one of them say her mother was meant to die young since it taught her self-reliance and how to survive being married to an alcoholic. He wants to give Delia's leg an appreciative pat, as he once would have without thinking. He pulls his cigarettes from his shirt pocket.

She pushes in the lighter and rolls down her window a bit. An old, familiar ritual that feels comfortable.

"What did Kate say when you called?" he asks.

"Oh, she said she'd be glad to see us."

"Well, God, what else could she say? Is that all?" The lighter pops and he inhales its metallic taste, his hand steadier now.

"More or less. But I'll be glad to see her." She sounds concerned.

Alarm bells jangle. Delia is not a worrier.

"Why? How did she sound? What's wrong?"

"Give me a chance, Matthew. She just sounded exhausted."

"Oh, God, I hope she doesn't –"

A small white car passes him too close to a narrow curve. He brakes and it skitters in front of him just in time to miss a huge logging truck coming around the bend, its horn blaring as they meet.

"Jesus, that was close!"

"Never mind, Matthew. Nothing happened."

He knows that, but suddenly the world is full of danger. Blood on the highway. Young women with breast cancer.

"Is she sick? Is that why she's on stress leave?"

"Matthew, stop jumping to conclusions. She sounded worried."

"Well, I'd damn well think so. What are they living on? It's two years since Michael quit teaching."

"I'm hoping she'll come back with us for a few days. Then we can talk to her."

"Maybe Sam could come, too. They probably both need to get away from Saint Michael."

"Now Matthew, don't say anything to make him angry. We don't want to upset Kate."

He sighs. "Don't worry."

"Is that a promise?"

He hesitates a moment, then raises his right hand.

The sun is struggling to break through, the passing scenery still dazzles him with its beauty, and the sugary doughnut and coffee have given him a bit of a lift. He might survive the day after all.

After a silence that doesn't feel too uncomfortable, he turns on CBC 2 and the opulent trees still dotted with red and gold and wine drift by to the Goldberg Piano Variations punctuated with Glenn Gould's little audible mutterings. He loosens his death grip on the wheel and leans back. He could almost believe nothing has changed.

They pull into Nanaimo for a nip stop and have coffee in a little restaurant with a view of the harbour. Some toast and three cups of coffee later Matthew starts to feel almost human. It's not far to Kate's, and he's looking forward to it now.

"I brought Sam the new *Star Trek* video for his birthday," he tells Delia.

"Oh, he'll like that. I got him *The Physics of Star Trek* book. It looked fascinating. And a Sony CD Walkman for Christmas."

"Oh, damn. I've never shopped this early for presents."

"That's for sure." She laughs. "You can send them on the bus. It's hard to believe our Sam is almost a teenager."

Our Sam. They've always called him that. They still have that between them anyway. Their children.

"Isn't it?" he says. "Remember when she told us she was pregnant?"

They both laugh. "It's a wonder we survived it," Delia says.

"Don't worry," Kate said, when she told them she was pregnant by a scary biker named Shadow. She was living in a dilapidated house down near the river in Saskatoon, having quit university to hang out with his biker gang. "Shadow will make a wonderful father."

"How do you know that?" Matthew asked the apple of his eye, the pale, thin little girl all in black, her beautiful wavy hair styled with a hunting knife, by the look of it, the butch cut hollowing her cheeks and making her eyes enormous.

"Because of his dog," Kate said reasonably, as if anybody should know that.

"His dog?"

"Yeah. His dog, Boh. Shadow's so good to Boh. You should see. He plays with him and looks after him like a baby."

"Oh."

And then one frigid January night Delia phoned Kate from work and got the message their phone was disconnected. She called Matthew in a state, and there they were, sitting in a car with the windows frosted up, peering at a squat, ugly, darkened house that gave Matthew the willies. A serial killer of a house, out of place between its tony neighbours. Ice fog off the river haloed the street lights all the way down Spadina Crescent.

"Maybe they went to bed early," Delia said, without much conviction.

"Don't be ridiculous. That outfit wouldn't all be in bed before midnight." He noticed the walk was all snowed in. "Well, maybe they've gone out. To a movie or something."

"I don't think they worry about saving electricity. Especially if they don't plan to pay the bill. It's deserted."

"You don't know that. You always expect the worst."

He couldn't deny it. Somebody had to do it.

They got out and floundered through the knee-deep snow up the front walk, slid on snowy boots across the large black skull and crossbones painted on the peeling porch floor, pounded on the door and listened. Silence. ...*naught there was astirring in the still, dark night.* Walter De La Mare? That one went way back.

The door was locked. Then Delia plowed through even deeper snow off the path to peer in the uncurtained front windows, faintly lit from the street light. She strained against the window, her red-mittened hands shading her eyes.

"See anything?"

"Just piles of clothes and newspapers, it looks like, and garbage."

"They're gone," Matthew said, his breath forming clouds of vapour. "Probably skipped without paying the rent." Reaching up to cover his numb ears with his stiff leather gloves, his boot slipped on the porch and he clutched a railing just in time, wrenching his back.

"Ow! My back! Ow! Goddamn it, Delia, why didn't she tell us she was leaving?"

"Oh, never mind your bloody back. We'd better look around the back. Maybe the door's not locked."

And in the moonlight, hunched over with pain, he followed Delia's disembodied, white-stockinged legs around the corner and along the side of the house.

Delia turned the corner and stopped.

"Oh. My. God."

"What?" Trying to peer around her, into the near darkness, his heart squeezing like a fist. "What?"

She moved aside and he saw it. The black Doberman frozen stiff by the back steps, all four legs straight out.

"Oh, Jesus," he said. "That must be Boh."

They fled back to the car, where Matthew hunched over

the steering wheel, inflammation spreading around his sacroiliac joint and pains shooting down his leg.

He moaned. "I think I slipped a disc."

"I don't give a damn what you slipped. It's Kate I'm worried about."

"Don't worry. Shadow'll be a great father, remember?"

"Matthew, are you laughing? It's not funny!" She smacked him a good one on the head and several more on his shaking shoulders as he shielded his head with his gloved hands. "Our pregnant daughter's run away with a biker who left his dog to freeze to death, and you're laughing?"

"It's nerves," he said. And it was.

She wrapped her arms around her chest. "Oh, my God, that poor dog! My poor baby!"

And she rocked on the seat, hugging herself and crying as he started the car and drove home at a crawl over the frozen, shining streets.

"Poor Kate. My poor pregnant little girl," Delia kept saying. "Poor baby."

And it suddenly came home to him that there would be a baby. Not just a pregnant daughter. A real, live baby.

"She'll come home," he said. "The baby will bring her home." For some reason he knew it.

And he was right. Five months pregnant she arrived on the doorstep one warm spring night with a cheap, ugly suitcase, flinging herself into Matthew's arms when he opened the door. She had come by bus from Vancouver, still in her black tights and black sweater. Without money. Sans Shadow, thank God. In the suitcase a baby blanket, second-hand baby clothes, and a tiny, yellow, half-knitted sweater. And in a shoebox with holes punched in the lid, a tiny calico kitten.

She lived at home, going back to university and finishing her teaching degree after Sam was born. Four great years in which both Matthew and Delia fell in love with and bonded with their only grandchild. Years he hardly drank and he and Delia scarcely said a harsh word to each other. When a little child brought out the best in all of them. The best years of his life.

Delia laughs now about that frigid night by the river. It's Matthew who wants to cry.

Chapter Nine

They turn onto the narrow logging road and the old Volvo almost rattles to bits.

"Slow down, Matthew," says Delia, jouncing around as she leans forward to peer into the small visor mirror. "I need to put on some lipstick." He slows down, watching her from the corner of his eye perform the rite he's seen thousands of times. She caps the lipstick and pulls a turquoise hair thing through her hair, which crackles with electricity, and inspects herself, first one side, then the other, before flipping the visor back up. As he picks a long red hair that's adhered to the shoulder of her sweater, her hair clutches his hand in a soft, magnetic embrace and his throat tightens.

"Thanks," she says, brushing herself off. "I don't know how they stand travelling this road every day."

"They're used to it."

As he gets out to open the farm gate on their property he sees a cabin in the trees past the house, its newness like a scar in the clearing where the weathered A-frame blends into the landscape. He'd forgot about the woman who's living here now.

Delia has noticed it, too. "I hope they know what they're doing," she says.

As he's parking the car, Kate and Sam, as tall as his mother, come out the side door and hurry toward them through the rain. With a pang Matthew remembers a small boy running to meet them and leaping up into his arms.

"Hi, you guys. Good to see you," she says. She hugs her mother. Matthew gives Sam a manly hug, and Sam grins as Delia grabs him and kisses him, exclaiming how tall he's grown. Kate reaches up to kiss Matthew's cheek. "Hi Daddy," she says, before turning away, arm in arm with Delia, towards the house.

Her willowy body is graceful in an ankle-length flowered skirt and red t-shirt. Delia was built like that once. Kate's hair is long, he's glad to see, a cloud of black, curly hair she must have got from his black-Irish ancestors. She called him Daddy so she can't be too angry with him.

Matthew puts an arm around Sam's shoulder and the boy leans into him for a moment.

"How're you doing, my friend?" Matthew asks.

Sam shrugs. "I'm okay." Every line of him saying he isn't.

"I hope you're hungry," Kate says, too cheerfully. "Lunch is almost ready."

"You bet," Matthew lies. There's a big pile of lumber in the yard, obviously intended for the un-germane addition he now sees growing onto the house. He's surprised at Michael building such a graceless extension, but perhaps A-frames don't take kindly to expansion.

"So what's this all about?" Matthew asks. "Surely you don't need that much more space?"

"I know. But Michael seems to think so."

"Well, you've always said the living room's too small." Delia says diplomatically.

Kate nods. "That's true."

"But you don't need to play hockey in it," Matthew says, and Delia gives him a shut-your-mouth look.

In the house, they perch on kitchen stools made by Michael, Sam between them, while Kate stirs something that looks and smells deliciously like chicken soup, and cuts thick slices of homemade brown bread. There is also the smell of baking apples and cinnamon. He should have passed on the toast.

Matthew likes this kitchen with its pine walls and cupboards, rag rugs on the bare wood floors, narrow open cupboards with jars full of dried peppers, tomatoes and mushrooms, and cats asleep in odd places. A matted old calico cat, the kitten that came with Kate from Vancouver, is sleeping in an open drawer.

"So Muriel is still with us, eh? She's pretty old."

"Yes. She might make it as long as Old Tom," Kate says. Old Tom had come home with her in grade two and died when Sam was three.

"I remember Old Tom," Sam says.

As Kate works, Matthew notices how thin her arms are, the tendons standing out as she cuts the bread. Her hands too, and her thighs, outlined by the flimsy skirt, look almost skeletal as she squats down to reach something in a low cupboard. His stomach clenches, and he glances at Delia but she looks relaxed.

"You're still baking bread. Good for you, Kate."

At the sound of Delia's voice, a large black and white cat stands up in the mixing bowl at the end of the cupboard, arching his back and meowing a delighted greeting.

"Felix! Come here you beautiful big boy." Delia loves cats.

Felix steps daintily over the rim and marches purposefully down the counter talking to Delia, long plumed tail waving, and butts his big face into hers again and again as cat hair rises and drifts.

Jesus. He never could understand Kate's laissez-faire with cats. He likes cats as well as anybody, but not in the damn dishes. But he must remember to tell Delia about Bo Peep's nocturnal visitor. Maybe it'll gain him some brownie points.

"Mom didn't make the bread," Sam says.

"Oh? It looks homemade. You make it, Sam?"

"Yah, right, Grandpa."

"Emerald baked it. She's a friend who's living out here now." Kate's tone is noncommittal as she pulls a bubbling apple pie from the oven. She smiles at Matthew's expression as she deposits it on a woven seagrass mat under his nose and he grabs a cat hair drifting toward it.

"So we heard. How do you like that?" Delia asks.

"It's all right."

"No, it's not," Sam says.

"Oh, Sam. She helps out. Sam's finding it hard to get used to sharing the place, that's all. She has a sweet little boy."

"I don't mind sharing it with Joey." You couldn't miss the stress on the word Joey. Delia and Matthew are both looking at Sam now, waiting for more.

"It's not that," he says. "It's..." he looks at Kate, "...everything."

The door opens and Michael comes in with a woman about Kate's age and a small, curly-haired boy. An almost aggressively plain woman who could be very attractive if she made any effort, Matthew thinks. Her skin takes on the hue of the khaki green shirt and pants that give her a slightly military air. Michael is also in khaki, his grizzled, chest-length beard shot with grey and speckled with what looks like breadcrumbs. They look like a couple of insurgents back from scouting the hills for enemies. All they need is AK-47s slung over their shoulders.

"Hi, Mom. Good to see you." Michael walks over and kisses Delia, pointedly brushing past Matthew to greet his mother-in-law. "Hello, Matthew," he says, barely glancing at him.

"Hi, Sam!" The little boy runs to Sam, clutching his leg and laughing up at him. "Wanna play Snakes and Ladders?"

He's a sweet-looking child with enormous chocolate brown eyes. Matthew notices the greenish faded remnant of a bruise on his cheek.

Sam pats the child's head awkwardly. "Later, Joey. Okay? My grandma and grandpa are here."

Kate is introducing them to Emerald.

"How do you do," Matthew says. He's damned if he'll say it's nice to meet her or shake her hand. He hates her on sight.

"Hello, Emerald. Hello, Joey." Delia sounds pleased to meet them. She would.

"They could, too," Joey says, pulling on Sam's arm.

"Who?" Sam says. "Could what?"

"Nice to meet you both," Emerald says, her indifferent tone belying the words. There's something unsettling about the way Kate is banging things around in the kitchen. She's nervous, Matthew thinks. Or angry.

"Could play!" Joey is jumping up and down now, hanging onto Sam's arm, "Your gramma and grampa could play Snakes and Ladders!"

"Never mind, Joey," Emerald says. "They don't want to play with you."

She doesn't even look at her child, as if his reaction to this blunt rejection is of no interest to her.

Matthew can't stop looking at her. She's sizing him up, too, a flicker of interest in her hazel eyes. A very unpleasant, very sexy woman he now realizes. One of those women who wear it like an aura.

"Lunch will be ready soon," Kate says. "Mom, would you mind setting the table?"

Delia leans down to the small, upturned face. "I'm going to set the table for Kate and then we'll have lunch and after that I'll play Snakes and Ladders with you, Joey. How would that be?"

"Awesome!" he says so emphatically they all laugh, the tension broken as Delia gets up and starts to set the table.

"He's picked up Sam's favourite words," Kate says.

Matthew, feeling hot and claustrophobic all at once, gets up to pull off his sweater and sit down in the living room. "Come over and tell me what you've been up to, Sam," he says.

But Michael gets there before Sam, taking the chair closest to Matthew's so Sam has to sit across the room. Ornery bugger, Matthew thinks. It suddenly strikes him that Michael looks like Fidel Castro.

"So, how's it going, Matthew? I hear you're on the wagon again." Michael smirks. He really does smirk, the supercilious idiot. An expression you don't see much once you leave elementary school.

"You heard right. And big changes going on around here, I see. Are you going into the motel business?"

"Hardly. We're not that hard up." By his tone of voice he's spoiling for a fight and Matthew would love to accommodate him but he promised Delia. A little flame of hope is flickering now since the drive up and he wants to hang onto that.

"Just asking. What's with all the construction?" He reaches for his cigarettes.

"Sorry, Matthew. We don't allow smoking in the house."

"Oh? Since when?"

"Since the last time you were here."

Matthew's blood pressure jumps several notches. "Obviously," he says, shoving the package back in his pocket while trying to look pleasant, an oxymoronic endeavour if ever there was one.

"So. What's new around here?"

"Plenty, but I doubt you'd be interested."

"Try me," Matthew says.

Across the room Sam is methodically cracking his knuckles. First one finger, then the other, finishing one hand and starting on the other like he's being paid by the hour. Something's far wrong, as the Scots say. He'll get him alone after lunch. Find out what's going on.

The dog barks at the door and Kate lets him in. He makes a beeline for Sam and puts his head on Sam's knee, who stops cracking his knuckles to stroke the dog's damp head. Buddy's eyes roll anxiously in Michael's direction.

"Phew, that dog stinks," Michael says. "And you know he's not allowed in when he's wet."

"Well, how can he get dry if we don't let him in?"

When Michael doesn't bother to answer Matthew says, "How's the soccer team doing, Sam?"

"I'm not playing," Sam says sourly, shooting an accusing look at Michael.

"Oh? Why not?"

"Mom doesn't have a car any more."

"What? What happened to it?"

"We sold it," Michael says flatly. "We don't need two vehicles."

"Well, I'd damn well think you would, living in the country. But why can't Sam get in for soccer?

"There are more important things in life than soccer," Michael says, in an end-of-subject tone of voice.

"Yah. Right." Sam's tone is belligerent. "Like the End Times."

Jesus. It's even worse than he thought. Matthew glances over at Kate, who is looking worriedly in their direction. Sam and Michael never really "took", as much as Kate wanted to believe they did. Sam has always felt constrained by Michael, his natural ebullience reined in. Now it's become a lot more than that.

"Well, what are you building these days, Michael?" Matthew asks. Surely that's a safe subject.

"Oh, this and that. Still a lot of pine stuff, just about everything people commission is pine or maple. Kitchen stuff, mostly." His tone dismissive.

"And you'd rather make something else?" The living room suddenly darkens, runnels of rain sluicing down the windows. "Like maybe an ark?"

Michael scowls.

It wasn't an innuendo, not a conscious one, though now he thinks of it he can see Michael at the helm. "I just meant it looks like we might need one soon," he says lamely, gesturing toward the window. Talking to Michael is like traversing a minefield.

"Let it rain," Michael pronounces.

Let there be Light, Matthew thinks.

Kate turns on the kitchen light. Emerald is planted on a stool leafing through a magazine on the counter. Why doesn't the ignorant damn woman leave Kate and Delia alone to visit? Good manners should dictate that, surely, but she gives off the kind of vibrations, even from the back, of someone who couldn't care less what people think of her. He feels suddenly smothered by the humidity in the room. Delia, however, is talking and laughing like it's a Walton family supper coming up.

Michael is saying something about some cherrywood he's going to make into a desk for himself, obviously bent on continuing a conversation neither of them wants.

And suddenly Matthew gets it, or thinks he does.

They're being chaperoned, he and Delia. Michael and Emerald have a pre-arranged agenda, to keep them from talking to Kate, who is looking pale and tense now as she dips soup into cheerful yellow bowls. With the kitchen light on, the black shadows under her eyes are alarming.

And the little flame of fear he felt in the car roars back, a conflagration now. It's cancer, or Lou Gehrig's disease or something else. He's got the feeling you get when something's gone horribly wrong, as if a trapdoor just opened inside you.

"Soup's on," Delia calls, like a cheery camp counsellor. His body heavy as lead, Matthew gets up and goes to the round pine table, where Kate is placing steaming soup bowls onto blue plates on woven placemats. He feels as white as she looks, but manages to smile as he gratefully drops into a chair.

"Mmmmm. This looks good, Katie." Next to him Joey, precariously perched on top of a stack of pillows, hugs a large plastic T. Rex.

"You're sitting on the leaning tower of Piza," Matthew says.

"Pizza? I'm sitting on a pizza?"

"No, you're not sitting on a pizza."

"But you said —"

"I know. I said something silly."

"Why?"

"Because he's silly. That's why." Delia, come to his rescue, sitting down on Joey's other side and shoring up his precarious perch. "Do you like pizza, Joey?"

"Yes I do!" And he sings "Je suis une pizza," waving T. Rex in the air like a conductor.

"I'll ask the blessing," Michael says when they're all seated, and they duck their heads.

"Jesus, bless your followers gathered here together. We thank you for family and for friends born again in you. We especially thank you for this opportunity to show others the way to salvation before it's too late. Help them to see that The Day is fast approaching when all unrepentant infidels will be..." his voice takes on a droning, almost hypnotic tone.

Unrepentant infidels? Matthew looks up.

Emerald's head is up, eyes closed, a blissed-out expression on her face. Kate's head bowed, shoulders slumped. Sam sits defiantly upright, eyes open, arms crossed, his little tight-lipped smile at Matthew saying, See? See what's happening here? Delia raises her eyebrows and rolls her eyes at Matthew. "Je suis une pizza," Joey sings under his breath into T. Rex's ear.

"...until the Rapture comes and we who are your chosen –"

Matthew clears his throat loud enough to get through to Michael in what looks like a fast approaching trancelike state.

He opens his eyes and looks straight at Matthew.

"You'll see," he says.

"Whatever happened to 'God is great, God is good, let's all thank him for our food?'" Matthew says in what he hopes is a light tone.

Smoothing his beard out of the way, Michael reaches for his spoon and Matthew sees a large wooden cross on a thong, which was hidden by his beard. "There are more important things to say. And not much time to say them."

Matthew knows he should let this pass.

"Oh? And just when is The Day arriving?" He pauses. "This time?"

Delia is shaking her head at him. Joey marches his dinosaur up Matthew's arm and onto his shoulder, half slipping off the pillows as he reaches over, and Matthew shores him up while looking at Michael.

Michael shrugs. "1999. I can't give you an exact date." He reaches a long arm across the table for a slice of bread.

"Why 1999 if I may be so obtuse?"

"Niney niney nine," says Joey, walking his dinosaur back down Matthew's arm.

Sam leans forward, looking interested.

"The signs are there for those who know how to read them," Michael says, slathering butter on a thick slice of bread.

"Niney niney nine," Joey whispers, marching T. Rex around his plate.

"We unrepentant infidels should have some warning, too, don't you think?" Matthew says.

"Why?" Michael asks. "Anyone can be born again."

"Christ," Matthew says, "once is enough for anybody. But," he persists, knowing he shouldn't, "why 1999?"

Michael takes a huge bite of bread, and starts spooning up his soup. "If you really want to know, the answer's in the date."

"It is?" Matthew asks. "You mean it's in code?" Emerald gives him an amused look.

Michael sighs, the sigh of the martyr, and Matthew has a sudden flash of what a nasty teacher Michael must have been. "If you turn the date upside down, what does it contain?"

"What? You mean 666?"

"Of course."

Matthew knows what he's getting at but wants to hear him say it. "And that means?"

"The mark of the Antichrist, of course," Michael's tone so matter-of-fact he might be saying pass the bread. "When he's going to claim his own."

Matthew, so obviously one of the claimees, decides not to touch that with a ten-foot pitchfork.

"So why didn't the world end in 1666?" he asks, as if they're having an intelligent discourse. "Or better yet, 666?

They didn't even need to turn it upside down."

"Yah. That's right," Sam says, in a why-didn't-I-think-of-that voice.

"Laugh if you want. It's encoded for a reason."

"And you born-agains figured that out, did you?" Face flaming, heart thumping, hand jerking as he tries to eat, this ludicrous conversation is making him mad as hell.

"I'd like to talk about something else," Delia interrupts in a firm voice. "This is lovely soup, sweetheart."

"Thanks, Mom."

Matthew feels the actual physical sensations of dragging himself away from the brink of a confrontation; muscles taut, gut quivering like jello. "Yes, Katie," he says. "Nice and spicy." He picks up his spoon, hand shaking, and lowers it. Michael notices and smiles.

"I'm glad you like it, Dad." Kate's drawn look vanishes when she smiles. She always had a smile that could light up a room. He mustn't let that deluded self-important idiot spoil this chance with his daughter.

"Kate makes wonderful soup," Emerald informs them, smiling fondly at Kate.

Sam rolls his eyes.

"We know," Delia says shortly, barely glancing at Emerald.

A flat, shuttered look drops over Emerald's face. Shuttered but watchful, Matthew thinks, not much gets past this babe.

Well, they seem to have done all they can with the soup and Armageddon. Now what are they going to talk about?

"Dad, how are you getting along at the Kensington?" Kate asks.

"Better than I expected."

"You should see the beautiful Christmas tree he put up," Delia offers.

"No kidding?" Kate laughs. "Good for you, Dad. Those old people would like that, I bet. Well, I guess they're not all old."

"They do, as a matter of fact. And they are, as a matter of fact."

"Maybe you could do your Santa act and give out presents Christmas Eve," she says, smiling at a shared memory. Warming his heart.

"Like when I was little, too," Sam says, laughing for the first time since they arrived.

Matthew enters into the spirit. "My long underwear is dying red as we speak." He feels himself starting to relax. Maybe Kate's just stressed out. Who wouldn't be? "So what are you working on these days, Kate? Got a new kids' book on the go?" He hasn't noticed any art clutter but maybe she's working someplace else.

Kate looks uncomfortable. "Oh, nothing right now, Dad." Matthew catches her look at Michael. Now what's that all about? Landmines everywhere.

Michael just keeps slogging away at the soup, some of it dribbling into his beard to drown or feed the organisms lurking there. Disgusting slob. Matthew hates to think of Kate having sex with the guy.

"We brought your birthday presents, honey," Delia says, smiling at Sam. "Grandpa will get them out of the car after lunch."

"Sweet. Can I open them?"

"Of course, Silly," she says, giving his ear a friendly tug.

Kate gets up and down several times waiting on them, and Emerald makes no move to help her. Neither Matthew nor

Delia speak to her for the rest of the meal and she must know they wish she wasn't here. Either that or she's stupid, and he suspects she's anything but.

Dying for a cigarette, he remembers the covered deck. "I'm going to have my coffee on the deck. Coming, Sam?"

"Sure!" That sounded more like the old Sam.

"We could all have our coffee on the deck," Michael says, as Matthew is getting his sweater.

"Brrrr, no thanks," Delia says. "I'll stay in and help Kate clear up."

"I'll help Kate with the dishes," Emerald says.

"No." Delia's tone brooks no argument. "Kate and I will do the dishes."

Out on the deck Matthew sits down, gratefully lighting up and inhaling deeply. The chair cushions and quilted tablecloth exude a musty smell, but he has to admit the view from the deck is striking, the rain now slowed to a misty sprinkle. The pines beyond the clearing splashed with gold and red and that wonderful maroon of the Japanese maples against the thickly wooded hill beyond. The air imbued with pine, cedar, woodsmoke. A squirrel runs up a tree by Michael's workshop and Buddy dashes madly after it.

"He always chases them," Sam says. "But he's never caught one."

He's just about to ask Sam what's been going on when Emerald comes out with a *Harrowsmith* magazine and flings herself into a chair. She's wearing a maroon padded vest that gives her sallow complexion a bit of colour. She lights a hand-rolled cigarette and starts leafing through the magazine. The chaperone has arrived.

Inside, he hears Michael suddenly transformed into a chatty Kathy. He's telling Delia something funny, judging by his tone of voice and her delighted laughter. Delia has always had a soft spot for Michael. He sure as hell hopes she's not giving him a hundred-dollar sweater and a bottle of good Scotch – their usual gift – for Christmas this year. He wouldn't put it past her. There's tolerant and then there's stupid, and Delia tips over into stupid on the Michael front.

"Where's Joey?" he asks Emerald. He slipped off his pillows and went out to get Snakes and Ladders while they were still eating.

She shrugs without looking up. "Around."

"Around? Couldn't he get lost out here?"

"No."

"Well, why not? He's only three or four, isn't he? And there's lots of bush back there."

She shrugs again. "He's probably in the cabin."

"Shall we go look for him?" he says to Sam. He wants to see if she'll get up and follow them.

"Yah. Sometimes he gets scared when he's alone. Or tries to play with matches."

Matthew looks at Sam with surprise. Here is a Sam he hasn't seen before. Too bad he's an only child.

"There aren't any matches," Emerald says, tight-lipped, pitching down the magazine and following them down the steps.

"Sam!" Joey comes running out as they approach the cabin, leaving the door open behind him. He runs over to Sam and hugs him around the legs. "Hi, Sam. I'm playing with my dinosaurs." The light rain wets Joey's face and spots his short-sleeved blue T-shirt. Goosebumps cover his small arms.

"You should have a jacket on, Joey." Matthew looks at Emerald and is met with an indifferent stare. Apparently Joey is on his own.

"I know the names of all the dinosaurs," Joey tells Matthew. "Sam told me all of them."

"No! Tell me," Matthew says. Joey is holding Sam's hand and now takes hold of Matthew's. Not since Sam was little has Matthew felt such a small, soft hand in his.

"I got tronasorus rex!" His beautiful dark eyes shine up at Matthew. How has Emerald borne this lovely child, he wonders. "And stegasaurus..."

"Right. I like that one."

"Me too!" Joey lifts his feet so he's swinging between their arms. Is there a child in the world who doesn't love doing this? His sleeve rucks up and Matthew sees an ugly black bruise on his small upper arm. Matthew touches it lightly.

"How did you hurt yourself, Joey?"

Joey glances at Emerald, who says shortly, "He fell."

Joey nods solemnly. "I fell."

They're still standing in front of the cabin. "Nice little place," Matthew says to Emerald. "May I have a look at it?"

"You're looking at it."

Her flat hostility jolts him after looking at Joey's bright, open face. He feels a small frisson of what you would feel if you met someone who might be a mugger on a dark street.

"I meant inside, of course." From the house comes the clatter of dishes, Michael still yakking it up.

She shrugs. "Whatever."

Matthew lets go of Joey and, with a hand either side of the doorway, leans in and glances quickly around. Crystals and

New-Age light-catchers hang in the three windows of the small sitting room and kitchen. The sink is full of dirty dishes and a grey dishcloth sours the air. Through a doorway he sees a small, messy bedroom with an unmade bed and a large crib in the corner. On a table near the door, piles of unfamiliar religious-looking magazines and two books of matches. He reaches in and scoops up the matches.

"Terra-dactul, Grampa!" Joey shouts, "that's the nother one!"

"Very good! That one flies, doesn't it?" He turns back.

"Satisfied?" Emerald says nastily.

"Are you always this unpleasant or are you making a special effort just for me?" he says, closing the door and handing her the matches as he starts back to the big house.

A surprised look pushes the mask aside.

"Well, you're invading my privacy," she says, glancing toward the sound of Michael's voice from the kitchen window.

"And you're not invading mine?" He stops. "I would like you to leave me and my grandson alone, please. I didn't come out here to see you." Only downright rudeness can get through to this woman. Sam, holding Joey's hand, stops, too, looking from him to Emerald.

"So why are you snooping in my house? And whether you like it or not I live here too."

"Since you mention it, no, I don't like it but I don't have to put up with it. It's my daughter I'm sorry for." His voice loud in the sudden silence from inside the house. Kate looking out the window.

"That's for her to say if she doesn't like it, isn't it?"

Michael is coming down the steps and across the yard. "What's going on?"

"Nothing," Sam says, hastily. "Grandpa and Emerald were just talking."

Emerald steps over and stands close beside Michael, her cupped hand reaching out to touch his, then dropping. And that one little step and one small gesture says it all.

"You son of a bitch," Matthew says quietly, looking from Michael to Emerald and back again. Michael's face flames as he moves a step away from Emerald.

"I don't have to take that from you or anybody else," Michael blusters, glancing at the house to make sure he's heard. "I'd appreciate it if you'd just leave."

"Aw, don't," Sam pleads. "Michael, don't, please!"

Michael sees Kate and Delia come out and his voice gets louder. "Stay out of it, Sam. He's nothing but an old drunk who's fucked up his own life and his wife's and daughter's too."

"Don't say that! Don't go, Grandpa!" Sam is crying, his mouth open in his rain-wet face.

"Who do you think you are, Charles Manson? Eh? Eh?" Matthew yells, like some crazed pensioner. "You fanatical, hypocritical bastard!"

Kate is hurrying across the yard.

"I won't be called that by anybody, Kate, not even your father."

"Oh, Dad," she says, the way she used to say it when he was drinking.

"Kate, I'm sorry but –" What can he say? Your born-again Christian husband has moved his mistress into your yard? Is

130

carrying on with her right under your nose? A shocked look-ing Delia is still watching from the deck, and the full signifi-cance of what he's done washes over him.

Emerald looks from him to Delia, her expression avid. She knows his predicament and loves it.

"I mean it, Matthew. And don't come back," Michael says.

"Fine, I'm going."

Sam lets out an anguished cry and takes off, past the house and onto the road to the highway, Buddy right on his heels.

Delia runs after him calling "Sam! Come back, Please honey, come back!" Matthew can't seem to make his legs move as Delia walks back, wiping tears from her cheeks.

"You don't have to go, Mom," Michael says.

Delia looks at Matthew, and if looks could kill he'd be face down in the mud. "I have to. I'm on days."

"I'll talk to you before you go," and Michael turns and lopes off toward his shop, as if afraid Matthew will blurt out his secret before he gets there.

"You know what I meant, you lying bastard," Matthew yells after him. Michael shrugs and throws up his hands as he walks. Delia goes back in the house and slams the door. Kate just stands there like someone in shock. "Aw, no," she says. "Aw, no."

"I'm sorry, Katie. I'm so sorry."

"I was looking forward to this so much," she says. And she walks away, head bent, shoulder blades outlined through her t-shirt like incipient wings. The painful yearning he feels as he watches her go is almost more than he can bear.

He rounds on Emerald.

"Fuck off Emerald." he says. "What's your real name? Madame DeFarge?"

And since the fun is over she actually leaves; not to her house where Joey might be setting fires or drinking poison or climbing and falling, but to her lover's workshop.

Leaving Matthew standing alone in the rain.

Chapter Ten

When it becomes clear that nobody gives a damn if he stands there all day Matthew goes and sits in the car. Hunched down behind the wheel he smokes and smokes and smokes, peering out through the windshield like an old turtle wondering whether to go back into its shell.

An old drunk who's fucked up his own life and his wife's and daughter's too. It'll take a long time to get over that one; it always does when the truth is applied with a branding iron. And did he have to say old? He could have said no good, or hopeless, couldn't he?

He frets about Sam. Where would he go? He wanted to help Sam and all he did was make things worse and break his promise to Delia. But Sam at least is defiant. Kate's meekness scares him. Where has all her spirit gone? At least she got to talk to her mother, the contretemps in the yard accomplished that anyway.

Oh, a contretemps was it? And a backhoe is a shovel. But maybe Delia will persuade her to come back with them. She must see that she's ill.

He hopes Sam didn't hitch a ride to town, he's a good-looking kid and you never know who's out there. If something bad happens to Sam it'll be his fault. He feels his bowel loosen at the thought and orders it to behave. Quite often that works. He saw Michael go back in the house and the stupid bugger is just mean enough to make him go in the bush. Come to think of it Emerald must use their bathroom. Poor Kate.

Where would Sam go? Maybe to the old barn. He used to play there when he was a kid.

What a strange thought. As if he isn't any longer.

He turns to get out of the car, almost screaming at a dribbly-bearded face inches away through the window. Matthew rolls down the window and cigarette smoke billows out.

The man backs away. "Oh, man," he says, coughing. "Whoo!" waving a skinny hand in front of his face, "I can't believe I useta smoke like that."

Matthew is speechless.

"I saw you standing out there in the rain," he says, in a surprisingly deep voice. His stringy, grey hair touches his shoulders.

"Yes?" Matthew says. He might as well have said So?

"I thought you might be moving in," he says, hopefully. He's wearing a faded black T-shirt, heavy, green plaid shirt and dirty suede, fringed vest. Jeans that maybe fit him fifty pounds ago.

"Moving in? Why? Where do you live?"

"Over there." The man waves a skinny arm beyond the house. "In a tent." Matthew remembers seeing a tent back in the trees and assuming it was Sam's.

"Good Lord. Isn't it too cold?"

The man smiles a sweet, gap-toothed smile, rain dripping off the end of his nose. "Jesus keeps me warm," he says.

Matthew can think of nothing to say to that. Nobody even mentioned this guy's existence. "Are you a friend of Michael's?"

"Yes, indeed. He's given me a home. My name is Jim." He sticks his hand through the window and Matthew reluctantly shakes it. A little bundle of cold twigs.

Matthew opens the door handle but the man doesn't move away.

"Please move, I have to go," Matthew says, pushing the door open none too gently. He steps out and slams the door.

Alarmingly, the man opens his arms as if to hug him and almost manages to before he backs up against the car.

He drops his arms. "Life can be hard."

"Thanks for telling me that. I thought it was a bowl of cherries."

His sarcasm is ignored. "Peace, brother. God loves you."

And he flashes the peace sign before turning back toward the house. He walks with shoulders hunched up against the rain, the seat of his old, colourless jeans drooping straight down, as if they cover unpadded bones, the heels of his boots run over on the sides. Without looking back he raises his hand in a wave, as if he knows Matthew is still watching him, and disappears around the side of the house.

Matthew shakes his head. Hard.

On his way to the barn he sees what he didn't see on the way in. In a clearing beside the barn is another cabin, one surely too small for anyone to live in. Nearby, a pile of lumber is covered by a tarp weighted down with tires.

What now. Who's moving into that one? One of the seven dwarves? Joey?

Maybe Jim. After a tent in the rain an eight-by-eight cabin might look pretty good. It might be a shed except for the windows and, now that he's closer, the fretwork. Like a playhouse. He tries the door but it's locked. He peers in the window and sees shelves loaded with canned food and bottled water. Huge rolls of black plastic in the corner. Duct tape. A straight wooden chair.

Pushing open the door of the barn, he steps inside.

"Sam?" he calls. It's dead quiet.

The first thing he notices in the dim light is a staircase on the end wall going up to the loft, its new lumber contrasting with the age-darkened grey walls, water-stained black in places. The place feels cold and damp, and smells of sawdust and mildew and the ghosts of long-gone horses. Above the old ladder on the side wall the egress to the loft has been filled in. Under a small window that lets in a grey mist of light a carpenter's table with a circular saw is set up, its heavy electrical cord neatly looped over a nail. Nearby something that can only be described as a manger about six feet long and wider than a single bed has been recently built. It's half full of packed down hay. Now what the hell is that for?

"Sam?" Silence. Maybe he's up in the loft. He calls again as he climbs the stairway but there's no answer from above.

Stepping out onto the loft floor he stops short.

He's in some kind of meeting room. Or church. A large plain wood cross is nailed to the far end wall, which is newly lined with plywood as are all the walls. Several rows of mismatched chairs, some metal folding, some wood, face forward. At the very back, against the wall, an oak church pew.

Matthew sits down heavily in the nearest chair. This is weird. And somehow scary.

It's several welcome degrees warmer up here, though, and he leans back and lights a cigarette. A large heater in the back corner will warm this place on the coldest days. A plywood ceiling hides the curved rafters and the hook and rope where Sam played Batman, landing in the hay, also no more. Even the smell of it gone. He smokes and gazes around.

An unpainted railing encloses about an eight-foot-wide space in front of the cross. In that space there is a wood table draped with a red cloth and set with candles on both ends, and to the left of it, an oak pulpit – obviously a real one salvaged from a church – and open on it a very large bible with a wide red ribbon hanging from it.

Definitely a church. Can't Michael find one extreme enough to suit him? He must not or why would anybody go to all this trouble? This is not ordinary Christianity, surely, where you try to live a good life, help your fellow man, don't covet your neighbour's wife or if you do, don't tell your neighbour, and look forward to your reward in Heaven, whatever you perceive that to be. People don't travel this far out of the way to go to church when there's one with the same message on the corner.

He counts the chairs. Twenty-five. Does this church really have a congregation or is it wishful thinking on Michael's part? "If you build it they will come?" Anyone can start a church, and after hearing Michael's bizarre grace at lunch he can almost believe it of him.

But not quite.

Michael has never been a leader. A searcher, yes, digging all kinds of holes in the desert and never waiting for any of them to fill before excitedly digging another. And each hole, while he dug, was always the only right way to dig a hole in the only right place to dig.

First he was a Buddhist, or professed to be. He even considered throwing everything up and joining a Tibetan monastery. If only. Kate just rode that one out. She was teaching at the time and quite capable of supporting her and Sam. Then it was Taoism. And some other ism. Then an ardent New Age phase, with crystals and magnets and books on loving yourself above all – that one fit like a glove – and sleeping on the floor when he came to visit rather than sleeping in a bed that wasn't set precisely north and south.

Michael invariably knew somebody who had all the answers, his enthusiasm taking him, always, onto the extreme fringe. But always a follower.

The warmth of the room is getting to Matthew and he yawns.

Now it's fundamentalism with a capital *F* and how far is he going to go with that?

Taking up serpents?

Drinking strychnine?

Kool-Aid?

Jesus! That woke him up.

Matthew realizes now the one consistent thing in Michael's life is this place. He lived here before he married Kate. And his work. Matthew has to admit he's very good at what he does. They had some lovely "Made-by-Michael" pieces. They cost the earth and then some, but they were worth it and Delia took them with her when she went, reminding him it was she who forked over the earth. Except for the cherry bookcases. They're his and he'd love them if Satan himself had made them.

He drops ashes in his turned-up pantcuff, then notices a tobacco lid on a table with a wooden chair near the back of the room and goes to get it. There's a homemade butt with a twisted end in the lid and he sniffs it. Pot. Apparently Michael still smokes where and what he damn well pleases. He sticks that in his pantleg, too, worrying Sam might smoke it.

There are some small-format newspapers on the table, and some periodicals that look, at first glance, like something you'd find in the narthex of any church. But aren't.

He rifles through them: *End Times News Digest; The Wanderers; Twin Circle; The Remnant;* and some Marian literature. Some apparently Catholic publications, though not, he suspects, church approved. And a small stack of paperback books: *The Beginning of the End; The Late Great Planet Earth; The Rapture Book; Guide to Survival; The Tribulation.* Writers like Tim LaHaye. Hal Lindsey. Pat Robertson. And this one, *Left Behind* – the unrepentant infidels, no doubt. How jolly. Where the devil do they find all this stuff? They should have left Sam's rope on the ceiling with a noose on the end of it for those who didn't feel up to it all.

He carries some papers and newsletters back to the chair and starts to leaf through them. A picture of a woman held on her knees by two uniformed men while another with a smoking branding iron with three raised sixes prepares to apply it to her forehead. The fact they haven't figured out the sixes will be backwards makes it more funny than anything.

In another, titled *The Rapture,* an astonished man with a lawn mower watches his wife soar heavenward in her apron with a wooden spoon in her hand, and other beatific people fly up as driverless cars crash and mayhem reigns below. One has a couple of evil-looking men in a hospital nursery full of babies, whatever that's about. Only one thing he reads makes sense to Matthew, that the Antichrist is a computer. That, he can believe. Fearing a computer-induced nervous breakdown at the *Colonist* office they'd let him go back to his old IBM Selectric.

He's still standing there scowling when he hears Delia calling his name. It sounds like she's down near the car, so she must be ready to go. Good. He can't wait to get the hell away from here even though he dreads the drive back with her.

He butts the cigarette and puts it in his pocket.

Delia is standing by the car, and when she sees him she gets in and buckles the seat belt. Kate is nowhere in sight. "Is Kate not coming?" he asks, through the window.

"What do you think?" she says. "She's in no shape to decide anything right now."

He decides to ignore that. "Should I go and say goodbye to her? And I have to pee," he says, rather plaintively.

"Well, go in the bush. You're not going back in the house. Michael is there and you'll just make matters worse."

She's right of course. He goes and takes a leak in the bush, his own silly parody of a John Masefield poem running through his head: "I must go down to pee again, to the lonely sea and the sky, and all I ask is a strong stream and a star to steer it by." His old drinking buddy, Bill, always found that hysterical. They were so easily amused, the two of them. Drunk or sober.

Back in the car he says, "I hate to leave before Sam gets back."

"He's in Parksville with a friend. Kate phoned."

He takes a deep, grateful breath. "Is he all right?"

"Yes, he's all right. Come on, Matthew. It's late."

"Well, did he hitchhike? He shouldn't do that."

"Stop looking for trouble, Matthew. You caused enough today without looking for more."

"You got that right," he says dismally, starting the motor. Though it's not true he caused it. How should a father react to a cheating son-in-law?

Anxious to put it all behind him he's driving too fast down the narrow, closed-in logging road when the car lights pick out the eyes of a yearling deer, standing close to the road. It's too late to stop but the deer doesn't move, just looks thoughtfully at them through the windshield as they pass.

"Ooh. That was close," he says.

"Yes. Slow down, Matthew. You're driving way too fast," she says. "Killing us both isn't going to help anything."

She's right. Who would rescue Sam and Kate then? Who's going to now? He slows down and they drive in silence until they turn onto the highway. He wishes she'd give him hell like she would have once. It's somehow depressing that she doesn't.

"How was Kate when you left?"

"Well, how do you think she is, Matthew? Michael is her husband, you still can't seem to get that through your head."

"Unfortunately I can." He pushes in the lighter and

reaches for his cigarettes. "He's having it off with that bloody Emerald woman. That's what that was all about."

"Oh, for heaven's sake, Matthew, what makes you think that?" The lighter pops and she winds down her window. "Brrr. That's cold. When are you going to quit smoking?"

He lights up. "I don't think it, I know it. I could tell the way she..."

"The way she what?"

"The way she looked at him when he came out in the yard. She put her hand out and touched him." It sounds lame, unconvincing.

"Oh, really?" She sighs. "There you go, making a mountain out of a molehill again."

"What I saw pass between those two was no molehill."

It's pouring rain again, cars spraying water as they pull out to pass him, one after the other. He gets over in the slow lane and at least a dozen cars zoom past in a steady stream.

"Is there never a time when this fucking highway isn't like the fucking Grand Prix? Why is everybody in such a godamn hurry?"

"Stop swearing, Matthew. Just – calm down. And could we have some heat? It's cold in here."

He turns on the heater and adjusts it. "Michael looked damned guilty," he goes on, "but he knew I couldn't accuse him in front of Sam. And Kate."

"Well, I don't like her, either, but I don't think Michael would do that right in their yard. At least I hope not."

"But he did. They are. You'll see. And did you know Michael's turning the barn into some kind of holy roller temple? Some damn weird thing."

"Yes. Michael said you were snooping around up there."

"Snooping around? I was looking for Sam. And somebody needs to snoop around there. Did you know some old hippie is living in a tent in the bush? Scared the hell out of me peering in the car window."

Delia laughs. "Yes, I saw him. Kate says he's just staying there for awhile."

"How many more strange people are going to turn up there, I wonder. They don't need all that extra room. And what's that little cabin for?"

"That's going to be Michael's retreat house. A place to pray and meditate."

"Oh, of course. Why didn't I think of that? Jesus. I guess praying makes him hungry. It's full of food."

Hot air is blasting up from under the dash. He yanks open his jacket and the velcro flap closers glom onto his sweater. "I hate this goddamn velcro crap! It ruined that good pullover you gave me."

"You're getting all worked up over nothing. Hasn't A.A. taught you anything, Matthew? Try saying the serenity prayer when you get like this. You're swearing worse than when you drank." She's wrestling out of her jacket and he gives her a hand. She settles back, buttoning up the rose cardigan.

"Never mind the serenity prayer. And I'm swearing because I'm upset. What's he up to, anyway? That's what I'd like to know."

"Nothing. And why would he tell you about it anyway? You'd only make fun of it the way you did about Al-Anon. I see nothing wrong with a group of people getting together for spiritual growth."

"Well why can't they grow spiritually in the house?"

"I don't know!" She sounds exasperated. She spreads her hands down where the heat is coming in. "Why? Was it weird up there or something?"

"Yes. Well – maybe not if you know it's a holy roller church before you go up." He knows he repeating himself but fundamentalist sounds too normal.

Now somebody's giving him the horn because he's driving too slow. He speeds up.

"Well, what then?" she asks.

He thinks hard, seeing the room in his mind. "There was a red tablecloth on what I assume was the altar. Is that weird?"

"I don't know. Probably not."

Neither of them had kept up more than a nodding acquaintance with church during their marriage. For all they know red tablecloths might mean a United Church Christmas or human sacrifice night at your friendly satanist service.

"It was a feeling more than anything," he admits. "He smokes pot up there. And there's a bunch of god-awful depressing doomsday literature."

She shrugs. "Well, you'd expect that, wouldn't you? His grace at lunch made that plain."

"His Grace? Is that what you called Michael?"

"Don't be ridiculous, Matthew." But she laughs.

"Okay, I'll drop it, but it's nothing like an Al-Anon meeting that Michael's into, I can guarantee that." He considers making amends about his Al-Anon-grudging days but decides he's not sure he's over it yet. Al-Anon gave her the courage to leave.

Three cars pass them like they're standing still while he

tries to steel himself to ask.

"Did you find out why Kate looks so terrible?"

"Yes."

His stomach contracts. "What. What's wrong with her?"

"She's hooked on pills. Poor kid, she didn't want to tell me. She's been taking Xanax and tranquilizers for more than a year."

Tranquilizers? Xanax? Not cancer or MS or Lou Gehrig's Disease? He could cry with relief. "What's Xanax?"

"It's bad stuff, Matthew. Addicting and depressing. It's meant to be a short-term anxiety drug, or muscle relaxant."

"How can you take muscle relaxants for a year and still stand up?"

Matthew is struggling to get his jacket off and Delia reaches over and helps him. "She's trying to quit but it's hard. I said she should go to a treatment centre but she seems afraid to leave."

"No wonder. So you admit it's not a good situation up there, even if you don't believe me about Michael?"

"Yes, I do. But even if you're right about that, you've got to let go of it, Matthew. We can't tell her Michael's cheating on her. If he is. And she knows she's got a drug problem and said she's going to cut down." She reclines the passenger seat, doing up her jacket and tucking her hands into her sleeves. "Turn it over, Matthew."

Turn it over to God, she means. Spoken like a true infuriating Al-Anon.

"Michael will get tired of this, too. It's not as if he's starting a cult or anything."

"No," he says. *"Michael* isn't." Then closes his mouth on

what he was thinking. Maybe she's right. Maybe he is overreacting about the religion thing. But not about Michael and Emerald. Just the thought of her out there with Kate and Sam, like a viper in a nest with baby birds, gives him a falling-away feeling in his chest. And his gut will be on the rampage tomorrow. He can tell. Damn it, he's getting too old for this.

"Can we just be quiet, Matthew? I'm exhausted and have to work in the morning." She puts her head back and closes her eyes.

And it's only when he stops talking that he realizes how desperately tired he is. Tired and wired at the same time, way beyond sleepy now in spite of his four hours last night.

Delia is already asleep. She could always do that, put her head down and be gone; he used to resent it like hell, up bleary-eyed popping valium in the bathroom. What he wouldn't give for one now – one, hell, a pailful – but killjoy Marty warned him about trading one addiction for another. He sighs and reaches for his cigarettes. Hard rain drums the roof of the car, and the cursed wind is getting up again, a hard gust almost pushing them off the road.

Delia's gentle snoring keeps him company as he drives through the dark night. Being this close to her warm body, the lovely, familiar smell of her, their legs touching at the knees, has caught the attention of the man downstairs, who begins to stir. Stop it, behave, orders Matthew, moving his leg away. He doesn't want to feel like a pervert. Delia called him that once over some drunken fumbling when she was asleep. He didn't even remember it.

God grant me the serenity to accept the things I cannot change, he thinks over and over like a mantra as the black night glides by and the rain pours down and the cars whoosh past, and it soothes him a little. He doesn't say "Courage to change the things I can," knowing full well he doesn't know what they are, maybe he'll never know. And wisdom to know the difference is still way beyond him.

Still, hearing from the man downstairs like that cheers him a little. It's been so long since the old fellow has shown an interest, he's wondered if he might be impotent.

At her apartment door Delia fumbles with her keys, so foggy she can't seem to find the keyhole. He takes the keys and opens the door.

"Thanks." She yawns. "Goodnight, Matthew. I'll talk to you later."

"Delia?"

"What?"

"Do you love him?"

"Who?" She frowns. "Michael?"

"No. Nick."

"Oh, for God's sake, Matthew. I'm not even awake."

"Well, do you? I need to know."

"I don't know!" she says, exasperated. And shuts the door behind her.

He raps on the glass panel beside the door and she turns around, frowning.

"I'm sorry about today," he calls, and turns away.

Cold rain trickles down his neck as he trudges back to the car.

She always did say his timing was lousy.

"Oh, that was fun." Sam is out of breath. They've been kicking around the soccer ball in the park behind Jeff's house. Him and Jeff and Chad, a flat-out free-for-all, charging around like crazy with a goal but no goalie, wrestling each other for the ball. Now they're flopped over the swings. Coming down. Chilling out.

"Yah. That was awesome, Sam." Jeff is puffing. "You got eight goals." He's draped over the swing on his stomach, his knuckles dragging through the sand.

"Well, it helps when there's no goalie," Sam says modestly.

"No. You're just good. You always were. We need you back on the team," he says.

Chad says: "Yah. We really suck. We're seventh in the league."

"Seventh?" Sam says. He's on the middle swing and feeling happy again with a friend on either side and staying over tonight. He didn't tell them what happened at home today, he's trying to forget it. "How many teams are there now?"

"Seven," Chad says. Even Jeff looks solemn. "Can't you talk your folks into letting you play?" Chad asks. He's twisting slowly around on the swing and then letting go and twirling back again.

"It's not my mom," Sam says. "It's Michael."

"Why? Why won't he let you?"

"I dunno. Who knows why Michael does anything?"

"Something to do with religion, eh?" Chad says.

Sam makes a face. "Yah. I guess —"

"Jesus never played soccer!" they all shout in unison, and fall around this way and that.

"Beat you up!" Sam suddenly yells, pumping hard.

"No way, Jose," Chad says, running backward and giving himself a huge push off.

"Hey!" Jeff yells, twisting himself onto the swing. "You guys got a head start."

They pump madly and soon they're flying through the air, almost up to the crossbar.

"See who can jump the farthest," Sam yells, flying off the swing. He lands with his stomach still floating up somewhere, then arcing down again. He likes that feeling.

They swing and jump. Swing and jump. Laughing like crazy. And it seems like something wonderful to Sam. Just hanging out with his friends. Doing stupid stuff.

Then they sit on the swings, slowly rotating this way and that, kicking the sand, catching their breath again. It's getting dark and the light near the swings and slides comes on, leaving the rest of the park in shadow. In the big spruce tree near the swings birds are making sleepy cheepy noises.

"I had a sorta cool dream last night," Chad says. "I dreamed I had the most enormous book and when I opened it up it turned into a big field full of words, like a crop all made out of words."

"Awesome," says Sam.

"Yeah. And Jeff and I were reading our way around the field."

"Cool," says Jeff, who never reads anything if he can help it.

"And there were all different levels, with bigger words and stuff."

"Hmmm. Verrry interrresting," Sam says, in his evil-psychiatrist voice.

"Yeah, it was. And when we were finished reading we looked back and the field was tramped down in a design where we'd been, kinda like crop circles?"

"Oh yeah? We made flying saucer designs like that?" Jeff asks. They're *X Files* fans and in total agreement that aliens are out there.

"No. We made a picture of the Beatles."

"Cool," the others say respectfully.

"Yah, a real cool dream. Wonder what it means?" Sam muses. Chad always has kind of intellectual dreams.

"Ah, probably something to do with Mister Barker talking about high school lately," Chad says.

"I had a dream, too," Jeff says.

"No kidding."

"Yah, I dreamt a man in khaki shorts and helmet came to the door delivering *National Geographics.*"

"Yah?"

"And he handed me the magazine and said 'We've changed the name of *National Geographic* to *Pee On My Shoe.*'"

"Pee on my shoe?" they all yell.

"Yah. It said that on the front."

Sam laughs so hard he falls off the swing. "They changed the name of *National Geographic* to *Pee on My Shoe?*"

"Yah."

"Oh! God!" Chad is hanging over the swing howling and kicking his legs. "What did you say when he said that?"

"'Oh, I can see that,' I said. It made perfect sense to me."

And that's funny, too.

"Oh, help, my stomach hurts," Sam finally groans.

"Mine, too."

"Mine three."

"Hey look at Jupiter," Chad says after awhile. They're all lying on their backs on the ground now. "It had sixteen moons in an old book I read, they probably found a bunch more by now. But they only knew about sixty-six in the whole solar system then."

"Awesome," they all agree.

"They've found more, for sure."

"What's the biggest?" Sam asks.

"Ganymede. It had water on it once."

"Ganymede. Sounds like the name of a knight, doesn't it?"

"Yeah. And Callisto and Europa are two more they think have oceans under ice crusts, too." And they all lie on the ground awhile and look at Jupiter, hanging there in the sky like the Christmas star. Sam resolves to read more. He doesn't want to grow up stupid.

"I wonder if the moon has frozen oceans on it," Jeff says.

"They think it might..."

"No way!"

"Yes way."

"Do you think people will ever live on the moon?"

"Nah. Just the Moonies." They laugh. "And Michael Jackson."

"And Juliet, I hope," says Sam. Fat Juliet, going around saying "Wherefore art thou, Romeo?" to all the guys in grade eight.

"Yah." Jeff laughs, "maybe Romeo is an alien. But it'd be weird, wouldn't it? Having people up there."

"Yah. Guys playing soccer and taking out the garbage."

"And looking at us through telescopes."

"And going to Michael Jackson concerts."

"I wouldn't want to go."

"I'd go if somebody gave me a ticket."

"What? To the moon?"

"No. To a Michael Jackson concert."

"Well, yah. But who'd want to live on the moon?"

"No way. They don't have any trees."

"Or birds."

"Or dogs. Or cats."

"Or anything."

"Except Michael Jackson."

"But getting there'd be awesome."

"Yah. Awesome."

"Yah."

It's ages since Sam felt so good. It'd be so great if they lived in town. Just him and Mom. Mom could teach school again. And he could get a skateboard. That'd be sweet.

Whenever he imagines his future, Michael isn't in it.

Chapter Eleven

"Michelangelo you're not, my friend," Marty says. He's leaning against the wall watching Matthew, up on the stepladder. "But who looks at the ceiling?"

"Inspector Funk. That's who." Matthew's face and arms and old green T-shirt are spattered with paint. He blobs peach paint on the white ceiling. "Shit. I can't paint with this skid row tremor."

"It's worse holding your arms up," says the voice of experience. "You need a break."

Needing no coaxing, Matthew lays the brush on the tray and climbs down the wobbly ladder. Marty proffers his pack of Exports and, cigarettes lit, they sit on the floor with the coffee maker in the corner between them.

"I couldn't rent you this apartment, could I?" Matthew says.

"What? With this lousy paint job?" Marty laughs. "Why?"

Matthew tells him about the visit from Liz Wright and her mother.

"Uh oh. That's what you get for trying to be a hero. Tell me about the trip with your wife."

Matthew runs a hand over his paint-spattered bald head. "You really want to know?"

"I asked."

So Matthew tells him the whole miserable story, about what went on up there, what's going on up there, why he's worried sick about his daughter and how he still feels about his wife. He even tells Marty about Michael's "old drunk" jab.

"Ouch!" Marty says.

As he talks, the sky outside the window darkens, Marty's white shirt blooming ghostly in the dim light, but it feels comfortable like that. He's not quite baring his soul, but it's still a lot more personal than any conversation he's had with another male since he was ten years old. Though he vaguely remembers some drunken, whiny even, god-forbid teary, episodes – there's nothing worse than a crying drunk.

"Whew! That was some trip, in more ways than one," Marty says when he's done.

"And to think I was going up there to make amends to Kate."

"Ah, the best laid plans eh? But hey, think what you'd've done if you were drinking."

"I'd still be drunk," Matthew says, his tone a bit wistful.

"Yes, and convinced it was all somebody else's fault, probably."

"Did I say it wasn't?"

They both laugh, Matthew's sounding a bit rusty.

"But I know how you feel about your daughter, Matthew. I got one, too." Marty's lighter flares, his strong, dark features illuminated as he lights a cigarette. "Write her a letter."

"I suppose. At least she can't talk back."

"A daughter? Are you kidding? Mine's in university and still thinks it's her duty to run my life. But that quack who kept your daughter on Xanax so long oughta lose his licence." He shakes his head. "And tranquilizers, too? Jesus. I knew a guy who got so depressed on that stuff he killed himself."

Matthew's scalp prickles as if his non-existent hair is standing on end.

Marty shakes his head. "That should never've happened."

Matthew closes his eyes. Oh, God, please don't let that happen.

"Stop expecting the worst, Matthew. You're such a gloomy bastard. She'll need some help getting off it, that's all. That poor guy had nobody."

"Delia says we have to let go of it. Turn it over to God, you know, that Al-Anon thing."

"It's not just an Al-Anon thing. They got it from us in the first place. Step three, remember?" He takes a thoughtful drag on his cigarette. "They just practise it better."

"Yeah, they do." Matthew's nodding acquaintance with God has always been during crises till now, but his short, tentative prayers are starting to feel more natural. "The hard part is believing it makes a difference."

"Yah. That takes longer."

"I have to phone Delia about Kate, and Nick will make sure I know he's there."

Marty puts his cigarettes and lighter in his shirt pocket and drains his coffee cup. "Maybe you better get used to it. Maybe he's always gonna be there."

Something about Marty's expression reminds Matthew that he lost his wife to cancer three years ago when she was just thirty-nine. And he's whining about Delia. "God, Marty, I'm sorry. This must sound pretty trivial to you."

"No, it doesn't. Loss is loss. Maybe you should take somebody out yourself? That Liz seems pretty nice."

"She is. We had a game of Scrabble last night. We might become friends."

"She must've let you win." Marty grins. "But that's good. You're alone too much." He butts his cigarette and pushes himself up off the floor. "Turn on the light and I'll cut in those ceiling edges for you before I go."

And he does the edges in no time, as straight as a die. "There," he says, climbing down. "You can finish with a roller now. And tell that old skinflint to buy a new ladder."

"Thanks, Marty. I appreciate it." Matthew can't quite straighten up. Sitting on the floor so long was dynamite on his arthritic hip. "And thanks for letting me sound off, too."

"Glad to lend an ear, Quasimodo," Marty says, wiping his hands with the paint rag. "I'll say a prayer for your daughter. But you should really get a sponsor, Matthew. You got a lotta stuff goin' on there." He drapes the rag over the stepladder. "I gotta run. Don's off tonight. He's got a new guy and I hope this one works out. We think we got problems, eh?"

He's halfway down the hallway when Matthew catches up with him. "Would you consider being my sponsor, Marty?" He says it fast.

Marty turns around, grinning. "I thought you'd never ask," he says. "Sure I would. But there's a couple of things you should know about first."

"What's that?"

"You gotta go to meetings. Two or three a week wouldn't hurt you at this stage, but no less than two. And you've got to promise to call me before you pick up a drink."

Matthew swallows. Marty's dark, knowing eyes are taking in his urge to back down, he's sure, but he says nothing.

"I don't think I'll go to three, but I'll try for two," he says finally.

"Try for two?"

"All right. I'll make two."

"We're on." Marty claps a hand on Matthew's shoulder, and they shake hands before Marty jogs off down the hall, giving him a thumbs-up before he disappears through the exit door.

Now he's done it. Marty's a funny guy but he's dead serious about Alcoholics Anonymous. But back in the room Matthew climbs the stepladder almost with alacrity.

Two meetings a week? He makes a face as he picks up the paint roller. Then shrugs. Oh well, in for a dime, in for a dollar.

He makes a long, sweeping, peach-coloured arc.

M atthew is offended by the sheer mind-numbing magnitude of ugly, useless junk everywhere, shouting buy me, buy me. He tries not to look as he wends his way to the Bay cafeteria. He's got to find somewhere else to eat till the seasonal insanity is over, it's a masochistic exercise to just walk in the door.

In the downstairs cafeteria he gets in the lineup of early

Christmas shoppers and accepts a roast beef, yorkshire pudding dinner from the tired-looking woman about his age he's beginning to feel he knows. She's wearing a Santa Claus hat, her tight-lipped smile saying yes, I know it's ridiculous but I need this job. What's ridiculous – no, obscene – is the retail world where the Halloween witch and Santa Claus shake hands in passing.

"Hi there," chirps the cheerful young reindeer-antlered cashier, ringing up his dinner for $7.25 including coffee, 10% off for seniors. "How are you today?" He's become a regular.

"Oh, can't complain," Matthew says, like the other old-timers, pocketing his change.

He's moved up in the world, deserting the Macsomethings for department store cafeterias. He's researched the cheap places that still make a decent meal, and the Bay's roast beef dinner is very decent. So is the turkey dinner, $6.50 with the discount.

As are Eatons' chicken pot pie, salmon steak, and fish and chips, $3.95 on Tuesdays. Seniors' Day. When it's not so busy he often gets a table by the window with a view of the water that would be the envy of the trendy restaurants.

So here he is with all the other seniors who hate cooking for themselves, eating by themselves, just plain being by themselves. It depresses him a little to be so obviously one of the lonely, but not enough to keep him away.

Over a few tables, he sees the familiar classic-featured man with the ebony-dyed hair without his ebony-dyed wife. They must live downtown near the *Times* office since he's seen them for years, walking arm in arm, like two stately black-headed waterbirds. They must have shared countless bottles of

Clairol, towel-draped in their apartment, applying the dye and setting the timer. A ritual he knows from Delia covering the grey in her hair.

He's seen the man so often he almost feels he could go over and ask about his wife, but he hasn't seen him lately and realizes he now has the look of a man without a wife. His longer than usual wavy hair, showing white at the crown and sideburns, lies over his collar in a dispirited kind of way – she probably cut it too – and his tan windbreaker jacket needs cleaning. He gazes into the distance, listlessly chewing his roast beef special.

And there's old Alec two tables over, sound asleep with his nose buried in the napkin dispenser he uses to prop up his head. The first time Matthew saw him like that he went and told the cashier he thought the man was dead.

"Oh, that's just Alec," she laughed. "He comes here to sleep." And indeed he does. Comes to sleep and read the Bible, which is open on the table by an empty orange juice bottle and half-eaten doughnut. One of these days Alec will die with his nose in the napkin dispenser and they won't know till closing time.

Five Chinese matrons at the next table are talking up a storm. Do Chinese people really say five times as much as we do in the same time or does it only sound that way?

At another table two old ladies cozily attired in mauves and pinks are out for lunch. They giggle like girls in pigtails, as old women often do, as if they've found some secret of life denied to the rest of them. To old men, anyway – the ones they're probably laughing about. He thinks again of that happiness graph, believing more as time goes on that it's true.

Outside, his stomach comfortably full, he sets off down the street. It's a mild, foggy evening. He needs some new pants and there's a menswear somewhere along here.

Walking by a rundown hotel with the door of the bar propped open he stops dead on the sidewalk, and breathes it in; the stuffy, closed-up smell of a seedy bar with its beer-stained carpet, smoky drapes, fresh booze and cigarette smoke and just a hint of eau de pissoir. He closes his eyes, like someone inhaling the scent of roses.

He likes the smell. Powerful as love.

Yes, his taste in bars matched his decline, but that doesn't make him want to march smartly away and have a cappuccino in the nearest upscale coffee house. No, indeed. It speaks to him, yearning there on the sidewalk as shoppers detour around him.

Come on, old friend, it says. *Stop trying so hard. Come in and sit in a corner. Wrap your hand around a drink, light up a smoke and relax, life is not such a serious affair. If you want to be alone to fig-ure things out with a glass of scotch to oil the lobes, nobody's going to bother you. We know that sometimes a man has to drink and be sociable, and sometimes he just has to drink....*

Move, Matthew orders himself, but his feet have taken root. A fierce physical craving clutches his throat.

What's that you say? You're an alcoholic? Hey, that's all right. No problem. We love alcoholics here. Where would we be without them? Lots of brilliant, creative people are alcoholics. But are you sure about that? You don't look like an alcoholic, you look like a fine, intelligent, interesting man, you look a lot like Patrick Stewart in fact. You would-n't need to get drunk. It's Christmas after all. You could just have one....

You could just have one.

And suddenly he's running as if it's after him, bumping into people like an escaping robber, tripping over a flower stall, turning heads. He wheels into a little old coffee shop with wine vinyl booths and orders coffee, his hands shaking so hard he has trouble lighting up. The table is set with two cups and, grateful for the privacy of the booth, he slops half the coffee into the other cup so he can drink without spilling. His shirt is damp with sweat.

When he's calmer he calls Marty from the pay phone in the entry, hunched around the phone and speaking low, like somebody setting up a drug deal.

"I wasn't even thinking of a drink, for God's sake, I was on my way to buy some pants." He was blindsided by it. "It was the smell. I felt like an old horse who's just caught a whiff of the barn."

"Oh, man, an open bar. You poor bugger. Maybe you better forget the pants."

"But I was feeling okay. It just came out of the blue."

"That it can. D'you want to come by for coffee?"

"No. I'm all right now, I think. Just feeling a bit – shaky." Actually, he's vibrating from head to foot, sweat still leaking down his sides.

And when Matthew convinces him he's all right, Marty says, "Get to a meeting tonight." Not, "Can you get to a meeting tonight?" Or "It would be a good idea to go to a meeting tonight." Or "Good for you, Matthew, you didn't drink." Just, "Get to a meeting tonight." Any other time his back would be up around his shoulders.

"Yeah, okay. Marty," he says, humbled by the experience. "I will."

Calming down over another coffee he remembers a scene in *Under the Volcano,* where the Consul is talking about the beauty of his favourite poor Mexican bar, the way the light came in the window, the old woman at the table in the back, his love for the place. And Malcolm Lowry said – or was it the Consul – that he saw nothing wrong in going down the drain, considered it a valuable experience, even, if the drain was interesting enough. Of course Lowry said it better than that. And did it, in the end.

At the meeting, he relates his experience to empathetic nods.

"That's all it took, an open barroom door," he says, still shaken by his inability to move away from it. "Like the little man in the *Grapevine,*" he says, and they laugh. In the A.A. publication there's always a cartoon of a little man in a hat, sweating by the swinging saloon doors, and always rescued by someone or something; a kid looking for a lost coin, a woman who drops her groceries....

What he doesn't say is that, standing there, he understood the almost irresistible urge to stop fighting it for good. The lure of complete surrender. The lure of the drain.

He understood his father.

Step Four Matthew types on his old IBM Selectric. Then, *Make a searching and fearless moral inventory of ourselves,* he adds bravely, underlining *searching* and *fearless.*

The A.A. step that separates the men from the boys, they say, or is that a different step? If you ask him they all separate the men from the boys. And which is he? He saw a birthday greeting in the paper that said "looks fifty, acts forty, feels seventy, must be sixty." He feels like he knows the guy.

Matthew is afraid, after his scare, that if he doesn't do this step he'll end up drunk. And he has to get into the program or out, he can't stay on the periphery forever. It'd be some easier if you didn't have step five rearing its ugly head right behind it: *Admit to God, to ourselves and to another human being the exact nature of our wrongs.* That baby can't be a walk in the park either, can it?

Searching. Fearless. Exact. He frowns.

Man, the language those people used when they wrote the steps didn't leave you any room to manoeuvre, did it? No interstices anywhere. Exact means exact, doesn't it?

Exact. Exact. If you say it enough times it has a kind of Nazi sibilance with that heel-clicking *T* spat out at the end. A word you don't mess with.

But about his defects – he's beginning to hate the damn word, why can't they just say faults? Everybody has faults. Only alcoholics have defects, apparently.

1, he types. He leans back in his chair and looks at the number staring blackly back at him. Now he thinks about it, he doesn't like the look of it. Too rigid. And weighted with that line on the bottom, like you couldn't budge it with a bulldozer. Not like 3, a number you could reason with, a pushover, even, with that rounded bottom; or 4, lopsided, can-tilevered out in space hoping for the best, a number you could identify with. But 1. Obstinate, unforgiving bastard of a number.

He doodles on a scratch pad on the desk, lights a cigarette. Looks at the paper. Picks up his pen and accentuates the little flag at the top of the number.

For crying out loud, he hasn't murdered anybody. Mugged

or robbed anybody. Stolen anybody's wife. Why is this so god-damn difficult?

Just write something down. Anything.

That jacket he shoplifted in grade ten and never took out of the back of the closet except to admire his acned fifteen-year-old reflection. That jacket did more for him than any-thing he's ever owned, before or since, and it broke his heart to carry it out to the garbage late one night. Fortunately he's managed to avoid a life of larceny.

But he's been a serial liar, hasn't he? The times he missed work with the "flu", skipped city council meetings because they bored him silly or he already had a snootful, wives he kissed a little too enthusiastically at New Year's parties, the two he more than kissed, he'll have to write that last down. That station wagon he crashed into in a parking lot and drove away because he was drunk and afraid to lose his licence again. The lies he told Delia. Those especially. About some of the places he ended up, the company he kept.

God, he's a pathetic human being. Just scratching the sur-face he can see that. Not fit to walk among the good people of the world. A tale told by an idiot.

He gets up and pours the last cup of coffee into his mug. It turns grey when he adds cream. He carries it back to his desk, pulls the chair in briskly. Sips.

It's terrible. Bilgewater. He's got to make a fresh pot.

He has to run the water for a long time before it runs cold. Sometimes it's like that. Delia used to make coffee with hot tap water when she was in a rush. He always told her she should know better, all those nasty organisms multiplying like rabbits in the hot water heater, but she only laughed, she was surrounded by nasty organisms every day. Including him, he supposes.

Filling the pot, he notices the thick, brown film built up inside. Vigorously attacking the stain with Comet, he rubs squeakily at the darker ring where the pot curves into the rim, scours it, then rinses and rinses.

The pot gleaming, he hesitates over the coffee canister. The stale smelling grounds will make coffee he wouldn't touch if A.A. coffee hadn't deadened his taste buds. He empties the canister into the garbage along with the soggy used filter, splattering wet grounds on his clean khakis.

He remembers Delia used to run vinegar through the coffeepot every few weeks. He fills the tank with vinegar and leans against the cupboard while it bubbles up and runs into the pot, a diseased-kidney-piss colour. But now he sees the whole coffeemaker is disgusting with spilled coffee and grubby fingerprints and wipes it thoroughly, burning his finger trying to get at the bit behind the burner.

Now the water. Two pots of it. As he waits, his suddenly critical eye roams over the small galley kitchen. At the spilled coffee grounds, bits of God knows what stuck on the cupboards, greasy smudges around the handles, on the canisters. Delia would be shocked.

Out with the Mister Clean, and by the time the two pots have gurgled and sighed their way through, he's cleaned the whole kitchen and is eyeing the floor.

He glances over at his searching and fearless moral inventory.

Searching. Fearless. Moral.

Coffee? Christ. Nobody should be asked to do this without a shot of Demerol. It's enough to scare the liver – what's left of it – out of you.

Why don't other people have to do this? Sit down and examine their defects. They're sure as hell not all perfect, why don't they have to examine their goddamn defects?

Because, of course, what's wrong with them or bugging them or makes some of them poor excuses for humanity doesn't make them drink like fishes, turn into Mister Hydes, lose their jobs. Kill themselves.

He's not tackling this thing without a pot of good coffee and that's that. No booze. No sex. A man has to have something, some little bit of pleasure in life. He'll get some really good Colombian at the coffee store, which just happens to be next door to Ye Olde Fish & Chips.

Then he'll get right at it. A couple of pages ought to do it. Not sixty-three pages like Susan in his group did. Short and sweet. Well, short, anyway. Succinct. That's his style. Think of it in newspaper terms. Who? What? When? Where? Why?

That might work, he thinks, shrugging into his jacket. Yeah.

"Don't number them, for God's sake. What are you, some kind of masochist?" Marty says. "Keep it simple. Start with fear and resentment."

"Fear? I don't think I —"

"Yah, right. How come you're here instead of home doing your fourth step?"

"All right," Matthew says testily.

"And you might think about self-pity."

"Are you saying I have that one, too?" His tone aggrieved.

Marty laughs. "Good Lord, why would I think that?"

"Gee, thanks, I'm ever so bloody grateful. I'm leaving with more defects than when I came in."

"Hey, I just did you a favour. Now you can start with resentment." And Marty claps him on the shoulder and laughs his way back to the kitchen.

Sometimes Matthew wishes Marty wasn't so easily amused.

Back at his desk, startlingly good coffee to hand, he starts over. On a fresh page, writes *Resentment:* He can get going with that one all right. Nick the Prick for starters.

The phone rings. His mother. Can he come for dinner? She's made her oven pork chops that he likes.

Likes? He salivates for them. "What time?"

"Come any time. We'll eat at six."

He looks at his watch. 5:15.

Too bad she phoned tonight, though, he thinks, washing up and combing his hair. Just when he was getting in the mood, he ruminates, changing his pants for a pair with fewer stains.

After dinner, Scrabble and a walk, he comes home tired. He was up early, painted all day. Not a good time to start something as important as step four. But he thought about it as he walked and thinks now he should probably write it out by hand. He heard someone say it worked better for him than typing. That way you can carry it with you and jot things down when you think of them, the guy had said, as if he'd just discovered the wheel.

How jolly. Like hanging a dead chicken around the neck of a farm dog to keep him from killing any more chickens. He's not carrying the damn thing around with him, that's for sure, he's liable to lose it somewhere, but thinks writing it by hand might have some merit. Not so glib.

Yeah. More personal, somehow.

Chapter Twelve

Another bloody Saturday. Mom upstairs again, to "just lie down for awhile," she said. Michael and Emerald gone to town for more lumber. Joey yawning beside him on the couch.

It's really starting to bug him. Why couldn't Mom look after Joey, or why couldn't they take him? Then he could've gone to town, too.

But he doesn't know what Jeff and Chad are doing today, they don't phone as often as they used to. And he can't ask them out here now. They joke about Jesus not playing soccer and stuff, but he hasn't said how awful it really is. If they saw the barn they might start thinking he's weird, too. He looks through his videos for *Jumanji,* thinking Joey would like the dinosaurs though maybe it's too scary for him, but it isn't there, and he remembers distinctly putting it back. He always puts them back. Who would have taken it out? He shrugs, picks out *Star Wars, Special Edition,* and presses play. He's been watching the *Star Wars* trilogy again because of *Star Wars, The Phantom Menace* coming out. It's not a sequel, but a prequel.

That'll be awesome. Obi-Wan will be a young guy. And they get to see Luke's father Anakin Skywalker before he goes over to the dark side and becomes Darth Vader. George Lucas is showing clips from the old movie his mom saw when she was a kid, telling how they've made it better with computer technology. He's seen it a couple of times before and fast forwards to the movie.

Star Wars confuses Joey. "Who are they?" Joey asks.

"Sand people."

"Are they made out of sand?"

"No. They live where there's lots of sand."

"Is R2-D2 a vacuum cleaner?"

"No. He's a droid."

"A what? Who are those funny little guys?"

"Jawas."

"Who is that big dog? He's funny."

"That's Chewbacca."

And so on.

Sam is relieved when Joey falls asleep in the middle of another question. He rewinds the film so he can watch it again from the beginnning.

Joey went to sleep leaning against him. He gets up carefully and Joey slides down the couch without waking up. Sam picks up his feet and deposits them on the couch and sits down again. He reaches for his sketch pad and starts to doodle. He likes to draw while he watches TV. And practise tags, trying to work out a cool one. Maybe he'll get some spray paint and practise on the back of the barn. Nobody goes back there. He wants a skateboard but there's no place to practise out here. It's just bloody boring.

It's not fair, damn it. As soon as they get back he's going to town, even if he has to hitchhike and Michael beats him up when he gets back. Then he'll have a reason to leave, and if Mom wants to stay here with a child abuser, then she can. He doesn't care any more. He's mad at her, too.

They had a fight this morning, her and Michael, and he saw her take two pills before she went upstairs. He's figured out that's why she sleeps so much. How could she let all this happen to them? It's like how he feels doesn't matter. Like she doesn't even care about him.

Joey's small feet twitch now and then, like Buddy's when he's dreaming. His greyish socks are too small, curling his toes under a bit. One pantleg's pulled up and there's a big bruise on his leg with a red welt in the middle of it. It makes Sam's stomach feel funny, the way it feels when he sees any kind of wound. Emerald did it for sure. He hates her now. But nobody believes him. Michael just said he was making it up about Emerald hitting Joey because he doesn't like her living there.

He hears Felix crunching catfood in the kitchen. "Hey, Felix," he calls.

Felix comes and lies down on Sam's lap, stretching his big paws over onto Joey's legs, stretching out his chin and purring his loud, happy purr.

Sam saw Muriel outside this morning, and he knows the way she walked, so slow and weak as if she hurt all over, that she's going to die soon. Muriel slept in his carriage when he was a baby. Tears slide down his cheeks and he wipes them away hard, hating how often he feels that way lately. Sometimes he wishes he was little again.

He watches Obi-Wan teaching Luke Skywalker to use the Force, telling him his father was a Jedi warrior, and he will be, too, when he learns to trust the Force. And he doesn't know why, but that makes him feel like crying, too.

Sam wants to be Luke Skywalker. To have someone like Obi-Wan Kenobi, who's so wise and cool and teaches Luke how to fight.

And to have the Force, that'd be awesome.

They finally come home, Emerald all smiley and Michael in a good mood, but when he tries to phone the guys they're all out. Jeff's mom tells him they have a soccer game. She sounds sorry for him and that makes it worse. Joey hugs his mother when she picks him up but cries when they leave for their house.

Sam just wants to put his fist through something.

Matthew is getting worried. An old gent on the top floor fell asleep with his tub running, flooding his own place and the one below. What a mess. Ceiling, carpet, one wall, all ruined. The workmen just left a couple of days ago. And just before that old Mister Findlay died of a heart attack and their daughter took her mother home. She must feel like half of her is missing, they were always hand in hand. Their suite hasn't been painted in years, trust old Funk, but people who can actually see might be looking at it soon.

Mrs. Salisbury's suite rented, thank God, so Liz isn't living across the hall from her mother. He really likes Liz's company, she's smart and fun and comfortable to be with, and that's all he wants or needs from any woman except Delia. There's something downright embarrassing about the thought of starting a love affair at his age. And exhausting, just the thought of it. Trying to look good. Reining in his natural irascibility. I yam what I yam and that's all what I yam. Like Popeye. And Delia is his Olive Oyl.

He wants her back, damn it, that's all he wants. And is afraid he wants too much.

He's hauling paint and equipment out of the painting closet when his cellphone rings and he drops a half gallon of paint on his foot. Shit! He can't get used to the bloody thing. Jumps out of his skin every time.

"Matthew!" he barks, bent over, clutching his foot. The pain is excruciating.

"You have such a lovely telephone personality, Matthew," Marty says. "At what finishing school did you learn that?"

"Well, I just dropped a pail of paint on my foot."

"Oh. I hope you're still mobile. Because, Matthew my friend," he continues in a buttering-up tone.

"I'll let you know if I'm your friend when I find out what you want." He leans against the wall, massaging his throbbing foot.

Marty laughs. "Okay. I won't waste any more time sucking up. Can you go on a twelve step call with me?"

A twelve step call. Answering a call for help. Carrying the message to the alcoholic who still suffers. He's never gone on one. "I thought you had to be sober a year first. And I think I just broke my foot."

"Excuses, excuses. You're sober long enough to go with somebody else. Two old geezers sober since the Stone Age came to see me when I yelled help and the identification factor was zilch. I even thought they were lying."

"But they got you anyway." The pain is abating somewhat and he gingerly puts his weight on the foot.

"Well yeah, but I was desperate. If they'd had tails and pitchforks or pointed white sheets I'd've still joined."

"I don't know, Marty...what could I say to anybody? 'I'm still thirsty' isn't too encouraging, is it?"

"I think it is. It's the truth, and you could tell about the open barroom door. You didn't go in."

"Well...."

"I'll pick you up in twenty minutes."

Matthew sighs, already putting the paint back on the shelf.

O n the way Marty fills him in. "The guy who called sounded desperate. He thinks he's dying which he probably isn't, but he didn't sound healthy."

Matthew has stage fright, frantically trying to think of something profound to say to a man who's hit the Crunch, the place where you know you can't drink and you can't not drink. In the jaws of a vise. Or vice, more aptly.

"His wife took the phone and said not to come. Said he didn't have a problem. Sounds like she might have one, too."

"So what are we going to do, crash in like the drug squad?"

"Don't worry," Marty says. "I'll do the talking."

The man's a mind reader, Matthew thinks, not for the first time.

Marty is peering at the house numbers in an upscale neighbourhood of handsome old houses and expensive townhouse developments. In front of a good-looking building with lots of windows and balconies they stop. In the foyer Marty looks up the number and enters the corresponding number on the keypad. When there's no answer the third time, he catches the door as a handsome old gent in a Harris tweed jacket comes out. He stops and looks back at them like he's worried he may have let in a couple of con men, or worse.

At number 32 Marty clangs the door knocker. Whoever's inside must think the gestapo has arrived. He would have given up when they didn't open the downstairs door. Marty hammers it again and partway through, the door jerks open.

"I told you not to come," says the small woman holding the door half open. "He's asleep now."

"He asked me to come," Marty says, pushing the door open far enough to step inside. "My name is Marty and this is Matthew. We're from A.A."

"I know who you are," she says, throwing up her hands and heading for the chair with a drink and cigarette burning on the side table. She sits down, picks up the drink and glares at them, as if daring them to comment. She's a very thin, sixty-ish woman with a dissipated, once-attractive face. Under her soft, blue velour track suit her body is thin, emaciated almost, except for a surprising pot-belly. Matthew notices a dusting of small cigarette burns on the expensive fabric.

"Where's Dave?" Marty asks, looking at a closed door visible in the wide hallway opening off the living room. The best of materials have been used here but the plushy cream rug is stained, the area around her chair spotted with dark cigarette burns and ground-in ashes.

Her lips tighten to a thin line. "Mister —" She almost gives his last name, stops, "– David is sleeping and I don't want him disturbed. Come back another time."

"He asked me to come tonight. He said he needed help."

"Oh well," she says, her tone dismissive, as if her husband always needed help. Or thought he did. She butts the cigarette and lights another with an expensive brushed chrome lighter.

"He's not an *alcoholic.*" Her tone saying axe-murderer. "He gets crazy ideas sometimes."

"Well, I think he should be the judge of that, don't you?" Marty says.

She lifts her chin and turns her head away.

Her inquisitor is undaunted. "Where would I find your husband?"

She doesn't answer.

"Is that his bedroom?" Gesturing toward the closed door.

Her chin goes higher.

Marty walks over and opens the door.

Matthew is having an anxiety fit. Surely Marty is overstepping the bounds.

"I'll call the police," she says, and he's not surprised, thinks maybe they deserve it.

"Go ahead," says Marty, closing the door and disappearing down the hallway. Another door opens.

The woman looks at Matthew. She picks up her drink and drains it. He smells good scotch. "Who do you people think you are?" she says.

"I'm sorry..." Awkward at not knowing her name. "We aren't here to make you uncomfortable."

"I told him not to call you. We're going on a cruise next week."

"Matthew!" Marty calls, and he hurries down the hall to an open door. "Look at this guy."

A heavy-set man in a white golf shirt and navy slacks is passed out on the bed, one leg bent under him, his black loafer streaking the pale, quilted bedspread. His white golf shirt is in sharp contrast to the sepia hue of his face. His breathing is loud, erratic.

"Christ," Marty says in a low voice. He lifts the man's hand, its splayed fingers swollen like sausages. "I think the guy's on the way out." He gently lays the hand down and touches the man's head. "Poor bugger," he says.

"They're going on a cruise next week," Matthew says.

Marty snorts. "This guy ain't cruisin' anywhere except maybe to the morgue. I think his liver's giving out. We've gotta get him to the hospital."

"Will she let us?"

"It doesn't matter, he's going anyway. Stay with him. I'll go talk to her." And he runs from the room.

Matthew looks at the man. He looks like a decent guy. One who's done very well, judging by the beautiful bedroom suite, his clothes, his thick silvery hair clearly not cut by the neighbourhood barber. He looks so uncomfortable with his leg bent under him and Matthew straightens it out, pulls up a soft, green blanket folded on the bottom of the bed. He hears Marty's low, urgent voice in the living room. Her monosyllabic answers.

He sits down on the edge of the bed. He looks bad, no doubt about it, an underlying yellow tone to his tanned face. He moans and his hand flops around on the cover like a dying fish. Matthew takes it and holds it and the hand grips his, then goes suddenly limp.

Oh, God, is he dead? No. Still breathing. This whole scene is making him very uptight. He lays the hand on the coverlet and goes out to the living room.

Marty has pulled up a large corded hassock in front of the woman's chair and is leaning toward her, his elbows on his knees. Black mascara tears slip down her cheeks, wrinkled like someone who's spent a lot of time in the sun. Tears of what? Anger, he suspects. Humiliation. Frustration at this pushy guy who won't go away.

"So Barbara, we're calling your doctor, right?"

The chin goes up.

"Okay? You want your husband to get well, don't you? If you don't want to phone your doctor, we'll call 911. Is this your address book?"

"What does it look like?" She swipes the tears away and finally points to a number in the book.

This chair with the view overlooking the city is obviously her nest. Cigarettes, drink, TV remote, telephone, address book. On the shelf under the table, the TV Guide, a carton of cigarettes and her purse. No doubt the cupboard is full of excellent booze. All the essentials. And a good security system downstairs, except for the likes of Marty. He recognizes her need to insulate, is stabbed with nostalgia. Part of him still thinks it's not a bad way to go.

He walks over and looks at a photo of a thirtyish guy on the antique, marble, art deco mantle. A younger version of the man on the bed. "Your son?" he asks and she nods, her face softening.

"He lives in Vancouver," she says, beginning to thaw a bit. "He's a lawyer."

Marty hangs up. "The doctor's ordering an ambulance," he says.

Barbara rolls her eyes and Matthew sees a flash of humour there. He'd enjoy it more if he wasn't wondering how many people they're going to piss off if the guy's just sleeping off a drunk.

The ambulance attendants obviously don't think so. They practically run him out on a stretcher with an oxygen mask clamped to his face and IV running. Barbara gets up out of her chair and straightens her back, trying to rise to the occasion, as they stop momentarily in the living room to ask which hospital to take him to. She reaches her hand toward the stretcher, then drops it.

"We'll be right behind you," Marty says.

"Make sure she has his hospitalization card," they call back from the vestibule as the elevator arrives and they're gone.

"Do you need anything before we go?" Marty asks Barbara, and she says she needs to go to the bathroom.

She almost falls over reaching down for her purse and walks to the bathroom as carefully as if she's walking a straight line beside a police car. She sways and reaches for the doorway.

"Damn it, she's pissed," Marty says, pulling a good-looking black cloth coat from the foyer closet, "but we'd better take her in case he doesn't make it."

"They have a son in Vancouver," Matthew says. "Should we call him?"

"Yah. Definitely. We'll get his number when she comes out. If she ever comes out."

Barbara finally emerges with hair combed and rouge and lipstick applied with a generous, albeit none too steady, hand.

Marty gets the phone number and then helps her into the coat. She motions to a pink flowered scarf in the closet and Marty reaches it and drapes it around her neck.

"What about shoes?" he asks and she looks thoughtfully at her slippered feet.

"Whassa matter withem?" she says, sounding friendly now.

"Nothing. No, they're a fine pair of slippers." Marty says, probably thinking how long it would take her to get her shoes. "Have you got your house keys? And your hospital number?"

She pats her purse. "Gottem...right.... Got everything." She looks down at her feet again.

"Are we ready to go then?"

"Yep. Gonna go in my flippers." And she falls against the wall, laughing. "I said flippers." And laughs some more, giving Matthew a nostalgic moment for that highly enjoyable state of mind. She bends over laughing and Marty has to rescue her from falling. "Oops, going in my – whatchamacallums?"

"Your kippers," Marty says, setting her off again. He rolls his eyes at Matthew. "So we're off," he says, offering Barbara his arm. Which, surprisingly, she takes.

"We're off to see the wizard," she says.

She's not off to see him, she's holding his arm, Matthew thinks, stopping to make sure the door is locked. He's relieved to be out of the place. Even more relieved to get out in the air, light a cigarette. He's finding this twelve step stuff damned stressful.

Barbara, it turns out, has a flask in her purse, and after a few trips to the emergency room washroom is drunk and disorderly but not enough to get them thrown out.

Marty gets her son on the phone. "He'll be over tomorrow

but I think the poor guy's got problem parent burnout. He didn't even ask to talk to his mother."

"Good thing," Matthew says.

Marty read it right. Liver failure. In the curtained emergency cubicle the doctor, a tall, balding, mid-fifties man with a likeable face delivers the prognosis as his patient is wheeled out to a hospital room. "I've been expecting this." Barbara is leaning at an odd angle in the cubicle's lone chair. Her head keeps falling over and she jerks it up, widening her eyes. She reeks of booze.

"There's another one for you guys," the doctor says, nodding at Barbara. He knows they're from A.A. "I've given up trying." He shakes his head. "Good people, too. Known them for years. David was a prince of a fellow." Matthew notes his use of the past tense, as if the real David has been gone for awhile. "They should be enjoying their retirement. They worked hard enough for it."

As he's leaving he says, "It's hard to say. If he lasts till morning, he may live to go home for a bit. But he'll never survive another go-round." He shakes their hands. "Thanks. I have great respect for A.A."

By the time they get her home Barbara has decided they are her dearest friends even if they won't stay and have "just a wee little drinky" with her. "Pour me a drink, honey. It's already dark under the house."

Marty laughs, "That it is. That it is," writing down the hospital number and their telephone numbers. He prints a large A.A. beside their names. "That way she'll remember who was here."

How could she forget? Matthew thinks.

She starts to cry as they say goodbye.

"Try not to worry," Marty says, patting her shoulder. "He might be a bit better tomorrow."

"I'm not crying about that," she says testily. "I'm crying about the cruise. Or do you think he'll be able to go?"

"You never know," Marty says.

"First things first, eh?" Marty says, outside the door. "Do they still bury people at sea?"

"So much for 'carrying the message to the alcoholic who still suffers,'" Matthew says as they get in the car.

"Yeah. It's hard when they're passed out cold," says Marty.

"Moribund, even."

"More what? You never know, though. It's too late for him but maybe she'll get the message instead."

Matthew thinks that highly doubtful. Isn't sure he'd wish it for her. She's even older than he is. "Alcoholics Synonymous, eh?"

"Kind of a witty bugger, aren't you?" But he laughs. "I'll phone the hospital tomorrow," Marty says when he drops Matthew off. "Let you know how Dave's doing. If he's doing."

So he's been on his first twelve step call, and a strange one it was. But what does he know, maybe they're all strange. As he undresses he sees his foot is swollen and quite black, but it's not too painful. Pawing around in the bathroom cupboard he finds the elastic bandage and wraps the foot before falling into bed, too exhausted to sleep.

He props himself up on extra pillows and smokes a ciga-rette, thinking. If it hadn't been for Marty's bulldozer tactics, Dave might be dead right now with Barbara still sipping away in the other room. Planning their cruise. Who knows, maybe that would have been for the best.

He's heard people talk about step twelve, carrying the message, how it helps you stay sober. Well, he doesn't want to end up like Dave, but Barbara's cozy nest had its attractions. He, however, doesn't have a pot to piss in, let alone a safe, endless supply of good Scotch. He'd probably end up in Vancouver's east side. In a room at the top of a long flight of stairs. He'll do step five as soon as he can. He's afraid not to.

He picks up the Nelson Mandela book. Maybe reading about a prison of a different kind will calm him down. But the wind is rising again, Virginia Creepy's bony fingers tapping the wall behind his head. *How do you know that pain in your liver isn't terminal?* inquires Virginia. Tap tap tap. *Once it starts there's no going back.* Tap tappety tap. *Neurosis. Psychosis. Cirrhosis.* Taptaptaptap.

He gets up and looks in the bathroom mirror, pulling his bottom eyelids down and scaring himself. Are his eyeballs more than faintly yellow? Yes, by God, they are. Even from the bathroom he can hear the damn creeper scrape and clatter on his bedroom wall. *Bare ruined choirs where no birds sing.* It's even crept into his dreams. Just last night he walked through a vine-covered barroom door, and trying to leave after just one drink discovered the door grown over with vines, as tough as a brick wall. *Little Shop of Horrors,* move over. He still has drinking dreams so real it takes him a few moments on waking to realize they didn't really happen.

At midnight he's dressed and roaming the halls again.

He's not getting away with it this time.

Tessie has settled herself in the lawn chair on the corner of her patio out of his sight when he comes back for his car, parked in *her* parking space just below her balcony as if he owned the place. Protected from the rain by the patio above, she waits. He's never here very long but that doesn't matter, it's the nerve of Mister Important Person in Government Dixon that gets her dander up. Somehow he must have figured out that she has no car and she knows who told him, that dipso caretaker; they say he's quit but he doesn't look like it. No doubt she's supposed to be honoured, seeing as who that man is. He's been doing this for way over a year, except for a couple of months when he must have been away, and she's not going to take it any more.

The Virginia Creeper is edging over onto her balcony again, it still grows a little in winter, and that useless Matthew doesn't keep it trimmed. He's from Saskatchewan, somebody said, and what would he know about anything. He's never going to do a darn thing about Mister Big Shot's car, so she wrote down the licence number a while ago and she's going to report him. But first she's going to tell him so.

Tessie jumps as the wind shakes rain from the creeper over her legs. There'll be hell to pay from her arthritis for sitting out here but she's not leaving if she has to sit here all night. The man has something to hide, she's sure of it, and a plan is forming in her mind.

She's cheered by the sight of the woman in the white car driving in. Something to watch for a while. The motor turns off and the woman remains sitting in the car, staring straight ahead, for a good five minutes. Then she backs awkwardly out and bends over, peering into the car. Goodness, her legs are like toothpicks, Tessie thinks, crossing her own large but shapely legs, her best feature, she thinks. Those skinny legs don't look strong enough to hold up a cat. She must starve herself. Now she's examining the front of her car as if she might have been in a car accident, then gets down and peers underneath, the same routine every time, so familiar Tessie could do it herself. What in the world is the matter with the woman. Crazy is what she is.

Shortly after White Car finally leaves, Tessie hears hurried footsteps approaching. It's him, and she struggles out of her chair to the balcony railing. He hasn't seen her, but in the light from the lower level suite she sees an odd thing as he rounds the end of his car and takes out his car keys. His legs are bare under his black raincoat, bare except for his socks, but definitely the man is not wearing pants. He has to stop to unlock the car, and she's so surprised he's halfway in it before she speaks.

"Good evening, Mister Dixon," she says in a loud voice.

He jumps, and stares wild-eyed, like someone who's just been caught robbing a bank.

"You are parked on my private property and I'm going to report you."

"Oh, don't do that. I'm sorry. Really, I am. I'm very sorry. It won't happen again." And he bends to get into the car.

"Just a minute," Tessie says, and he stops, standing on one leg behind the open car door as if that will hide him, but it only accentuates his bare leg. She looks pointedly at it. "You're going to catch a chill, Mister Dixon," she says.

"Now see here," Maurice blusters.

"No. You see here," Tessie replies, but he's in and the car starts and leaps back, crashing into the white car. The loud bang, a moment's stunned silence, and he throws the car into gear and speeds out of the parking lot. The white car's twisted bumper drops to the pavement with a metallic clunk.

Her legs are so shaky she stumbles and falls into the recliner chair, her heart almost jumping out of her chest. She's going to call the police, all right, all right, as soon as she's sure she shouldn't call 911 in case she's having a heart attack.

No. Wait. *Think,* she tells herself, think about it. Don't be in too much of a hurry to phone the police. Maurice Dixon was plainly terrified at being seen with no pants by someone who knew who he was.

And leaving the scene of an accident. Oh, my. She smiles with her plump hand over her gradually slowing heart. The more she thinks about it, the more interesting it gets.

People from the building are gathering around the white car, White Car herself in shock and being held up by a man from downstairs, the caretaker using his cellphone, phoning the police, probably. She'll talk to the police about witnessing the accident but won't know the licence number when they ask. She was watching TV when she heard the crash and only saw the car speeding off.

And then, not today, but soon, she has an important phone call to make.

Really, she couldn't have planned it better herself.

Well, that shook him up all right. Tessie waiting there on her balcony like a big old fat spider and Maurice caught in her web without his pants. I couldn't resist the symbolism. And when he told Liz he hardly knew me I decided that losing his underwear wasn't enough. Knowing someone in the biblical sense apparently doesn't count in Maurice's little mind.

I don't know if it was me, or Maurice in his panic, who hurled his car back into Joyce's. That poor suffering soul, I hope she sells the damn thing and starts taking the bus. Bad enough she washes her hands till they bleed. I'd rather be dead.

I can't wait to see how this is going to play out now that Tessie's got the bit in her teeth, but I suspect that Oscar will soon be eating gourmet goldfish. It almost makes me feel sorry for Maurice.

I couldn't have planned it better myself. Or did I?

Anyway, it's given me a whole new lease on – well, whatever.

"Want to walk out to the end of the breakwater?" Matthew asks. "Or are you too cold?" The light is fading, the red light at the far end blinking in the half dark.

Liz likes being with him. They enjoy doing the same things and he makes her laugh, but she mustn't get too fond of him. She's pretty sure he still loves his wife. He's careful, anyway, not to give the wrong impression.

"No. I'm fine." She's dressed warm. They both are. Toques, scarves, gloves, windproof jackets. "Hey, I grew up in Winnipeg, remember?"

"Right. A prairie girl." He smiles. He's starting to feel comfortable with this woman. But then, he's always liked women. Had women friends. Still has a couple from his university days.

A wicked wind is getting up and the breakwater is deserted except for the occasional intrepid soul, hair and clothes whipping about. Below, on either side, is a cement ledge where two men are putting away their fishing gear.

"What do you catch here?" Matthew asks.

"Pneumonia," one of them says.

VICTORIA PEOPLE ARE ALL BEING CONTROLLED BY ALIEN RADIO WAVES someone has printed in large black letters on the walk.

"That explains a lot," Matthew says.

The little shelter at the end of the breakwater is covered with graffiti. Beside JESUS SAVES someone added CANADIAN TIRE MONEY. AND STAMPS, another wag added. TAKE JESUS WITH YOU, advises an earnest soul. Below that a pentagram and some cabalistic signs in red paint. JESUS IS COMING. SO IS SATAN. Michael must have been here. ARE YOU PREPARED? THE END IS NEAR. Someone has replaced the *R* with a *T.*

"Maybe it's neat, I don't know," Matthew says.

"In Winnipeg there was a church with a neon JESUS SAVES sign with the SAVES written down from the s in JESUS. The last s on SAVES was always burned out so of course we called the street Jesus Avenue."

Matthew laughs. Spray-painted tags abound. *Schizoid, LikwidSoul, Loner,* and *Snot* are the only ones they can make out. Matthew likes LikwidSoul.

They stop for coffee at the hamburger joint across from Beacon Hill Park, one of Matthew's favourite haunts. Thinking about the eschatological graffiti, he tells her about what's happening up at Kate's. "I'm worried," he says.

"That's the way cults begin, isn't it? With two or three people who need to belong to something."

"And who need to know something the rest of us don't."

"I hope you're wrong. We haven't had any cults around here for awhile. There was a famous one on an island near Nanaimo. Wealthy people came from the States and the UK.

There's a book about it in the library."

"Interesting. I'd like to read it."

"Matthew, have you heard about any odd occurrences at the Kensington?"

"Odd how?"

"Well, I think I have a poltergeist. There's definitely a presence in my apartment. I've always been tuned in to those things."

"No kidding? You mean you see spirits, or feel them?"

"Feel them mostly. And see auras. I always have." She looks out the window at Beacon Hill Park where men in blue and white shirts are playing soccer in a heavy fog. "My father came to me the night he died. I smelled his cigarette smoke first, and then I saw him. He asked me to look after my mother."

Matthew wants to say he's glad he'll be able to smoke, but doesn't. "I know that happens to some people. Are you okay with it?"

"It was upsetting when I was a kid. But I'm used to it."

"I had a psychic girlfriend once. She had prescient dreams sometimes."

"I've had a couple of those, too, and wish I hadn't. I don't even like to think about them."

"That old girlfriend read my aura," Matthew says, to change the subject.

"Oh? What did she say about it?"

"She said it was full of holes."

Liz laughs and laughs.

"Well," he says, "I was hung over at the time. But you know, since it's a senior building I'm sure several people have died there. It seems a likely enough place for a ghost."

Chapter Thirteen

Sam wakes up in the night to go to the bathroom. He drank too much Coke watching the movie today, and fish and chips for supper always makes him thirsty. He stands watching the water swirl in the toilet, remembering when he was little going to visit Grandma and Grandpa in Saskatoon and being fascinated by the blue water swirling in the airplane toilet. When the stewardess knocked on the door people were lined up all down the aisle.

Now the toilet's quiet, he hears a sound that wakes him out of his semi-conscious state. A pounding, like someone hammering nails. But it's the middle of the night. He opens the bathroom window and listens. That's what it is. Somebody hammering. It must be coming from Michael's workshop but he can't be sure, the bathroom window is on the back of the house. He shrugs, not surprised by much any more, and starts back to bed.

But wait a minute. He stops in the hallway. That's weird, even for Michael. Maybe somebody else is out there pounding. Maybe he'd better make sure.

Outside Mom and Michael's bedroom door he stops. Their door is shut. Usually they sleep with their doors open; the upstairs bedrooms get cold if you shut the door.

He puts his hand on the knob, then hesitates and knocks softly. When there's no answer he opens the door partway and sees, from the bathroom light they leave on, that only his mom is in bed.

So it must be Michael. He closes the door.

It's still going on, the sound of long nails being pounded into wood, the different sounds they make when you start, and as they're driven farther and farther in, and that final thud when the hammer hits wood.

Through the window at the end of the hall he sees a thin line of light around the window in Michael's shop. The blind is pulled down. He must be doing something he doesn't want anyone to see. Or maybe he just doesn't like the dark window, the feeling that someone could be looking in. He wouldn't like it himself.

A shadow crosses the window blind. It's Emerald, or it looks like her, he couldn't swear to it in a court of law. He thinks about that sometimes. Like if he hears something that sounds like a gunshot in the distance, he will look at the clock to see what time it is in case he's ever a witness in a court case.

They must be making something to do with the church, something they don't want anybody to know about. Like what? He can't imagine. When he asked Michael what he built that big manger thing for, he muttered something about being born again, which didn't make much sense, but he's getting used to things not making sense, has quit wondering about most of them.

Then he gets it. Of course. Michael is making Christmas presents. That's why the blind is down. Making something for Mom. Or something for Joey. Maybe a grownup bed so he doesn't have to sleep in that crib any more. Joey would like that.

Just as he turns away to go back to bed the light in the workshop goes out. For a moment everything is dark because he's been looking at the lighted window, then it comes back into focus in the moonlight. He can clearly see the shop, smoke rising from its chimney, Emerald's house, the trees where Jim has his tent, the thicker trees behind the shop that go all the way back to the mountain. Sam wonders if Jim heard the pounding, but there's no light in the tent and Jim "sleeps like a log, Master Samuel, the result of an untroubled conscience, though it was not always thus." Sometimes Sam wonders what the heck Jim is talking about. If Jim knows himself.

Then he sees a light moving through the trees behind the shop; they must have gone out the back door. The light is dim, like someone holding a hand over a flashlight, or else the batteries are just about dead.

The light bobs along between the trees, on and off like Morse code as it passes behind the large and small tree trunks. Then, almost at the back of the trees, the light stays in more or less the same place, bobbing up and down and back and forth, and Sam's eyelids droop.

Oh, who cares? He yawns and goes back to bed. He's asleep in seconds.

Driving Sam to school in the morning, Michael hardly says a word. He looks like he was dragged through a knothole backward, as Grandpa would say. And he keeps sighing.

Probably tired, Sam thinks, remembering last night. He almost asks about it but doesn't really care.

After school Joey's not around, and Emerald and Joey don't come for supper. When Sam asks where they are, Michael says Joey has gone to live with his father and Emerald feels too bad to eat.

"What?" Sam drops his spoon. "I didn't know he had a father."

"What do you think? They found him under a toadstool?" Michael can't pass up an opportunity to be sarcastic, but his face is suddenly pale.

"No. You know what I mean. Where does he live? Mom, did you know about this?"

She's stopped eating too. She shakes her head, looking at Michael.

"Somewhere in Ontario. He moves around a lot." Michael mumbles.

"Jeez, we didn't even get to say goodbye," Sam says. But that's just what Emerald would do. Send him away, just like that. "And two of his dinosaurs are in the toybox in the hall-way. T. Rex is there. That's his favourite."

"That's odd." Kate frowns. "When did his father come?"

"Late last night." Michael has spooned beef stew over a thick slice of bread on his plate but isn't eating.

Sam is too upset to eat. He liked having Joey around even if he was a bother sometimes. It feels funny without him up there on his pile of pillows, waving his spoon, asking questions.

"I've never heard the father mentioned. But maybe this will be nice for Joey." His mother is giving him a kind of meaningful look and Sam thinks oh yah, it will be nice for him not to have Emerald beating on him, won't it?

"I hope his dad is nicer to him than Emerald was," he says. And for some reason, Michael doesn't get mad. He pushes his plate away saying he doesn't feel well, and goes up to bed.

Sam and his mom talk about it for awhile, and then she goes over to see Emerald because she'll be feeling so sad without Joey.

Sam sits on at the table, deciding to have some stew after all. He's hungry and Mom's stew is deadly good.

Yah. The more he thinks about it the more he's glad for Joey.

Envies him, even.

Sam used to hate driving to school with Michael but now it means escape. School is the best part of his days now. The best part of the week. Weekends are even more deadly with Joey gone. Another boring, depressing Saturday tomorrow.

He's doing better at school, that's one good thing, scoring almost all Bs and B+s, even a couple of As because homework is his escape at home. His math average has gone up from a C to a B, Mr. Barker said yesterday. He's discovering he actually likes math.

It's raining again. Pouring bloody buckets, and of course that puts Michael in a good mood because Jesus will be coming soon to separate the wolves from the sheep, he says. Sam would rather be a wolf any day, living wild and free, howling at the moon. They have families, too, wolves do, so it wouldn't be lonely. Sheep all just follow the leader.

"You've got too much of a mind of your own," Michael says, giving Sam a jolt. Is he turning into a mind reader? Nah, he's always saying that.

"Why? What are you talking about?"

"If you'd listen, you'd know. I'm just saying that schools are dangerous."

"What do you mean, dangerous?"

"I saw that science homework you were doing. All about evolution."

"So?"

"So. There was no evolution."

"No evolution?" Sometimes Sam can't believe his ears. The truck hits a pothole and they're thrown around inside the cab. Sam does up his seatbelt.

"Shit! Goddamn road. Yes. God made the world and everything in it in seven days. Not billions of years. We were talking about that at the meeting last night, how you kids are all being brainwashed."

They're being brainwashed? "Oh yeah," Sam says noncommitally. Arguing with Michael only brings grief later on.

"You're damn right 'oh yeah,'" Michael says.

Sometimes you can't say anything to please him. And Sam doesn't like the direction of this conversation.

"We all agreed we might have to do something about it," Michael says.

Sam's stomach tightens. "You're gonna do something about evolution? You're a little late for that, aren't you?" Sometimes he can't keep quiet.

Michael actually throws back his head and laughs. He has moments like that. When you can't help liking him. Sam wishes he wouldn't do that. It mixes you up. Like Emerald, being so nice when she first came. Nice in a way that started to feel uncomfortable. It's easier just being mad at them.

"So what are you gonna do? Barge into the school and burn the science books?"

"Maybe." Michael says it in a thoughtful way, like Sam just might have put a good idea into his head.

Sam laughs. But he can almost see Michael doing that. Emerald for sure. In her red gunnysack dress and her big wooden cross, pouring gas on all the books and throwing in the match. Kids cheering. But of course Mister Barker wouldn't let her get past the door. He's strong even if he is skinny, he once picked up a big kid with one hand.

"Yes, we're definitely thinking about it." Michael scratches his crotch. "Somebody has to do something. Especially if they vote against having the Lord's prayer in school."

Oh, God, maybe they are gonna do something really stupid. Embarrass him even more than he is now.

Finally, there's the pink brick school with the big grey heron on its side. Michael gives the school a narrow-eyed look when he lets Sam out.

Walking down the art hallway makes Sam feel better. He has three pictures up there now and, even if he does think so himself, they're pretty good. He's anxious to take them home and show his mom. One is a still life which was boring to do but turned out okay. One is a picture of Felix sleeping in the mixing bowl, and the other is a picture he drew of Joey watching TV. It's the best and he's going to frame it. Mrs. McCormack offered to buy the Felix one, she has three cats, but he wants to send it to Joey. Looking at Joey sitting there with his arms around his knees, he thinks how he must be missing Emerald. He loved her so much even though she was mean to him. Funny how that works.

Somebody punches him lightly from behind. It's Jeff in a new black *X Files* t-shirt. "Hey Sam. That's an awesome picture of that little kid."

"Thanks. Where'd you get the shirt?"

"My dad got it for me."

"Sweet." Jeff's dad likes *X Files* too. The only kind of t-shirt Michael might give him would say BEAM ME UP LORD, or something equally stupid. His mom likes *X Files* though.

"We're playing soccer in the gym at noon," Jeff says.

"Oh, yeah. I forgot." Sam brightens.

"I play goal today."

"Brilliant," Sam says. "D'you have a game tomorrow?"

"Nah. It'll be cancelled for rain. Ya wanta come in and hang out?"

"Sure. Cool." If he can get in, he thinks.

They move down the art hall toward the classrooms. And school swallows them up for another day.

But Sam can't stop thinking about what Michael said. Mr. Barker has to tell him twice to pay attention.

The rain hasn't let up even a little.

"Good morning, Sheila!" Kit McCormack calls as she passes the school secretary's station. "Another lovely day, eh what?" Her raincoat is wet, her short blonde hair blown to smithereens just from walking in from the teachers' parking lot. It rained cats and dogs all weekend.

"Yes, aren't we fortunate?" the caustic Sheila replies. "We don't have to worry about skin cancer today."

Kit laughs. "Or yesterday. Or all last month." The briefcase she sets down outside the principal's office drips water on the floor as she unlocks the door. Inside, she turns on the ceiling light and the desk light before taking off her coat and hanging it on the coat tree where it will drip a ubiquitous puddle onto the dark grey tiled floor. The school is almost new, you'd think they'd know enough to pick something light in a place with so little of it.

But in all the years she's lived at the coast she's never seen a year like this one. Like the sky's sprung a huge leak over Vancouver Island while some malevolent force is attempting to blow it out to sea. It's getting to the kids, too. More shoving in the halls, fights in the schoolyard, though they run a pretty tight ship when it comes to that.

She's just going to the staff room to make a pot of coffee when Sheila comes in with a brown paper-wrapped package addressed to her in black felt pen, the letters threateningly large, it seems to her. A book, obviously.

"This arrived yesterday after school when Charlie was cleaning. He said someone threw it between the doors."

"Really? That's odd, isn't it?"

Sheila isn't making a move to leave. "It smells funny, too."

"Yes, it does." She smiles up at the secretary. "Would you mind making a pot of coffee, Sheila? I haven't had my quota yet."

"Sure thing." Sheila hovers at the door with a backward glance at the parcel.

Kit smiles at her. "Thanks. You're a love."

As soon as the door is closed, Kit opens the end flaps of the package to a strong burnt smell. She pulls the paper away and burnt paper bits fall out on her desk.

It's a grade eight science book, its cover scorched, its spine broken. More burned paper drops out as the book falls open where pages ripped out forcibly enough to wreck the spine have been burned almost completely and stuffed back inside. Someone started to burn the book and then decided to concentrate on these few pages. She closes it, then opens the cover searching for a name. On the flyleaf someone has printed: THE DAY IS COMING. PURVEYORS OF BLASPHEMY PREPARE YOURSELVES. THIS A WARNING. Then a word heavily blotted out.

Kit turns the book sideways under her desk lamp and makes out the word BITCH. She closes the book with black, shaking fingers and, fumbling badly, rewraps it and puts it in her bottom desk drawer.

When Sheila returns with the coffee in the largest mug in the staff cupboard, Kit's just sitting at her desk, her hands in her lap. She feels a bit faint, actually.

Sheila sets the coffee down on her desk. "Just the way you like it, boss. You could float your spoon on it." She sniffs curiously. "Sure smells funny in here."

"Thanks for the coffee. I need it."

Sheila knows when a subject is out of bounds, but can't help hovering a moment. Obviously what was in that package has upset Kit a lot, something burned, obviously, but just as obviously it's private.

"Oh, I thought you'd like to know, the flu bug's struck again. Jodi Little just tore into the washroom with her hand over her mouth."

"Oh, great." Kit rolls her eyes. "Would you tell Jim and Ken I'd like to see them before class?"

"Sure thing," Sheila says cheerfully as she leaves, closing the door behind her.

What could have been in that parcel to upset her cool-headed boss? A poison-pen message of some kind, maybe something of hers burnt and sent to her from the husband she just broke up with. Or something she gave him, maybe. It sure upset her whatever it was. Men. She hopes he's not planning to visit the school with a shotgun. You never knew nowadays. She slides back into her desk and looks up at the spiky-blue-haired boy before her. "Cool haircut, Chris. What can I do for you?"

At her desk, a shaken Kit takes out the package and looks at it again. The missing pages are on evolution. It figures. Those sections in science texts have already been reduced to a pathetic few pages, in some cases none, since religious fanatics insisted their children were being exposed to heresy. In the new U.S. texts, at least in some states, creationist theory must have equal or more space than evolution – if evolution is mentioned at all.

She shakes her head. Who ever decided that a group of ignorant people who cavalierly dismiss millions of years of the earth's history have the right to deny it to our children? It's the best part about science for the kids and has fostered more than one budding scientist she taught in grade school.

She gets up and opens the window and stands staring out at the rain.

After school, Kit and her two grade eight teachers meet again in the principal's office.

"So, was anybody missing a grade eight science text?"

"Unfortunately, yes," Jim Barker says. "Sam."

"Mike Taylor." Kit's voice is flat.

"Yep. No surprise there. I told them our story about Charlie accidentally throwing it in the incinerator when he cleaned the yard."

Ken Wilson, sandy haired and still freckled as a schoolboy, says, "Do you think Sam knew about it?"

"No, he didn't know. But he looked like he might be putting two and two together."

Kit leans back in her chair, rolling a pencil thoughtfully between her hands. "I don't have much use for Michael but I must admit I'm shocked by this. What do you think? Should we talk to him?"

"I think we should ignore it," Jim says. "At least for now. We can't prove it was Michael anyway." He gets up and moves his chair back so he can stretch out his long legs. His six-foot-four frame never looks comfortable unless perched on the corner of a desk or table.

Ken nods. "I agree. The less said about it, the better. We've got a hot enough issue with this Lord's Prayer human rights thing."

Kit sighs. "Yeah. That's what prompted this, for sure. Mike was wild at that meeting."

"No kidding." Ken says. "And when he hears the school board's decision it'll send him right over the edge."

"Send him over, did you say?" Jim raises his eyebrows.

"I worry about Sam," Kit says. "Keep an eye on him, Jim, see if he needs counselling. From what I hear, the situation out at his place is pretty bizarre."

Jim nods. "I definitely will. His schoolwork hasn't suffered anyway. Not so far."

"That's surprising. Rumours are flying around town about a cult, but that's pretty far-fetched, I think. Mike isn't exactly a charismatic character." Ken loosens his Bart Simpson tie and undoes his top shirt button. His tie wardrobe is legendary. No wonder the kids like him, Kit thinks, he's just one of them with a couple of university degrees.

"He's starting to look the type, anyway. I saw him and a hippie-looking woman driving by in the truck. He'll be falling over his beard soon."

Kit shakes her head. "I can't imagine Kate putting up with his nonsense. Has anyone seen her lately?"

Neither of them has.

"I'm going to talk to her about taking over during Jill's maternity leave in the spring. She might be ready to come back by then."

"I'll ask around," Jim says. "See what I can find out about the situation."

"Good." Kit stretches. "Lord, I'm tired. Does anybody feel like going for a drink? Tis the season and all. It scared the hell out of me when I opened that parcel. Now I'm mad."

"Attagirl," Ken says. "You don't even have to buy this time." He pauses at the door. "Well, at least not all of them."

Two days later when Charlie Russell opens the school he finds a back window smashed and the library and grade seven and eight classrooms ransacked. On their blackboards the messages: EVOLUTION IS HERESY. VENGEANCE IS MINE SAITH THE LORD. THE DAY IS COMING. EVIL WILL BE THROUGHOUT THE EARTH. In the incinerator science books are still smouldering.

"Stupid assholes," Charlie mutters, and, fortunately finding nothing heavy to hand, wings blackboard erasers at the messages. By the muddy tracks in the school there were at least two people. Teenagers, probably. A guy and a girl. The kids are dismissed, except for the few who'll spend the day in the preschool till their folks get home from work.

Charlie, a lanky, balding man who loves his job, pulls a heavy table over two sets of clear footprints, muttering threats not fit to be heard in a school. He takes any hint of vandalism in his immaculate school highly personally. "Stupid, goddamn fanatics," he's saying as Kit pokes her head in the door.

"You got that right. The kids are all gone now, Charlie. We've called the police and they'll want to talk to you."

"I'll be here."

Chapter Fourteen

There's a powerful burned smell hanging over the kitchen and his mom looks like she's been crying as she pours milk into her glass from the old brown jug she made when she did pottery.

"I know, Michael, I said I was sorry. I just sat down for a minute and fell asleep."

Sam's stomach growls.

"Beef is expensive, you know," Michael says. "To say nothing of just about setting the house on fire."

I wish she had, Sam thinks. Burned the damn place down. Then they'd have to leave.

Emerald is looking at Michael with a little secret smile. She gets up to get the salt and pepper, tripping on her long Jesus dress and Sam laughs before he can stop it. She turns and throws him a furious look, then carries on into the kitchen.

"I know, Michael. I'm sorry. I think I need to go away for awhile."

"Why?" says Michael.

"To try to get myself together. I know I'm not...." She

stops, like she's forgotten what she was going to say. Michael looks at her with narrowed eyes.

"You don't need to go anywhere to get yourself together." He picks up the tuna macaroni dish and scoops almost half of it onto his plate.

Sam is hungry, too, and he loves tuna macaroni with brown cheese on top and lots of ketchup. And salad. He's hungry all the time lately, in another growth spurt, everyone says. Sometimes it feels weird to look down and see his feet so far away. He trips over things a lot, and his pants are too short.

"You can get yourself together right here," Michael says, plunking the bowl down on the table, not bothering to pass it to anybody. "There's nothing the matter with you anyway, it's all in your head."

"I don't think so."

"Mom and I could go to Victoria on my Christmas holidays. See Grandpa and Grandma and Gran. That'd be awesome."

His mother brightens. "Yes, I haven't seen Gran for ages, and she's getting old, you know. That's just what I need, Michael."

"That's just what I need, Michael." He mimics her in that hateful singsong way that makes Sam want to punch him in the mouth. Someday he will. He's started working out in his room with weights.

"If I went somewhere else for awhile I could..." She stops, looking at Emerald.

Fucking Emerald, Sam thinks. Always *there*. They're not a family anymore, like they used to be. Or were they ever? Not like Jeff's family, who laugh a lot.

"You could what?" says Michael nastily.

"Think," she says.

Sam pours milk into his glass. She's saying all the wrong things. Michael doesn't want her to think, to have "a mind of her own." That weird expression. If your mind isn't your own, then whose is it? And she never used to ask permission like that, like a little kid begging. Sam hates that.

Michael is giving his mom a kind of measuring look, then glances at Emerald.

"I'll think about it," he says, starting to shovel in macaroni, dropping a piece in his beard. Emerald laughs and reaches over to pick it out, leaving a little trail of cheese and tuna in the hair. Sam is so turned off by Michael's beard he knows he'll never grow one. It kind of turns him off the macaroni, too, like finding a hair in it.

"I'll think about it," Michael says again, looking at Sam.

Sam knows what that means. It means you're supposed to ask him again and he'll say he hasn't had time to think about it yet, to ask him later, and the same the next time, and you keep asking even though you hate it because just maybe he'll let you but in the end he says no anyway, or almost always, and you realize he never intended to let you in the first place, he just liked making you ask. Liked saying no.

Sam remembers something. "Could I have Joey's address?" he asks Emerald. "I want to send him his dinosaur."

Michael stops with his fork halfway to his mouth and looks at Emerald.

"He doesn't need it," she says flatly.

"But he left T. Rex here, that's his favourite. Did he take his other ones?"

"Yes."

"Well, I want to send him the picture I drew of Felix sleeping in the bowl. He liked Felix."

"Yes, Emerald," his mom says, "we miss Joey. And he must miss Sam. We'll want to send him a Christmas present."

Emerald goes white around her mouth, a sure sign she's mad. Michael reaches a hand out to her, then picks up a piece of bread instead.

"Yah," Sam says, excited. "I know what we can send him! I saw a really cool dino –"

"Aaaah!" she screams, throwing down her napkin. "Mind your own fucking business! Just...*leave it alone!* Quit trying to stir things up."

"Well, of course we don't want to upset Joey, but I don't think sending him a Christmas present would do that," his mom says, sounding mad, too. "He must think we've forgotten about him."

"Yah," Sam says. "Where does he live now? Whereabouts in Ontario, I mean?"

She jumps up from the table, kicks her chair in and yanks her jacket off the hook by the door. *"Just drop it!"* She glares at Sam. Kate, too. "Can't you two take no for an answer?"

"Stay and finish your supper, Emerald," Michael says.

"I'm not hungry!" She charges out, the door bangs like a shot, making Kate jump. Running footsteps on the deck and steps, then silence.

"Jeez. Why is she so weird about Joey?" Sam says. "What's wrong with sending him a present?"

"That's what I'd like to know," Kate says. "Sometimes..."

"Sometimes what?" Michael says.

"I wish she didn't live here."

"Me too," Sam says. "All the time."

"Well, she does," Michael says. "And you'd better get used to it. Both of you. She has her own house, which she paid for, and she helps out financially."

"Lucky her," Kate says. She jumps up and takes a blueberry cobbler off the stove, banging it down hard on the table. The whipped cream, too, which jumps up the side of the bowl. "Get some plates, will you Sam? You can help yourselves."

It's Sam's favourite dessert. Michael takes a huge helping, of course, and starts wolfing it down, a thread of whipped cream garlanding his beard. Only Emerald bothers to tell him anymore.

"Well, why *is* she so weird about Joey?" Sam asks his mom.

Kate, staring into space with her arms crossed, sighs. "I don't know. Ask your dad."

"She's just upset," Michael says. "She misses Joey."

"Well, it's stupid," Sam says. "She just doesn't want him to get a Christmas present. She always was mean to him."

"I know how you feel, Sam, but we can't do anything about it. What Emerald says, goes," his mom says, giving Michael a dirty look he chooses to ignore.

They finish supper in silence, and Sam gets up to clear the table. Thumbing through the Bible, Michael asks Sam to take some cobbler over to Emerald.

"Couldn't somebody else?" he asks. "She's mad at me."

"Do as you're told," Michael tells him. "Honour thy father and thy mother."

"How can I honour my father when I don't even know him?" He doesn't care. He wants Michael to get really mad and kick him out. He hates it when Sam mentions his real father.

"Watch your mouth," is all he says. "And take it over while it's warm. She's feeling bad."

Oh, he doubts that.

He carries the blueberry cobbler over to Emerald's under an umbrella. The warm cobbler and whipped cream smells delicious out in the fresh air and he'd like to sit down and eat the whole thing. He's still hungry.

She opens the door and Sam is surprised to see she's been crying. She looks over his shoulder like she's expecting to see Michael there. Her place is a mess and it stinks, too. An ugly smell like rotten potatoes, which in Sam's opinion, is the worst smell in the world.

"Mom says I'm to bring the plate back."

As she rummages around in the sink full of dirty dishes for a plate to put the cobbler on, he sees a large cardboard box full of stuff by the door.

Joey's stuff.

Joey's jacket. Joey's rubber boots. Joey's blue sweater.

His dinosaurs.

Sam's heart misses a beat. All thrown together in a tangled bunch, all Joey's dinosaurs. She said he took them with him.

He turns to see Emerald watching him. She knows he's seen.

"Tell your mother thanks for the dessert," she says, her face expressionless, "and thanks for bringing it over." She hands him the plate covered with purple smears and mauve whipped cream.

"Sure," he says, "no problem," tripping over the doorway in his haste to get out.

Back on the deck he leans against the house, his heart jumping in his chest like a frog in a jar. Why are Joey's dinosaurs still there? And why wouldn't she send his clothes with him? It doesn't make sense.

He sees Emerald standing in front of her window, eating the cobbler, looking out. She can't see him here, he hopes. Inside, he hears Michael droning on.

He stands there so long, trying to think what it means, that his mom comes out looking for him.

"What are you doing, Sam?"

"Nothing," he says. "Just thinking." And she goes back inside.

Just thinking all right.

Thinking why did Emerald lie? Where was Joey? Why wouldn't she tell him? Why did she get so mad when he asked.

Thinking why would she?

Maybe she lied about the dinosaurs because she hadn't sent them but was going to, he's told that kind of lie sometimes. Lots of times, actually. Maybe Joey was asleep when he left so he didn't take his toys. And maybe she didn't send his rubber boots because it doesn't rain much in Ontario.

And maybe not.

What about his blue sweater, he wore that all the time. And his *Lion King* jacket? He was so proud of it.

He shivers in his jeans and sweatshirt. It's cold out and dark, with no moon and no stars, just rain pattering on the deck roof, and wind, the dark trees swaying and sighing. Through the black trees the yellowish light in Jim's tent glows. He's playing the mouth organ, that mournful, beautiful song Mom said was an old Black spiritual. His mom told him the words, *Sometimes I feel like a motherless child, a long way from home.* He wonders if Jim feels that way. He does himself, sometimes, and that doesn't make sense. But he's a fatherless child, for damn sure. He's glad he never called Michael Dad.

Inside, Michael's voice rises and falls. He can't hear the words, but he can tell by the way he's reading it's Revelations, and just thinking about it makes a falling-away feeling in his chest. The sun turning black, the moon and seas to blood, black, bottomless pits spewing smoke and those hideous locusts with stingers in their tails, and earthquakes and everything dying. How did seven ever become a lucky number? And those terrible horsemen, especially the fourth, *Behold, a pale horse, and his name that sat on him was Death.* That line is the scariest of all.

The one thing that makes him laugh is one of the seven churches being in Philadelphia. Like hearing the word Chicago or Nanaimo in the Bible.

He's just thinking about going over to visit Jim when Michael stops reading so he goes in and watches *X Files* with his mom. She made Michael put back the TV, anyway. She makes popcorn, the first time in ages. Michael goes out to his shop or so he says. Probably to Emerald's.

He tells his mom about seeing Joey's stuff.

She frowns. "That is odd, isn't it? I think Emerald feels guilty about Joey and that's why she gets upset."

"Maybe."

"But if she's packing his things now she must be going to send them, so he'll have them pretty soon."

"Yah, maybe," he says. Wanting to believe.

He doesn't want to think about it any more. He just wants to eat popcorn and watch *X Files* with her.

Matthew paints and paces. Paints and paces. All day he's done it and only half the suite is painted. He drags the stepladder to a living-room corner, ascends like someone climbing the gallows steps. If only, he thinks. Drop the hood. Please.

He woke up this morning with a powerful inexplicable sadness.... And then he remembered.

Parking on Dallas Road yesterday to go for a walk on the first sunny day in memory. Lots of people out on the promenade, a gentle breeze ruffling the sea, kites climbing a clear azure sky. His spirits lifting, he started out. In the fresh sea air, the sun warm on his face, his arms stiff from hours of wielding brush and roller were loosening. Till he rounded a bend and saw them.

Up ahead, Delia and Nick, walking hand in hand, her bright hair cut shorter now, lifting in the breeze as she laughed up at him. Matthew was close enough to see his Eddie Bauer corduroys, the rose pattern on the skirt that swirled around her shapely calves, almost close enough to hear what they were saying. He mustn't hear. Mustn't be seen.

Stepping off the path, he watched. A woman meeting them turned to look at the attractive couple so obviously in love.

Legs trembling, he dropped like a stone onto a bench facing the sea.

Nick is no doubt considered handsome, with the regular-featured, sleekly padded face of a man who feeds on good steak and lobster and success. They're a type, these men, usually fair. Nick's hair is cut short on the sides and longer on top so that a lock of it falls cunningly over his insipid vanilla pudding face. The son of a bitch would have enough hair to stuff a mattress, Matthew thought, the wind skipping merrily over his naked dome. Just before they disappeared behind an avenue of trees, Nick pulled Delia toward him by her shoulder and kissed the top of her head.

A rush of longing and hate and despair took Matthew's breath away, leaving him jackknifed on the bench like someone shot in the midsection. At a touch on his shoulder he looked up into a woman's kindly face. The woman who had turned to look at them.

"Are you all right?" she asked.

He nodded.

"Are you sure?"

"Yes. Thank you. I'm – I'll be fine."

And he managed to get to his feet and to his car, the woman still worriedly watching.

Trembling on the stepladder now, the tumult still rages. After painting three square feet of ceiling he gets down again, lights a cigarette, paces. He'd felt bad when she left, but nothing like this. She'd come back if he just stayed sober, he believed. She'd left him twice before; first holing up in a hotel for a week; then living a month with an Al-Anon friend.

But then he'd had his medicine, enough to dull even the potent pain of rejection. The first time he tried to quit, the second time made no promises, knowing he probably wouldn't, or couldn't keep them. But she still loved him then.

This is different and he knows it. Knew it, really, but stuffed it down. Yesterday it leapt out at him like one of those spring-filled snakes in a can and he can't stuff it back in.

But what in God's name do you do with this awful turmoil, this revved-up feeling that won't let you stay still, suffused with the knowledge you've killed the love that mattered most to you in the world? Have no one to blame but yourself? When the only thing that would help has turned on you?

The balcony door rattles in the fierce wind that's blown all day, warnings on the radio to stay away from Dallas Road where huge waves are climbing the breakwater, washing over the road and up to the Chinese cemetery. The police are out to keep the curious away.

He stares out, not seeing. Thinking of the men he reads about who commit murder, kill their wives, their lovers, themselves. Of course it's monstrous, unforgivable; but now he understands the kind of torment that could possess a man to do that.

Unspeakable, but not unthinkable.

He paces from the end of the L-shaped dining room to the balcony door and back again, back and forth, like a big key between his shoulder blades is wound tight. His neck and back muscles screaming with tension, he hugs his chest. Through the streaming glass the rain barrels down, the sodden trees across the parking lot swaying and shaking like hula dancers, leaves and twigs flying, branches littering the parking lot.

He goes into the bathroom to pee. Then sits down on the toilet lid with his head bowed and hands clasped between his knees. He wants to cry. Needs to cry. "Cry, you stupid bastard," he says aloud. Cry for what you've done. Become. Lost.

But he can't.

What should he, *can* he do? The inexorable answer comes back. Nothing. *Of all the sad words of tongue or pen, the saddest are these, it might have been.* Jesus, how long has that one crouched in the starting blocks ready to leap out when the moment was right? He wishes he'd killed off a few more brain cells.

On the way out he kicks the door and grabs his foot with both hands. How do people punch holes through walls, for Christ sake?

Finally he feels a little calmer. Enough to go back out and mount the stepladder again. To pick up the roller and, instead of flinging the full paint tray at the wall, start painting again. God grant me the serenity to accept the things I cannot change, he says, over and over and over, every time he wants to start pacing again he says it, and eventually he finishes the room.

He should call Marty, he thinks, cleaning up and putting away the painting gear. But he doesn't want to whine, and what did Marty say about Nick? Maybe you better get used to it. Maybe he's always going to be there. And he was right. It's reality, isn't it, something he's never been very fond of. Why else try to blot it out as often as possible?

As he's heading outside to clear the parking lot for tenants returning from work, the perennially cheerful Mister Reilly stops to chat, then blows forth to do whatever he does out there, rain or shine. Matthew envies him. Envies everybody old enough to not feel like he does anymore.

But when is that? He's sixty, an old man himself, and still undone by love and loss. Burning with jealousy like a sixteen-year-old.

Maybe it never ends.

His phone is ringing and he groggily comes to. He lets the answering machine kick in. He turned it down after clearing the parking lot, and through sheer force of will or an intense longing for oblivion, fell asleep.

He gets up and makes a pot of coffee, turns the TV on to the six o'clock news. Sits without turning on a light. Before he slept he was tired, wired, and crazy with grief. Now he feels hung over, lonely, hungry, and very, very sad.

What is that A.A. acronym? HALT? Hungry, angry, lonely, tired. You're supposed to be careful, then. He should go to a meeting tonight but won't, he decides, with a little stab of unease. He's been missing meetings, pressured by all the painting, and tonight it feels like the last thing he wants to do. He hasn't got the energy it takes to get there. To talk. Even just to listen.

He stares blankly at the flickering screen. More rain in the forecast. Gale force wind. The Trans-Canada closed. White Rock washing down to the sea. God, it's enough to make you think Michael might be right.

Then the commercials. Mom and Dad and the kids, and the dog. Of course, opening presents. A Nick clone draping a diamond necklace around his wife's neck. He changes the channel.

The phone rings again. He'd better answer it though he feels incapable of fixing even a leaky tap. Hearing about another leaky balcony. He's a man in a leaky boat, after all, with nothing to bail with.

He tries to sound pleasant. "Matthew here."

"Hi Matthew. It's Liz."

"Oh, hello Liz."

"I was just going to have a drink before dinner and wondered if you'd like to come by."

His hand holding the receiver starts to shake. "Oh. I uh – well I'm –"

216

"If it's not a good time, that's fine. We can do it some other time."

"No, it's not that. I just woke up. Bad night last night."

"Oh, I'm sorry. I hate being woke up by the phone."

"No, you didn't, really. Can you give me twenty minutes?"

"Sure. See you then."

He drops the receiver trying to hang it up. He's never told her he can't drink.

I'll have a soda or juice, he tells himself, soaping up in the shower, scrubbing at paint spatters, I need the company. I'll tell her I can't drink, and get to a meeting later tonight, he decides, brushing his teeth and what there is of his hair. I won't stay long.

You've got to tell her, he lectures himself, climbing the stairs to the second floor, standing outside her door, hands clenched in his pockets. Tell her before she asks what you want to drink. No, that sounds prissy, she'd probably think she shouldn't have one either.

He takes a deep breath and knocks on the door.

It opens to an attractive smiling woman, a warm, lamplit room, rose floral drapes cozily closed against the wind and rain.

He closes the door behind him.

Chapter Fifteen

The grade eight room is empty except for Jim Barker seated at the teacher's desk and Sam, slouched in his desk at the back of the room. The rest of the kids have gone in a boisterous Christmas holiday exodus, the last heartfelt "yesss!" still echoes in the room. It hurts Sam to hear it.

"Yesss!"

Jim Barker finds it hurts to look at Sam, whose head is bent, fair hair hanging down in front of his face, flushed with the effort not to cry. His shoulders inside his navy sweatshirt are slumped, his slim, ink-stained, adolescent hands limp on his desk. Jim Barker wants to go to him and hug him but knows he mustn't.

Outside, the cacophony of shouted plans and laughter and slamming car doors gradually subsides, the last car pulls away with its buoyant passengers, and all is quiet.

"Come up to the front desk, Sam. It's easier to talk." Then, when Sam is facing him, "I'm concerned about you, Sam, and wondered if you'd like to talk about what's bothering you."

At the kindness in Mr. Barker's voice, tears fill Sam's eyes. He opens them wide to keep the tears from falling.

Jim Barker reaches over the desk, handing Sam the box of Kleenex. He's more than a little concerned. He's seen the signs of a growing depression in Sam. He's in another world half the time lately.

"Is it because you had to quit soccer?" he asks, going around to sit on the corner of his desk. He knows the coach offered to have Sam picked up for soccer but was told by Taylor to butt out. He also knows there's a lot more than that going on with this kid.

Sam blows his nose, wads up the ink-stained Kleenex and shakes his head.

"No. Well, yah, that's part of it but..." The tears spill over and he pushes at his runny nose with the wadded tissue.

Jim Barker waits, and when Sam doesn't continue says, "Do you want to tell me what else is troubling you, Sam? I want to help if I can."

The lengthy silence is broken only by the sound of Sam sniffing and the furnace cutting in. Perhaps he isn't going to talk about it. Not a good sign. Jim waits.

"My –" he's suddenly sobbing, he can't help it, "my whole – everything – just sucks." He blows his nose noisily, snot stringing out when he takes his hand away, and he grabs some more Kleenex and blows harder, throwing the used ones into the wastebasket by the teacher's desk and awkwardly wiping his hand on his pantleg.

The teacher waits. Sam isn't exaggerating, he's sure, and he's almost afraid to hear what's going on in the boy's life. His stepfather is a mean, sarcastic, self-righteous jerk who should never have been a teacher. The staff and the math and shop students celebrated when he left. And since the book-burning spree he's pretty sure Taylor's gone off the rails completely.

"I believe you, Sam. Do you want to talk about it?"

Sam looks at him, wondering how much to say. He's stopped crying.

Another silence. Jim waits.

Sam takes a big breath. "Michael's taking me out of school." He says it fast.

"What?" Jim yells. "He can't do that." He jumps up from his desk, starts to pace back and forth.

Sudden hope surges through Sam. Is it true he can't?

"Why? What's his reason?"

"He says I've got to have home-schooling because I need a *Christian* education." His voice full of contempt, more for Michael, Jim suspects, than for Christianity.

Of course. After Taylor's performance at the meeting about the Lord's prayer, he should have seen this coming. He picks up a piece of crumpled paper and fires it into the wastebasket.

"Well, your mother doesn't want that, does she?"

Sam shrugs. "No. She thought we shouldn't say the Lord's prayer because of the Padmanab and Solomon kids." When he showed her the school letter she threw it away so Michael wouldn't see it. But he heard about it anyway and him and Emerald went ballistic. "There's gonna be some little kids, too. And some other kids, I think. I don't know."

Juliet, the teacher thinks. Her parents are mixed up with that bunch, he's heard. Michael's welcome to the silly little twit, but that would finish Sam. "So Michael proposes to teach you, does he?" His teaching degree might make his application more attractive to the school board, Jim thinks, except for the burned science books. If they can prove it was him, of course. He stops prowling around the room, perches again on the edge of the desk, waiting for Sam's answer.

"No, not him. This woman who lives out at our place," Sam says, his tone scornful, scathing. *"Emerald."*

Oh. The one who's seen everywhere with Mike.

Sam is inking in the o's and a's and e's on the cover of his English notebook. "I won't do it," he says. "I'll run away."

"Where would you go, Sam? Do you have family on the island?" He doesn't say don't go.

"My grandma and grandpa live in Victoria."

"Sam, listen. He can't do this against your will. Or if your mom doesn't agree. One parent can't make that decision. He knows that."

"He's not – he doesn't care." Sam's knuckles are white as he grips the pen.

"Maybe not, but he's not above the law."

Sam looks up. "I wouldn't do it anyway, even if Mom wanted me to. I hate her."

"You hate your mom?" Jim is shocked.

"No. Emerald." The expression in his eyes is painfully bleak.

The room is almost dark though it's not yet four o'clock, and Jim gets up, striding to the door in about five steps to flick on the lights. He picks up a piece of chalk from the floor, fires it in the basket with a loud ping. Puts one foot on his desk chair, elbow resting on his knee, and looks at Sam.

"Nobody can make you do that, Sam. Even if a student agrees to home-schooling, if he or she won't co-operate and do assignments, that's called non-compliance, and the school board will take away permission for the home school."

Sam has put down the pen, is hanging on his every word now. "So if I won't go, nobody can make me?"

"That's right, Sam, and don't let anybody tell you different. You can tell your father –"

"He's not my father," Sam interrupts.

"No, right, you can tell Michael I said so. This Emerald, does she have children, too?"

"No. She has, had – Joey, but he's too little to go to school. Well, preschool, maybe, but he doesn't live there any more."

"Oh? Where did he go?"

"I dunno. She won't say." Sam frowns. "Somewhere with his dad, I guess. She was mean to him."

My, don't they sound like a lovely couple, Jim thinks. Taylor's found his soulmate. He steps down and shoves in the chair. Leans against the blackboard, covered with happy holidays messages the kids wrote on the board today. All except Sam.

Sam smiles faintly, thinking Mr. Barker's dark jacket will be all chalk dust again. He's always doing that, it's one of the things the kids like about him.

"How's your mom, Sam? I haven't seen her for a long time."

At the question Sam looks worried, rolling the corner of his English exercise book back and forth, leaving blue ink smudges on it. Then stops, as if suddenly realizing he shouldn't do that. But he doesn't look up. "Oh, I don't know, she's...sick a lot. I don't know what's wrong."

"Oh? I'm sorry to hear that, Sam. Say hello for me." He walks down and squeezes Sam's shoulder just as Michael's truck roars into the yard, the horn blaring.

Sam rubs his face with the palms of his hands, leaving ink stains on his cheeks. He'd hate Michael to know he was crying. He's leaning on the horn, and Mr. Barker marches over and shuts the windows, then slams the door so hard Sam jumps, and the beeping is fainter. Back at his desk he picks up a big brown envelope. "Here are your pictures from the art wall, Sam, you'll want to take them home." He pulls them out. "This one of the little boy is especially good. Is that the boy you mentioned? Joey?"

"Yeah, that's him." Sam frowns. Looking at the picture gives him the worried feeling he gets every time he thinks about Joey.

"I can tell the way you drew him that you really liked him. Good artists can do that. You've got a lot of talent, Sam. And the cat in the bowl is great." He laughs. "Were you having chicken CATchatori for dinner?" Sam laughs, too. Mr. Barker is famous for his puns.

"That's Felix. He sleeps there all the time," Sam says, reaching for the envelope. He loves Mr. Barker ignoring Michael as if he wasn't sitting out there hitting the horn continuously now beepbeepbeepbeepbeepbeepbeep like an idiot. It reminds him of when they play shinny, their room against Mr. Wilson's room, and how sometimes when the bell goes if it's a tied game they keep on for a few minutes till somebody scores.

Jim Barker seethes at the horn still beeping without a pause. He doesn't dare go outside with Sam for fear of punching Mike Taylor right in the middle of his ignorant hairy face. Sam is gathering up his stuff. "He told me to clean out my desk," Sam says.

"No, don't. You're coming back, Sam. They couldn't get permission that fast. And tell Michael to call me if he has a problem with that."

"Okay."

"We'll see you after the holidays. And don't worry," he says, as they start for the door, "they can't take you out of school against your will. There's no way."

He walks Sam out to his locker for his backpack and all the way out to the front steps, ignoring Michael in the truck still honking the horn.

"Thanks, Mr. Barker." Sam wants to throw his arms around him. He clatters down the stairs where he turns and smiles up at him before climbing into the truck and slamming the door. The beeping stops.

Jim Barker stands there as the truck grinds into gear and roars out of the yard. He can't lose this kid. He's bright, sensitive, funny, one of his best students. The talk seemed to help him some. For now. But he fears greatly for Sam. He definitely does.

Back in the classroom he stops, frowning, then abruptly gets his coat and leaves without clearing off his desk. He's going to the gym before dinner to punch the hell out of the punching bag when what he really wants is to beat the shit out of that asshole, Mike Taylor.

It's quiet in the truck cab except for the rain on the roof, neither of them talking, the air charged with what they're not saying. Michael mad he had to wait. Sam mad at Michael. He hugs Mr. Barker's words to him. *They can't make you. There's no way.*

But he still has to get through the holidays. Ten days at home alone. He might as well be, the way Mom is. And Michael and Emerald hoarding canned food and water and rice like squirrels is starting to freak him out too, it's up past the windows of that new little cabin. And those big rolls of black plastic. That's spooky as hell but he's not asking. He asked Michael if the food was for the sinners since Michael's going to heaven where presumably they don't need to eat, but he just said you won't be laughing long.

He can't see out. The side windows are foggy. But through the windshield he sees the signs even before Michael stops to open the gate: KEEP OUT. NO TRESSPASSING. GOD'S CHILDREN And under that, in smaller letters, Gather Together For Safety, And I Will Protect You.

God's Children? Oh, no way. No fucking way. He's getting out of here all right.

Him and Buddy.

Tonight.

Matthew opens his eyes, Michael's cluttered bookcases across the room coming slowly into focus. What's he doing on the couch with all his clothes on? And surrounded by crumpled Kleenex, like someone on a float in a parade.

How long has he been here? He's got a fierce palpitating headache. His eyeballs feel peeled. For a moment he tries to tell himself it was just another drinking dream but the sinking feeling in his gut tells him otherwise.

"Oh, no," he says aloud, struggling to sit up, a wave of

225

dizziness driving him back down again. Oh, no.

What time is it? What day? He can't see his wristwatch, too gloomy in the room. He reaches the TV remote and programs the channel that gives the date. It's 5:15 p.m. December 16th but he's still too foggy to relate that to what he thinks was yesterday, had to be yesterday, No, God, the last day he remembers was the 14th. Though he has no recollection of anything after Liz handed him his what? Fourth drink? Fifth?

At the memory, a wave of nausea sends him lurching for the bathroom where he collapses on his arthritic knees to find the toilet reeking of vomit, the floor around it littered with crumpled Kleenex. Christ. Who said skid row had to be an alley? Oh, this is bad. This is very bad.

He heaves and gags, heaves and retches, hanging onto the toilet lid, pulling it hard against his excruciating throbbing head, bellowing his misery as his stomach turns inside out again and again to bring up nothing but burning green bile. Delia always said she'd never heard anyone make so much fuss about throwing up. Well, there's no one to hear it now. He blows his nose and flushes the toilet, drops the surrounding litter in the wastebasket and reaching for a facecloth dampens it under the tap and slowly wipes the toilet and the floor around it. Then throws the cloth away, too, shakily tying the plastic liner bag. Standing up, he nearly tips over into the tub. Well, maybe a good crack on the head would cure his headache, cure everything. If he had the strength, he'd give himself one. Shuffle off this mortal coil. *A consummation devoutly to be wished, for damn sure.*

Now the toilet's stopped running, he hears something alarming. The sound of the Beast in the hallway. He stands still and listens. What the devil? There's no mistaking that snarl, but who's running it, that's what he'd like to know. Or not.

Is it Liz? Jesus, what a mess. What did he *do* at Liz's? What did *they* do? He remembers taking the first drink and trying to look like a social drinker, the second one not coming fast enough to suit him, the knot in his stomach when she didn't offer a third. He must have asked for it or she saw his humiliating need. He doesn't want to think about it.

He turns on the ceiling fan and washes his hands. Then leaning down, splashes his face with cold water, which, except for his fevered brain colliding with the front of his skull, feels wonderful. He avoids the mirror, can't face himself, pisses, and leaving the bathroom light on, heads back to the couch where he hopes to pass out.

"Feel better?"

Matthew jumps and squawks. A ghostly white shirt is suspended in his living-room chair. Marty. His glow-in-the-dark friend.

"How did you get here?" he asks, almost losing his balance turning to sit down where he hopes the couch is. He's still drunk. Or his body is. His body always got drunk before his mind and stayed drunk longer. The rest of Marty is coming into focus. Well, let him be there, it saves him having to confess.

He reaches for a cigarette and Marty gets up and lights it for him. In the flare of the match Matthew sees a large rip in the thigh of his mud-spattered pants.

"Hey, that must've been quite a night," Marty says.

Matthew falls back on the couch. "I guess. I don't remember. I don't suppose you'd believe I have the flu."

"Yeah. I hear it's going around. Johnny Walker flu."

"Please, Dewers. How did you get here?" he says again. "Without me hearing you?"

Marty snorts. "The Russian army could've come in with the noise you were making in there. I dropped by to see you earlier and heard you talking to Ralph on the big white telephone. I thought you must be dying."

"You heard me *what?*"

"On your knees in the bathroom talking to Ralph on the big white telephone. You know, 'RAAAAALPH RAAAAALPH' How is old Ralph? It's a while since I've spoken to him myself."

A ghostly smile is all Matthew can manage.

"Wanna tell me what happened?"

"I wish I knew. Or maybe I don't." His clothes smell like that bar on Douglas Street. But he knows this isn't what Marty is asking. Just then the Beast comes roaring past his apartment, bumping the wall a few times. "But wait a minute. How did you get in here without any keys? And who the hell is out there vacuuming?" His hand lifting the cigarette to his evil-tasting mouth jerks as if palsied, and he butts the cigarette out before it makes him sick again.

"First things first, my good man. I have taken the liberty of pouring out a very good bottle of scotch, or what was left of it, except for a hair of the dog. With the case of shakes you've got, you probably need it."

Matthew has a flashback of pawing around in the cupboard over the sink for the hidden bottle, stuff falling everywhere. Looking in the toilet tank, too, presumably, when the first one was gone. His joy at finding half a mickey Delia must have missed. "Are you serious?"

Marty answers by getting up and coming back with a couple of ounces of neat scotch in a glass which he hands to Matthew.

"No ice?" Matthew jokes feebly.

"Ice? You're not talking to your neighbourhood bartender, my friend. This is purely medicinal, as my father used to say."

At the words "my friend," Matthew's eyes tear up. He tips it up and downs it in two swallows. His stomach heaves mightily and then a beautiful calm begins to settle.

The Beast roars past the door again, going in the other direction.

"Marty, who the hell is —"

"Well, since you insist on knowing, that is Mr. Desmond Funk."

"What? Who?"

"How about why, when and where? What kinda newspaperman are you? And yes, it is the old skinflint himself. Came by and found me trying to break into your place with a credit card." Marty laughs. "He let me in."

Matthew sets down the empty glass and leans back, closing his eyes. "Oh, Christ," he says. "There goes the job."

"Not so. Apparently he got into it pretty good himself after the war."

"You're kidding. He told you that?"

"Yah. He quit when he lost his wife and a whole lotta money in a poker game."

"He lost his *wife* in a poker game?" They both laugh and Matthew clutches his head with both hands.

"Say, is your condition too delicate or can I turn on a light? And *by the way* how did this happen? And you know what I mean."

"Leave it off," Matthew says. "My head's falling apart." He sighs. "I don't know. Liz asked me up for a drink and I was going to tell her but..."

Marty isn't going to make this easy for him.

"I didn't. I don't know, I was uptight and..."

"And you haven't..." Marty prompts.

"Been going to meetings. I know. Maybe I just needed to get drunk one more time."

"And maybe you didn't."

"Delia's not coming back."

There. He's said it. And it doesn't hurt quite as much today, though it probably will tomorrow. Sometimes his drunks were very cathartic, left him peaceful and happy in some strange way he never tried to analyze. Full of acceptance. Good intentions.

"Ah," says Marty. "I'm sorry. What, did you see her or did she phone to tell you that?"

"No. I saw her hugging Nick on Dallas Road. She's not coming back."

There's a knock on the door and someone steps in, says "Jeez, it's dark in here," and turns on the ceiling light. Edwin is standing there with bottles of Mister Clean and Windex clutched to his scrawny chest. He's growing his hair out and it's in a short ponytail today.

Matthew, who was expecting maybe Mr. Funk, or Liz, gapes.

"Hi Matt. Howya feelin, buddy?"

Marty laughs at the expression on Matthew's face. "Edwin dropped in for coffee just as I was leaving for your place. He's been cleaning the laundry room."

"And the laundry room washroom, before I escaped. Is that old guy ever bossy," he says, going into the kitchen to put the cleaning stuff away. He comes back and sits down by Matthew, who tries to thank him.

"Well, I don't know how good a job I did. There he goes now," Edwin says, as the Beast buzzes past again and down the hall. "He reminds me of my ex-wife." Marty laughs his maniacal laugh, Matthew his feeble one.

"She had a vacuum cleaner with a light on it and she useta clean in the dark. It was spooky," Edwin says. "Actually, she was too."

"I didn't know you were married," Matthew says, feeling guilty for all his mean, superior, dismissive thoughts about Edwin.

"Weren't we all?" Edwin says.

"Thanks, you guys," Matthew says. He wants to say more but truth to tell, he's feeling perilously close to tears. Maybe the beginning of his sentimental, filled-with-love-for-everyone hangover phase. *How many goodly creatures are there here.*

Edwin reaches out and pats his knee. "Hey, you don't need to thank us, Matt."

"Yes, he does," Marty says. "And whataya have to do to get a cup of coffee around this joint?"

"I'll make it," says Edwin, and goes off to the kitchen.

Marty gets up, turns off the ceiling light, and sits down again, flicking on the lamp beside his chair. His feet on the cluttered coffee table, he nudges aside a badly wilted plant and leans back in his chair, hands behind his head. "What's that poor spotted thing on the table?"

"Delia's prayer plant."

"Well, I think it's giving itself the last rites. If you're just gonna kill it, give it to me." Marty's restaurant windows are full of plants. He gets a glass of water and waters it. "She probably left it here to pray for you." He returns the glass to the kitchen, stands looking around. "Why don't you brighten this place up, Matthew? Hang a picture, for heaven's sake, buy some cushions, no wonder you're depressed. And get somebody to clean the place up. It looks like nobody lives here."

Nobody lives in an ugly how suite.

"I know. Delia took all that stuff."

"Well, get some more. You'll feel better." Marty sits down again.

"So? What're you planning to do about this, Matthew? Are you gonna beat yourself up some more?"

"No, I hope not. God, no. I feel terrible. In every way."

It sounds like Edwin's washing dishes in the kitchen.

"And you look like death warmed over in case you didn't know. If you mean it about staying sober, there's some things you've got to do."

"I know," Matthew says. "More meetings."

"Yeah."

"Step four," Matthew says. "I started it."

"Well, finish it. And you better have a good look at the first three. Especially the first."

"I'm not doubting my qualifications if that's what you think."

"You sure about that?"

"Positive. I'm pretty sure social drinkers don't lose track of two days like I just did."

"Not unless they're in a coma," says Marty.

After coffee, which Matthew can't touch, Marty arranges to pick him up for a meeting, and they leave. He'd rather have gone back to bed, he's starting to feel rocky again, but to a meeting he will go. And tell what happened, he doesn't look forward to that. Telling how unbelievably easy it was to reach for that first drink. It shouldn't have been that easy.

A knock at the door and Mr. Funk walks spryly – springs, almost – through the door. The place has turned into Grand Central Station.

"Just seeing how you are, Matthew."

"I'm all right." Matthew is mortified. "Just embarrassed, and sorry as hell. I'm grateful for what you've done."

"Yes, well, everything's shipshape with some help from your friends, unless something untoward happens. I'll overlook it this time, but not again."

"Thanks. I quit awhile ago but –"

"Ah, I know about the demon drink. A long time ago, but you don't forget. You're doing a good job around here, Matthew, and I was skeptical. In fact," he looks regretful, "we might have to talk about a raise soon."

"Thank you."

Mr. Funk sighs. "Of course Delia was wonderful. How is that lovely woman?"

"She's fine, Mr. Funk. Just fine."

Mr. Funk sighs again. "Oh, well." He turns to leave. "Call me Desmond."

When he's gone Matthew says something he hasn't said since he was a teenager. "Holy Cow!"

He manages to keep down a poached egg on toast, and by the time he showers and puts on clean clothes for the meeting, he's starting to feel a bit better. Good enough for a drink, pops into his mind, and he pushes it out.

But maybe he planned it all along. There was some reason he never got rid of that bottle of scotch. Hid it away in that cupboard when there was no one to hide it from, the hiding habit so strong, but there wasn't a day he didn't think about it being there.

Well, now it's not.

He rinses his dishes and leaves them in the sink. He lifts his jacket from the answering machine, where he must have thrown it, annoyed by its flashing message light. He presses the button.

Two messages from tenants with minor, thank God, problems. A toilet that keeps running. A woman who wants to talk about her refrigerator. A message from Patrick inviting him up for coffee. Too bad he hadn't got that one before Liz's. The poor woman must have been horrified. He shudders. He's got to apologize, he just wishes he knew what for besides lapping up everything in sight.

A staticky message, just static, really, someone on a cellphone with a dying battery, or out of range.

Then, "Grandpa?" he hears. "Grandpa?" A loud roaring sound. And another. Like cars passing nearby. Then, "Grandpa, I'm —" more static — "come and stay with you?" A dog barking. Buddy. Another car, he's sure of it now. More static with Sam talking behind it but he can't understand it, except for the odd word. "crazy," more static, "hate it," another car, "Mom's not," Sam's voice breaking — God, when did this message come in? "Somebody's stopped, Grandpa," he hears clearly, Buddy barking, then just static before the beep.

He drops into a chair. When did that come in?

One more message, maybe Sam calling back. Please, God, let it be Sam, let him be all right. But it's Liz, saying she hopes he's all right. She was worried. Telling him not to worry about last night. She "didn't know." Presumably that she gave drinks to a raging alcoholic.

End of messages.

He calls Kate's number. No answer.

Sam needed him and he was drunk. And when did he call? Last night or the night before? Who stopped and picked him up on the highway? The trapdoor inside is opening.

Where is Sam?

Chapter Sixteen

Cutting the bread thick, Sam makes two big peanut butter and mayo sandwiches and sticks them in a bag with an apple, a granola bar, and a bottle of water. He needs to get out of the house before Michael, who's showing some people around the place, realizes he's up.

He'd better check on Mom first. See if she needs anything. She caught the flu awhile ago, with awful cramps and throwing up, but she didn't get much better, it seems like, better some days, worse the next. She's hardly been out of bed this week, with Emerald bringing her soup and stuff. He taps on her door, hears her tired "Come in."

Her room smells stuffy. Sick. She's propped up on two pillows, a hairbrush in her hand, her black hair accentuating the whiteness of her face, the terrible black around her eyes. Looking at her scares him. "I'm going out with Buddy. D'you need a sandwich or soup or something?"

She smiles weakly and shakes her head. "No, sweetheart, thanks anyway. I don't feel like eating."

"You should go to the doctor. Nobody else was sick this long."

"I know. I was kind of stressed out when I got it and that maybe made it worse."

"Make Michael take you." If only he could drive, he'd make her go. "If he was as sick as you, he'd've gone long ago. He's such a wimp when he's sick."

"That's for sure." She smiles a bit.

"Then make him, Mom." There must be something really wrong with you, he wants to say, but can't.

"Don't worry, honey. If I'm not better by tomorrow I promise I'll go." She squeezes his hand. Hers feels thin and hot.

"Want me to open the window?"

"Just a little. I'm cold all the time."

He opens the window, then leans down to kiss her. She smells different as she reaches up and hugs him. "You're sweet to worry about me, Sam. How are things with you?"

"Okay." What's the use of saying more? She can't do anything about anything. "We're going for a picnic."

"Let me guess," and she smiles, bringing out new lines on her cheeks. "Peanut butter and mayonnaise sandwiches."

"Right. Seeya later, Mom."

Downstairs, he looks out the patio door to check the lay of the land. He doesn't want Michael to see him. Jim is ambling across the yard with some scraps of lumber. Buddy is sitting on the deck watching two women and a man talking in the yard. Their truck has a huge gas tank on the back. That's the second or third one he's seen out here and he wonders what that's about. Where they're planning to go. Now and then Buddy woofs softly in their direction and then looks away. He's ignoring a little boy younger than Joey who is standing beside the deck looking up at him.

"Doggie," he says, sounding proud of knowing the word. "Nice doggie." Buddy pretends he hasn't heard. Laboriously, the boy climbs the steps, his small hand reaching up for the railing and, as Sam watches, he stretches his hand out and pats Buddy's head gently with his hand flat out, then moves in and puts his arms around Buddy's neck. Buddy stares straight ahead for a bit, as if the boy isn't there, then turns and licks him on the cheek. Sam smiles.

"Oh, be careful, honey. The doggie might bite." A woman breaks off from the group and hurries over to the deck, and the others start walking toward Emerald's house.

"He wouldn't," Sam says, through the screen. "He likes little kids."

But the woman has motioned the boy to the side of the deck, securing him with an arm around his waist. "You must be Sam," she says, smiling up at him.

"Yes."

She's wearing jeans and a big red T-shirt. Under her open rain jacket he sees a leather-thonged wooden cross like Emerald's, only smaller. Michael must be making them. Her blonde curly hair is pulled back like Emerald's too but with bits curling around her face. She's pretty. She's the woman he saw in church last night, crying and babbling some weird language. He snuck up there when he came back from the highway and nobody even noticed him by the back wall. Emerald was up front with her eyes shut and her arms waving in the air, Michael and everybody else standing up waving their arms slowly back and forth, like seaweed under water, and chanting something. Or everybody chanting something different, he couldn't tell. Then a very fat woman with long grey hair went up to the front carrying a sheet of paper.

"Friends, I have received another message," she called, and an excited buzz replaced the chanting. "I received it last night, just in time for our meeting." And, when they were quiet, she read "Satan has no power over God's Children. For you, my faithful ones, have heeded the warnings others are ignoring about the coming evil and terrible destruction. Not even the fowls of the air or the creatures of the land and sea will find refuge." She stops reading to look at them. "But you are safe, my children. I will protect you."

"Hallelujah!" someone shouted, and then others joined in, "Hallelujah! Hallelujah!"

Then another woman started speaking some weird language, it sounded like a language, anyway, and someone led her to the front, her eyes closed, those strange sounds coming from her mouth, and a man started doing it, too, and people shouted hallelujah some more and two women started dancing, or running around anyway, holding up their long dresses, one of them was Juliet's mother, and other people were crying and laughing and hugging each other. A woman fainted and two men caught her.

"Get the serpents, Moses!" someone called, and Sam ran for the stairs, falling down the last three steps and didn't stop running till he was in the house.

Today she looks like a nice ordinary person, like the mother of somebody you'd know. And he thinks now they said, "get the service," he was so freaked out he heard it wrong.

"What a lucky boy you are," she says, "living in such a beautiful place with such beautiful people." She suddenly lets go of the boy and twirls around and around laughing, her arms straight out, palms up, like she's waiting for rain, her face tilted up. "I can't help myself, this place does that to me. God is so close here. I can feel Him." She flings her arms skyward. "Can't you just feel Him here?" she says and Buddy stands up and barks an enthusiastic bark.

Sam doesn't answer. What he feels here he hopes isn't God.

"My name is Emily," she says, scooping the boy up in her arms.

"Hi," Sam says.

"And this is Luke."

"Hey, Luke."

"Though I guess we'll all have different names pretty soon. I wonder what mine will be."

What the heck is she talking about, they'll all have different names? Bible names, he bets, that sounds like something Michael might do. Luke already has one. Well, Sam's not changing his name. Or is there a Samuel in the Bible?

Luke is watching him, the top of his head pressed against his mother's chest, his neck bent to see Sam and Buddy, a shy little smile on his face. "Ouch." Emily shifts him up over her shoulder and rubs where the cross pushed into her collarbone. "Doggie," Luke says, struggling to get down. "I want to pet the doggie."

"Later, honey. You'll have lots of time to pet the doggie when we're living here. Remember, Michael told you he'll be your dog too. Won't that be wonderful"

Sam's stomach tightens. He snatches his lunch and clatters down the steps. "Come on, Buddy." And he runs rudely past the woman, who says, "See you," in a surprised voice, and giving Michael's shop a wide berth he jogs into the woods behind. Buddy is his dog and nobody else's. His best friend in all the world. He got him for his fifth birthday and he loves Sam more than anybody.

When he almost gets to the mountain, he sees a fallen log in the small clearing, his favourite place. Not a dead one, one cut not long ago, its thick, evergreen branches lopped off with an axe and thrown on the ground a few feet in front of it, its wounded trunk filling the air with the good, sharp smell of pinesap and pine gum. Where the trees have always met overhead there's an empty space now. Michael must have cut it to make something, but did he have to cut that one when there's a whole forest to choose from?

He sits down on the ground, his back against the log, and opens his lunch. First eat. Then plan his escape. He's surprised Michael didn't drag him out of bed demanding his cellphone. Probably thinks he just misplaced it. He wolfs down the sandwiches as Buddy sniffs around, peeing on several trees, then sits down with his head cocked to one side waiting for the crusts.

He's got to leave before dark tonight. Last night was no good. People can't see you when it's dark and raining and the traffic from the ferry is heavy.

But the man in the big car saw him, and as he pulled over his passenger window rolled noiselessly down. Sure, he said he'd be glad to give Sam a ride to Victoria, but not his dog so Sam said no, he wouldn't leave Buddy there, and anyway there was something about the way the man kept looking at him through the open window that creeped him out.

"I could make it worth your while to leave the dog behind," he said, but Sam shook his head.

"He'd probably get hit by a car trying to catch up." Besides, what did he mean, he'd make it worth his while?

He thinks now maybe he knows, and shudders as he bites into his apple. Buddy is sniffing around the branches in front of him.

And then the man had said, "You gotta good-looking cell-phone there, kid. Who'd you steal it from?"

"Nobody. I didn't." He tried to sound indignant.

"Well, d'ya mind if I make a call on *your* cellphone? There was an accident back there and I want to phone the police."

"Ah, I don't know," he said, but the fat man was climbing out and coming around to them, and Sam's heart started thumping hard. When he reached for the phone Buddy growled and took the guy's arm in his mouth.

"Holy shit, call off your dog, all I wanta do is borrow the phone. There's some people back there needing help."

So Sam called Buddy off and reluctantly handed him the phone.

"Thanks, you're doing the right thing. One of those people was hurt bad. Mind if I make the call in the car, it's too noisy out here. Thanks, won't be a sec," and before Sam could answer, he climbed back in the car and punched in a number, then he put the phone to his ear and took off, leaving Sam yelling and swearing and Buddy barking till the tail lights disappeared.

He has to phone Grandpa, he suddenly remembers, he'll be thinking he's kidnapped or murdered or something. But he's not going back to the house and he'll be seeing Grandpa today anyway. He'll just surprise him. That'll be sweet.

He finishes the apple and tosses the core onto the freshly

cut branches where Buddy pounces on it but it's fallen through the branches and he starts digging, scattering the branches every which way trying to get it. But when the apple core flies out he doesn't stop, just whimpers and digs faster, his white paws almost a blur, leaves flying everywhere.

"Whatcha got there, Buddy?" Sam says, getting up. "Got a mouse or something?" Buddy moans and yelps, digging furiously, soft black earth shooting out behind him. Sam's never seen him like this. Frantic, almost.

"No, Buddy! Stop it! Buddy, stop that!" He doesn't want him digging up something dead and eating it, he did that once and the smell hung on him for ages. "Stop!" Buddy ignores him and when Sam wades in to get hold of his collar his foot sinks down and he falls over backwards, dragging Buddy with him by the collar.

"Come on, boy. Stop it!" and he rolls back onto firm ground. Buddy starts backing away from the place moaning and yelping, howling, almost, looking at Sam like he wants to tell him something. Sam starts throwing handfuls of earth and leaves back where they were, almost as frantic to cover the spot as Buddy was to uncover it. Then starts throwing the branches back, too.

"What are you doing?"

Sam jumps. It's Emerald, standing there across from the branches.

"I dunno. Just having my lunch, I guess."

"It didn't look like that to me."

"Buddy dug a hole. I was just covering it up so nobody would trip." He'd never really have thought about somebody tripping. Nobody comes back here but him and Buddy.

But somebody did, didn't they?

"You're a nosy little brat, aren't you?" she says.

"I am not. And why are you spying on me?" Sam yells. "It's none of your fucking business what I'm doing!"

Her eyes narrow to slits, her mouth scrunching in tight and white.

"Don't you talk to me like that! I'm telling —"

Buddy growls suddenly, startling both of them. He's looking at Emerald, another low growl rumbling deep in his throat.

"Oh, come on, Buddy." Emerald reaches a hand toward Buddy but he growls louder, showing his teeth, and snaps as she jerks the hand away.

"Come on, Buddy. Let's go," Sam says, and starts back toward the house, trying to walk as if he doesn't feel her eyes boring into his back. He glances back.

She's still there, looking down at that place now, and Buddy, following him reluctantly, is looking back there, too. Sam feels the hair go up on the back of his neck.

"Come on, boy!" he yells and starts to run, dodging trees, tripping and falling and leaping up again, and pretty soon Buddy is crashing along behind him. Then he's on the path, running flat out, Buddy running ahead of him now, looking back to see if he's still coming.

The yard is empty of vehicles including the truck and he heads for the barn, climbing the ladder as if the devil is after him, crashing his head against the floor above before he remembers. "Ow! Fuck!" He jumps down and runs up the stairs, Buddy almost knocking him over to get up ahead of him.

He flops into the chair by what Michael calls the literature table. Sam rubs the top of his head where a bump is rising. Buddy leans into him, pushes into him.

"You were scared, too, weren't you Bud?" He kneads Buddy's neck. "What were we so scared of anyway?" he asks. "Just stupid Emerald sticking her ugly nose into everything. Just mean, fucking Emerald."

But why did she want to know what he was doing there? She must have seen and followed him, and that's kind of funny, isn't it? She's got even weirder since Joey left, and there it is again, that bad feeling about Joey, only worse. For sure now he's out of here, as soon as Michael's back, so they don't run into him on the road.

He glances over at all the Armageddon stuff on the table, wishing he had something to read. There's a hand-rolled cigarette there, too, a joint, he's sure, sitting in an old tobacco tin lid, a book of matches beside it, like an invitation, and every time he turns his head he sees it. Michael must have rolled it and forgotten it. He can't stop looking at it. He's never tried it. A couple of guys he knows have, but not him or his friends.

Oh, what the heck, maybe it'll relax him so he can quit worrying so much. And he's curious. He picks it up and lights it. Inhales and coughs it out, inhales and coughs. Then gets the hang of holding it in, and after holding a few more puffs he feels super loose and relaxed.

And then he looks up and the weirdest thing, Michael is hanging up there on the cross and Sam can't figure out how he did that, got up there without him seeing, he's not nailed on or anything, he's just hanging there with his feet crossed, talking.

"We're all going to have new names," he's saying, "new names for all God's children. You," he says, pointing at Sam. "Your new name will be Jeremiah." Sam snickers, that could be worse, it could've been Nebuchadnezzar. "Jeremiah Obadiah Jackanorry Jones for short," Michael says, and Sam falls off the chair laughing. That was his favourite picture book when he was a kid, all about Jeremiah Obadiah Jackanorry Jones trying to find his granny's stolen tarts and meeting four bears drinking beer and playing poker in the woods, it makes him laugh and laugh and laugh, Michael just hanging up there saying in his stern bible reading voice, "Jeremiah Obadiah Jackanorry Jones" over and over. And it makes him like Michael again and Buddy thinks it's funny, too, smiling from ear to ear then laughing, "arf arf arf" his head thrown back and that's hilarious too. "And you, you big hairy critter," Michael says to Buddy and Sam spews out a mouthful of smoke, "your new name is Charlie Chaplin!" and Sam rolls around, holding his stomach, "Charlie *Nebuchad-nezzar* Chaplin" says Michael and ohmigosh, Buddy's wearing a round black hat and a bow tie like Charlie Chaplin in that old movie they watched one night, and he's up on his hind legs dancing, smiling and kicking his legs out sideways as Sam kicks his own legs, howling with laughter "oh, ooh, my stom-ach!" tears streaming down it's funnier than the funniest movie he's ever seen. Buddy dancing, it's so brilliant, it's so fucking *brilliant!*

He's dropped the joint somewhere and crawls around gig-gling till he finds it and reaches up to lay it on the table, and when he looks up, Michael is slowly fading so he can see the cross right through him and Mom is there instead, all limp and pale, her blue jeans hanging so loose they're almost falling off, her T-shirt pulled up and her ribs sticking out, her head hanging to one side like Jesus on the cross, her hair hiding her face and she whispers "help me," so faint Sam almost can't hear and she starts to fade too as he stares, her bones showing through her body like an X-ray, she's turning into a skeleton with black hair and he can't look, mustn't look, crawling under the table hiding his eyes, hiding his head with his arms, crying now as hard as he laughed, harder than when Muriel died, harder than he's ever cried like tears are pouring out of him everywhere....

When he finally peeks, Joey is up there in his *Lion King* outfit, his green-sneakered feet twitching like they did when he fell asleep watching *Star Wars,* and Joey looks straight at him and says "I want my T. Rex, Sam," and Sam crawls out from under the table to talk to Joey. "Your mom won't tell me where you are, Joey, so I can send your T. Rex and a picture I drew of Felix," wanting him to know he's been thinking about him, "Felix in the mixing bowl," he says but Joey doesn't smile or anything, doesn't answer, his feet stop twitching and his eyes are closing and bright leaves are falling down on him, covering his feet first and then his legs, drifting over the picture of Simba on his chest, over Simba's big long-lashed eyes, leaves covering Joey like a blanket. "Where are you Joey?" he says, feeling desperate as the leaves fall faster and thicker, the blanket a quilt now, and Joey's eyes open and he looks right at Sam as if he wants to tell him something but now leaves are fluttering onto his face, gently, lovingly almost.... Sam screams at Joey's suddenly staring eyes and covers his own but can't help looking between his fingers as pine needles catch in Joey's hair and leaves settle thick over his white cheeks and forehead and empty open eyes. Pine branches dropping flopping on the leaf-covered mound till it's hidden, and "OhGodohGodohGod," Sam babbles, crawling around the floor, "Oh God, Joey, oh God, no, oh God I've gotta get out of here." Not knowing where "here" is anymore. Only knowing he's terrified.

He curls into a ball with his arms over his head as Buddy lifts his nose and sniffs the air. On the table, the cover of *The Late Great Planet Earth* begins to smoulder.

Matthew's stayed by the phone as much as possible all day, but no further word from Sam and he's almost crazy with worry. Delia says he's overreacting and if Sam was missing Kate would certainly have phoned to see if he was here. He said he supposes she's right but he's not convinced. Nobody answered the phone up there last night or today and that's kind of strange. If only they could get through to somebody. Even bloody-minded Michael.

After dinner he can't stand it any longer and heads out through the cold rain to Marty's place. He's made just a quick call to tell him what happened, afraid to tie up the phone, and now he has to talk to somebody.

Stopping across from Jimmy's Inn with its warm, welcoming bar, he thinks about a hair of the dog. But now he knows that dog is mighty pissed about having his hairs pulled out one by one and bites like a pit bull. Stuffing his still vibrating hands in his pockets, Matthew walks on.

"No word from the kid?" Marty says, sliding into the chair across from him.

"No. And I'm damn worried. If I don't hear anything by tonight I'm going up there tomorrow."

"Want some company?"

"Oh, God, do I? Can you get away?"

"Sure. If you can wait till after lunch. In the meantime, turn it over to God. I'm sure Delia's right. If anything bad had happened, they'd let ya know."

"I suppose."

"Hey listen, Matthew. Maybe he was gonna leave home but changed his mind. He's a teenager, for God's sake."

"Well, just." But that does help a bit.

He's exhausted. He only slept about three hours last night after hearing Sam's message. But he knows he won't sleep, and doesn't want to walk the halls in case there's news. After a desperate search he finds two sleeping pills left over from his drinking days, and downs one. He can't get hooked on two pills, surely. He'll save one for the next emergency, trying not to think what that might be.

Please God, let Sam be safe. Let him be safe. *Please,* he says, climbing into bed.

He gets up and plugs in the phone by his bedside table and turns up the ringer in case it rings after he goes to sleep. Afraid it might not.

Afraid it might.

Chapter Seventeen

Sam wakes up to the smell of smoke in his room and people shouting outside. He feels so relaxed he doesn't want to get up and see what's going on. He doesn't remember going to bed with his clothes on. Even his shoes. That's funny. He doesn't remember going to bed at all. And Buddy's in bed with him, his big, warm weight pressing all along Sam's back. He hardly ever does that unless there's a thunderstorm. Sam yawns and snuggles into Buddy, who smells like an old moccasin, for some reason. He winces at something sore on his back, like his T-shirt's sticking to his skin. Awkwardly toeing off his shoes with his eyes shut, he starts to drift into sleep again.

"Over here!" someone shouts outside. More answering shouts. What's going on out there? Are they having church outside? But the green numbers on his clock radio click from 12:30 to 12:31 a.m. Too late for church. And something is burning. He can hear the crackling now. Can smell it.

He drags himself out of bed and goes to the bathroom window. The noise of people yelling is louder there and from the window he sees flames licking out through the church wall, sparks flying up, the heat making the spruce trees wavy. He sees an arc of water, hears the crackle and hiss as a fireman hoses the barn. People are milling around and standing in small bunches. Michael and some of the church people are kneeling in a circle, and a fireman yells "Get back! Give us room." Some neighbours looking on shake their heads. A man laughs.

Jeez, the barn's on fire, Sam says. He yawns and goes back to bed.

When he wakes in the morning he's very foggy, then remembers the fire, just a flash of Buddy dragging him somewhere, connecting it with his sore back, he must have dreamed that. Buddy isn't there now. He lies for awhile, feeling super relaxed all over, starting to drift off again. Then jolts awake.

The joint.

Michael on the cross.

Joey.

Joey is dead. He knows it now. And if somebody dies you can't just bury them in your back yard like a cat or dog. Why would you?

But they did. It all fits. The light in the woods the night Joey left. Why she won't say where he is. Everything.

His heart beating slow and hard, he gets up and goes to his mother's room. The door is open but she's not there, not in the bathroom, either. She must be downstairs. He looks out and sees Michael's truck is gone, the air still smoky. He grabs all the money from his Borg bank, about fifty dollars, shakily stuffing it in his jeans pocket. Looking frantically around as he pulls on his shoes. He has to take Buddy, he can't leave him here with Emerald, not now. He grabs a sweatshirt, that's all he needs. His legs feel wobbly, and he stands a moment, eyes closed.

His mom's not in the kitchen, or the living room. As he comes back from checking the downstairs bathroom, Emerald is standing in the hall, barring his way. The back of his neck prickles, like it did in the woods.

"Excuse me," he says, "I want to get past." Hating how his voice sounds.

She doesn't move. "Where do you think you're going?" she says.

"I'm just going to get some breakfast," he says "Where's Mom?"

"Your dad took her to the doctor."

"What? Is she worse?"

Emerald shrugs, and finally moves aside to let him pass.

"That's good, though." He sounds better now, almost normal, actually, though his insides feel like jello and his heart is thumping. "She's really been sick," he says, taking down the Cheerios and bread. Don't look at her. Don't look at her.

"Psychosomatic, mostly," she says.

"No, it's not. I hope they put her in the hospital."

He puts two slices of bread in the toaster. "Say, did the barn burn down last night or did I dream that?"

"As if you wouldn't know," she says, sitting down on a stool at the counter.

"What d'ya mean? Why should I know?" Looking at her now.

"You set it on fire." She says it like she might say pass the Cheerios. Shaking her hair away from her face.

"I did not!"

"You went up there yesterday. I saw you."

That silences him. Holy shit, is there any way that joint started the fire? He can't remember what he did with it. Felix comes in and meows at his empty dish. Sam pours some food from the bag, spilling more than he gets in the bowl.

"You can't go out till Michael gets home."

Oh fuck, she's guarding him. The toast pops, and he jumps, stepping on the end of Felix's tail, who scolds as he wraps his tail around him and keeps on eating.

"Nerves bad?" There's a mean little smile on her face.

"No. Where's Buddy?"

Now she's really smiling and it looks odd. As if Felix suddenly smiled up at him.

"Gone to the vet's."

"The vet's? What for? What's wrong with him?"

"He's getting vicious. He probably has to be put down."

He lunges at her across the counter but she steps back. "You liar!" he screams. "Buddy's not vicious!"

"Yes, he is. Don't worry, they'll just put him to sleep. It doesn't hurt." She laughs.

"Stop saying that!" he screams. *"I know where Joey is."*

She goes very still. "What are you talking about?" She gets up and blocks the kitchen entrance.

"You know! He's buried in the woods, that's where he is and I'm telling!" He charges her, head down, like a bull, knocking her over backwards, and he's out the door, leaping off the deck and through the yard, then he's over the gate and hits the road running like the wind, tears flying off his face. He's got to get to the vet's.

He doesn't hear the car till it's right behind him and he swerves out of the way, into the neighbour's grassy field. The car swerves too, he should've turned the other way; there's no fence here and there are car tracks all over the place from kids coming out to party, and she's barrelling down on him – *Jesus, she's trying to kill him,* and he zigzags wildly, the car does too, twice, in a kind of crazy dance, then he sprints toward the party place, leaping over logs, beer bottles, firepit, more logs, and she has to go around as he heads full tilt for a grove of trees, the last bit downhill, he stumbles, rights himself, the car so close he feels the heat from the motor as he takes a giant leap into the grove, hears a horrendous crash behind him, metal buckling, glass breaking, and he's out past the trees and in the open running again, fearful she's following but as he scrambles over a rail fence he glances back at her still in the car. He sprints across the road, through a barbed-wire fence catching on his shirt, his head, a sharp pain and he's running and bounding like a rabbit till he finally drops into a hollow in a thick grove of trees about a mile up the road, his heart pounding so hard he's afraid it might stop. Sticky wet running down the back of his neck, his hand coming away bloody. Gasping for breath he starts to shake, goosebumps everywhere, it feels like, his T-shirt soaked, his sweatshirt back in the kitchen and it's starting to rain. "Ow!" A vicious pain in his head makes him howl like a baby.

Stop it! Stop crying. She tried to kill you and you're still here. And maybe she lied about Buddy. Michael wouldn't do that would he? He likes Buddy too.

It stings something awful when he warily touches his head again. A chunk of it must be on that fence back there. It's still bleeding down his neck but not as much.

And he's amazed at himself, too. He didn't know he could run that fast. Emerald's car must be history. It'll be evidence when he tells the police.

He hears a car and ducks down, raising his head just high enough to see, through the long yellow grass and trees, Emerald driving slowly up the road. Her grille is bashed in, headlight gone, left front side crumpled, her head turning from side to side, her face chalk white. Looking for him. He can't believe the car still works.

And she keeps doing it. Up and down, driving slow. Lying face down in the hollow he can still see that white face swinging back and forth on her long neck like a snake, eyes boring into the bushes till the sound of the motor dies away. Three times she goes up and back and another car goes by, too, but he doesn't lift his head again till he hears the truck motor and crawls up where he can get a really good look through the bushes. And there's big old Buddy, just sitting up looking out the window. Like a tourist on a bus, his mom used to say.

"Yesss!" he says. There's lumber sticking out the back of the truck, a red rag fluttering on the end of it, banging around as the truck hits a pothole. Mom's not there, though. She must be in the hospital. Where else would she be? He stares out at the road long after the truck has gone. If she's in the hospital, he could leave now.

No, he can't. Emerald will do something terrible to Buddy to get back at him. Poison him. Or shoot him and say she thought he was a bear or something. He's got to get him out of there. But he can't till they're all asleep. It'll be easy as long as Buddy's on the deck.

It's getting colder, and darker. He lies down on his side with his arms wrapped around his chest, willing himself to stop shaking. It's worse because his ᴛ-shirt's damp and his back still sore, like he's got slivers in it. He could cover himself with leaves and he'd be warmer, but thinking of Joey he can't bring himself to do it, instead pulling more leaves in on the cold ground under him, and spotting some old, still dry newspaper caught in the thicket, he retrieves it and covers himself with it. It's surprisingly warmer. With a huge, shuddering sigh, he closes his stinging eyes.

He's scared. Scared about Mom, and Buddy, scared of what Emerald might do, knowing now she'll do anything. He wipes his nose on his damp ᴛ-shirt and curls up on his side.

He wakes to the stealthy sound of footsteps rustling.

Through the leaves, coming very close, then stopping. He's afraid to open his eyes, but when there's no other sound, he does. A young deer, almost hidden by the brush, is inspecting him. He can see its face clearly, the curious look in its large, dark eyes. Maybe this hollow is where it sleeps.

"Hi," he whispers. "Am I sleeping in your bed? I'll be gone as soon as it's dark." The deer turns and walks away, obviously not too frightened by him. He's glad he saw it. He doesn't feel so alone.

It won't be long till dark now, and the moon will be full.

It's cold in the tent and Jim can't sleep. He is more than somewhat worried. The church burning last night. Young Samuel tearing off this morning like the devil was after him – he was going for water when he saw that – then Emerald roaring out of the yard after him and now her car's a wreck.

And still no sign of Samuel. He's been watching most of the day and is feeling more anxious by the minute.

He lies on his cot in the dark, his hands under his head. There's a full moon, and even inside the tent, with the screened window he leaves open on clear nights, it's not completely dark.

He has more than the boy on his mind. Michael's already buying lumber to rebuild the church and Jim isn't sure he wants to. He takes the fire, especially the cross burning, as a message from God. And Emerald telling everyone Samuel set the fire. He doesn't believe that.

The way things are going around here troubles him more than somewhat, and he can't sleep for mulling it over and over in his mind. Michael's good to him but he long ago figured out who's running things.

He sighs, and sitting up in his long underwear and wool socks, pulls on his old Siwash and boots and feels for the tobacco tin where he keeps his smokes. He thinks better with a cigarette. The wooden match won't light on the side of the matchbox, too damp, so he lights it with his thumbnail, a trick he learned in a lumber camp once.

A rustling sound outside the tent stills his hand halfway to his mouth. They had a cougar around not too long ago. Michael shot it and that really upset him and Samuel; it was just passing through, not bothering anybody, but that doesn't mean Jim wants to share his cot with its mate.

More rustling and he thinks bear. Jim is more than somewhat scared of bears. He sits absolutely still, listening with all his might. A twig cracks right outside the tent and he feels his pubic hair stand on end, a strange sensation if ever there was one.

"Jim? Are you there?" a voice whispers, and he almost screams.

"No," he whispers back, and hears somebody laugh.

"Jim. It's me. Sam. Let me in."

"Samuel! Oh, thank God."

Fumbling with the tent zipper, he opens the flap to see a shivering, bedraggled Sam who steps quickly inside and puts his finger to his lips.

"Just whisper, okay?"

"Okay. What's happened to you?" he whispers. "Is that blood on your shirt?"

"Yah. I'll tell you what happened, but I'm freezing."

Minutes later, on the cot with Jim's wool socks on inside the warm, flannel-lined sleeping bag, Sam finally stops shivering, but bathed in warmth he can hardly keep his eyes open. And he knows he must.

Jim lights a small gas burner and makes a pot of strong tea, the only thing he can think of for shock, and hands him a ham sandwich made in the light from the gas flame. Sam sits up and wolfs it down, just ham and slightly dry bread, no mustard, no mayo, no pepper, the most delicious thing he's ever eaten. He drinks the strong, hot tea with milk and sugar, feels it warming him, waking him up, as Jim lights a match to apply antibiotic salve to his head. "You got blood on the back of your shirt," and he gently tries to pull it away but it's stuck. "How did you get slivers in your back?"

"I dunno." Sam takes the aspirins Jim hands him and swallows them with the cooling tea. Jim refills the cup and, pulling a folding lawn chair up to the cot, sits down. "Now," he whispers, "what happened today, Samuel."

"Just call me Sam, okay?" And the dam breaks. Jim doesn't interrupt once as Sam, in a low rush of words falling over themselves, tells it. Everything he's had no one to tell all this time, the things he knows and those he can hardly bear knowing. Even about the joint and seeing Joey – Jim cries when he tells that – ending with Emerald trying to run over him with her car. "And I had to come back to get Buddy."

When he's finished there is silence in the tent. Jeez, Sam thinks, what will he do if Jim doesn't believe him? Some of it sounded unreal, even to him.

"Oh Lord, save us," Jim says into the dark.

"Oh Lord save us said Mrs. Davis," Sam says. It's a line from another kids' book he loved. And he laughs. And once he starts he can't stop, especially now. Jim laughing, too, and trying not to, his hand over his mouth, Sam burying his face in the sleeping bag, they laugh and laugh, both of them scared out of their ever-loving wits.

"Do you believe me?" Sam says, when they stop.

"Unfortunately, I do. I saw Emerald take off after you. I thought when I saw you she'd hit you with her car."

"She tried. She sure tried." If he lives to be a hundred he'll never forget that last terrified leap, the car buckling behind him. Will still remember Emerald sitting in the car glaring straight ahead, like she was willing the car to go crashing through the trees after him. Like she couldn't believe it wouldn't.

"I saw her come back with the car all smashed up. Real upset about something she was. Chewing nails and spitting tacks."

"If anybody could, she could." Relief is flooding through him. He has a witness.

"I hope to God you're wrong about Joey, poor little tyke. But the police will find that out soon enough. I used to hear him crying so hard sometimes when he was alone with her but I didn't know. We've gotta get you out of here, Sam."

Oh, the wonderful sound of "we."

"I know. But we can't go without Buddy. She hates him, too. She'll be so mad I got away she'll do something terrible to him. Poison him or something."

Jim doesn't say she wouldn't. "Where does he sleep at night?"

"On the deck, or in the house, by the back door, usually." He's worried that Buddy didn't bark when he came back, but it might just be Buddy getting deaf. They've noticed that lately. "But he's not on the deck, and the house will be locked."

"Ooooh," says Jim. "In the house, eh?" A little shiver runs down his spine. "I think she's there too. Emerald." He says it like he wishes he didn't have to.

"Oh, probably." She would be, with Mom gone. It doesn't take a rocket scientist to figure that out. Did Mom just go this morning? He never knew a day could be that long.

"So, will you help us get away?" Sam asks, only then realizing what this might mean for Jim.

"Yes. I been thinking about leaving anyway." Jim sighs in the dark, and Sam wonders where he'll go. He hopes he won't be a homeless person. Playing the mouth organ for quarters.

"Thanks," Sam whispers, with feeling.

And they put their heads together, whispering.

Later, as Sam sleeps, Jim packs all his belongings, which doesn't take long. Then, giving the house a wide berth, he unlocks the gate.

At 8:30, Jim, truck motor running, knocks on the door of the house.

All is quiet. No answering bark and Sam, under a blanket in the truck box, almost stops breathing.

Jim can see the patio door's secured with the two-by-four like Sam said. He knocks again, louder, and Buddy starts barking.

Sam starts breathing again.

Then the sound of the sliding door, Michael's just-woke-up voice. "Jim? What's up?"

Sam, listening hard, doesn't hear Buddy come out. The screen must still be shut. And it will be locked inside, as he told Jim.

Jim thinks Michael looks like death warmed over and can't help feeling a bit sorry for him. He's not the first guy to get his brain caught in his zipper.

"I'm just goin' to town for some supplies and wondered if you wanted anything from the lumberyard."

Brilliant, Sam thinks. Jim sounds just right.

"No, I don't think so, Jim. Thanks anyway. Say, you haven't seen Sam, have you?"

"Samuel? No. Isn't he at home?"

In the truck Sam hugs his knees, head down, *open the screen, open the screen, open the screen!*

"No. He knows he's in trouble over the barn and he's skipped."

"Oh, that's too bad." Buddy starts whining, then barking to get out but Michael doesn't open the screen.

"Okay," Jim says. Emerald has appeared behind Michael in her nightgown and Jim feels his balls shrivel a bit. "I'll keep an eye out for him."

Oh no. They can't leave. Sam pulls off the blanket, listening. Jim sounds nervous suddenly.

"What are you doing here?" Emerald says, her voice accusing. "Do you know where Sam is?"

"Uh, well, I might," Jim says. "Can I come in?"

Michael opens the screen and Buddy bounds out. "Here, boy," Sam yells and the dog makes a flying leap through the open tailgate just as Jim slams the truck door and steps on the gas.

"Hey!" Michael yells after them. "Hey!" The truck heads for the gate and through it, Michael and Emerald running into the road.

Sam grabs Buddy around the neck and hangs on tight. "Yesss! Oh yes!" as they bounce crazily around, Jim driving like a maniac over the potholes and ruts in the road.

Jim floors it when they reach the highway, all the way to Parksville, where he pulls down into the seaside park, stopping behind a grove of trees out of sight from the road. Buddy bounds out and into the trees to pee, and Sam jumps down and up into the truck cab, launching himself at Jim, punching his shoulder. "Oh, that was awesome!"

Jim, white as a ghost behind his beard, manages a weak smile.

"Saying you knew where I was, that was brilliant!"

Jim's gap-toothed grin widens. "Well, I couldn't tell a lie, could I?" And Sam laughs so hard he almost falls off the seat.

"You shoulda seen Emerald when she saw me in the back. She was so mad!"

Jim nods. "I knew she would be."

"Can we get out for just a sec?"

"Well, that's all."

The park has the beach smell Sam loves. Seagulls swoop and squabble over the grey, white-capped waves, and he runs as fast as he can up the beach a ways and back, the wind almost lifting him off the sand. Jim is hunched over by the truck, trying to light a cigarette in the wind.

"Come on, you guys, let's go."

Sam pitches a stone as hard as he can into the choppy waves and heads for the truck.

"Come on. Don't let Buddy get wet." Buddy, damp from the spray, shakes himself hard, ears flopping, collar jingling, before jumping up into the cab.

"Do up your seatbelt, Sam," Jim says, lighting the cigarette and taking a few deep drags before pulling out and up onto the highway where he puts the pedal to the floor.

"I bet she's chewing nails and spitting tacks!" Sam yells, over the roar of the ancient muffler.

They're rocking down the road now, Buddy scrabbling to stay on the old torn plastic seat, Sam's arm around him. Jim suddenly knowing, too, how great it feels to be away from that place.

"It was brilliant though, wasn't it, Jim?" Sam yells. "It was fucking brilliant!"

And, though he doesn't approve of Sam's language, Jim has to admit it. It was "fucking brilliant."

"Don't talk anymore," Jim says. He is more than somewhat worried, and needs to think.

It's not too far to Nanaimo, and Sam's head needs attention or it might get infected. It might be too late for stitches but it should be properly cleaned. Sam thinks his mom's in the hospital in Nanaimo but Jim's afraid maybe she isn't. And is afraid of what he's thinking. He wouldn't put anything past

Emerald now. If they stop at the hospital and Kate isn't there, what will they do?

Sam's just looking out the window. Coming down from his high.

"How's your head?" Jim asks.

"It hurts."

"A lot?"

"Quite a bit."

That decides things. "We'd better stop in Nanaimo and get it fixed up."

"Can't we wait till we get to Victoria?" His stomach is suddenly tight. What if Mom's not here? What then? But Jim is already turning the truck at a sign that says HOSPITAL.

"No, I think you need your head examined." Now he's slowed down they can talk without shouting.

"Yah. For staying there so long, I do."

"Me, too," Jim says. "I need mine examined, too." Pulling into the hospital emergency parking.

Fortunately Emergency is almost empty. Sam goes off to get a coke and then a nurse takes him in right in. Jim sits there a moment. He feels suddenly faint, the way he often does in hospitals. And he's scared to ask but makes himself find the information desk.

"Kate Taylor?" says the young woman with a headphone on over the brightest red hair Jim's ever seen. "Yes. Room 315." She smiles up at him. "Just take the elevator to your right and ask at the third-floor desk. It's not visiting hours but they can tell you how she is." Relief washes over him and he feels even weaker.

"Are you all right, sir?" The receptionist asks. "You're awfully pale."

"I know. I can tell," he says, turning away, his legs almost refusing to carry him to the elevator. He should take the stairs (he's claustrophobic too), but doesn't think he could climb three flights.

He leans against the elevator wall as the door closes and it starts up. At the second floor the door opens and an orderly rattles in a patient on a bed, a deathly pale old man with tubes running in and out of him everywhere. The bed stops with the old man's head right under Jim's nose, a strange smell wafting up, and Jim crumples against the wall and disappears down behind the bed.

"Holy shit," says the orderly.

Kate is awake when the nurse wheels him up to her bed. He is speechless at the actual sight of her. There could be another Kate Taylor.

Alarmed, she struggles up. "Jim! What are you doing here? Why are you in a wheelchair?"

"Passed out in the elevator, poor fellow," says the muscular male nurse, patting Jim's shoulder. Then to Kate, "He should stay put for a bit. It's not visiting hours but he said he had to see you. It was important." He pours a glass of water and hands it to Jim. "Call if you need anything," he says and swishes out.

"Jim. What's going on?" A magazine slithers off the bed as she reaches out and grips his hand.

"I brought Sam in to emergency." At her terrified look, he hurries on, "No, no, it's all right. He just needs a few stitches." The girl in the next bed is looking at him.

"Stitches where? How did he do that? Why didn't Michael bring him?"

She's asking too many questions. "He just caught it on a barbed-wire fence. That's all," he mumbles. To tell her what really happened would upset her too much. "Don't worry."

He feels flustered by the teenage girl in the bed by the window. Her short, black, spiky hair, white face, nose and eyebrow rings alarm him. She stares at him.

"We're going to Victoria, to Samuel's grandfather's." He takes a nervous swallow of the water. "I hope that's all right. With you, I mean. Sam had a fight with Emerald and he wanted to leave."

She nods. "Oh God, yes. It's wonderful. Now I don't have to go back home." She closes her eyes a moment and the tension seems to leave her body. But she's so pale, and black around the eyes, it scares him. "Please tell my father to come and pick me up, Jim," she says in a low, urgent voice. "I was just going to phone him. They might discharge me tomorrow and I can't go home. Tell him to come in the morning."

"No. You shouldn't go back there." Jim whispers. He shakes his head and feels dizzy again. "Neither should Sam."

They look at each other for a long moment.

A young guy with porcupine quill hair tiptoes in and pulls the curtain shut around himself and the girl. At the rustly, smoochy sounds behind the curtain Jim blushes.

"I gotta get downstairs now. Should Sam come up and see you?"

"No. Get him to my father's. Tell him I'm all right and I'll see him tomorrow." Jim is relieved. "And tell Dad to come early. I don't want to see Michael before I go."

"Yes. Yes, I'll tell him." He just wants to get out of the room now. Out of the hospital.

She presses the button for the nurse and squeezes his hand. "Thank you, Jim." She puts his hand against her hot cheek. "Hug Sam for me."

"Ready to go, are we?" The same nurse hustles in, and the sounds behind the curtain stop.

"Would you please take my friend down to the emergency ward?" Kate says. "And make sure he's all right before he leaves? He has to drive to Victoria."

"Don't worry, we'll see he's all right. Probably just another case of hospitalitis. We see a lot of that around here." He releases the brake on the wheelchair. "He'll be fine as soon as he's outside."

When they're gone Kate lies back against the pillow, then turns on her side and closes her eyes.

Chapter Eighteen

Matthew prepares a sandwich, deli ham, mayo and lettuce, and with a fresh coffee sits down to his noon meal. He hasn't eaten much for two days and he's hungry.

It's another windy day, the moribund cedars swaying slowly from side to side, like a tired old chorus line. He feels the same. So afraid for Sam, it was two before the sleeping pill kicked in, and his bowel is on the rampage. *The thought thereof doth like a poisonous mineral gnaw my innards.* Now which play from his long-ago Shakespeare class was that from? William must have had IBS, too.

When he's finished eating he pours another coffee and goes into the bathroom to get ready. The buzzer goes and he pauses, toothbrush in hand, to look at his watch. Marty must have got away early. He buzzes him in, shrugs into his jacket and opens the door.

"Hi, Grandpa," Sam says, launching himself into his grandfather's startled embrace.

"Sam. Oh, my, God, Sam!"

The shock of it, the surprise and the joy of it, the intense relief hits Matthew in the legs and he drops onto the arm of the couch. Buddy and that old hippie from their place are smiling in the doorway.

"Come in, come in," he says. "I was just getting ready to leave for your place. I was worried about you, Sam. Scared shitless is more like it."

Sam grins. Perched on the coffee table in a dirty, bloody T-shirt and an ancient matted cardigan that must be the old guy's, he's never looked so wonderful.

"Are you hungry?" Matthew asks.

"Starving."

"Okay. Wash up. Food first. Talk later."

Matthew quickly makes more sandwiches, gets coffee for Jim and himself.

"There's a coke in the fridge, Sam. And what about Buddy? Is he hungry, too?"

"For sure," Sam says. "We left in kind of a hurry. Didn't we, Jim?" He smiles at Jim, who, perched on the edge of the lone kitchen chair, looks like he's been dragged through a knothole backward, and then dragged through it a couple more times. "You could say that," he says, with a sickly smile, like someone just cast ashore by a hurricane.

With sandwiches between them on the coffee table, they sit down, Sam beside Matthew, Jim across the table, Buddy, with a half pound of expensive deli beef inside, passed out on the floor.

Thank you, God, Matthew belatedly remembers to think. He touches Sam's bandage. "What happened here?"

"Emerald happened," Sam says.

"That's the truth, man." Jim nods his grizzled head. "She sure did. They fixed him up at the hospital."

"Yep. Had my head examined." Sam gulps down the last bite of sandwich and reaches for another.

Matthew is shocked. "Emerald hit you there?"

"No. But she sure tried."

Matthew lights a cigarette and proffers the pack to Jim. "Oh, I forgot. You don't smoke, do you?"

"I do now," says Jim, rolling his eyes.

Fresh coffee poured, Matthew says, "Okay. Tell."

And Sam does, with Jim backing him up about the car chase.

Then, in a very quiet voice, Sam says, "Grandpa, that's not all."

Oh God. Matthew's heart sinks. What else?

"What?"

"I smoked a joint that was in the barn, and that's how I saw Joey and knew he was dead and buried in that place in the woods."

"You saw him?"

"Yah. I did. Promise me, Grandpa, you won't tell Mom about the pot."

So. Is this all a marijuana trip? Matthew feels a momentary relief. No. The rest all fits. And now he'll be worried sick about Sam and pot. He's got the genes. He could throttle that goddamn Michael.

"I know it's true, Grandpa. Michael and Emerald were back there that night they said Joey's dad came for him. Promise you won't tell about the joint?"

Matthew raises his right hand. "I promise."

He sits a few moments, thinking. "You know, I'm still going up today. You guys are okay here and I want to see your mom." He wouldn't be surprised by anything Emerald would do now.

About half an hour later, when he and Marty leave, Sam is in Matthew's bed already drifting off, and Jim, sitting on the couch made up with a blanket and pillow, won't be far behind.

"Don't answer the door or the phone," Matthew says.

"No way, man," Jim whispers.

In the car Matthew fills Marty in.

"That's a hell of a story, Matthew. Do you think your grandson might be –"

"Exaggerating? No, I don't think so. I believe she's capable of trying to run him down. Jim does too."

"Jim looks like somebody ran over him. Are the police gonna believe a kid and a guy who looks like Charles Manson on valium? And what about the boy? D'you think Sam could be right about that?"

"Well, I certainly hope he's wrong, he's pretty freaked out about that woman. But I saw a nasty bruise on the little guy's arm that day. And she was a supremely indifferent mother." He reaches for his cigarettes, remembers he's in a non-smoker's car.

"Go ahead," Marty says. "I think you need it."

"Thanks." Matthew gratefully lights up, opening the window a bit. "But I can't understand Kate not reporting it if she thought the child was abused."

"I don't know. You can miss a lot when you're addicted to pills," Marty says.

"I guess. I hope the police will check it out for Sam's sake. He's convinced the child is buried out there. And Emerald's actions seem to back that up. Sam smoked a joint that idiot Michael left in plain sight, and he says he saw the little boy dead."

"Oh no. Poor kid. Maybe the pot was telling him what he already knew. It can do that."

"Could be. Could be something else. Who knows? Liz tells me there's a ghost at the Kensington."

Marty laughs. "Several, I'd say."

"No, really. And Liz is a sensible woman. Didn't somebody say, 'There are more things in heaven and earth than we can imagine.'" Or are dreamed of in somebody's philosophy, he can't remember.

"I could have told you that."

In spite of everything, he's enjoying the drive in Marty's car, "More comfortable for your daughter," he said last night. He drives the winding island highway with ease, not swearing and sweating like Matthew, the new Nissan Maxima indeed a luxury ride compared to the old Volvo.

"Jesus. Your poor daughter," Marty says. "Finding out her husband's mistress tried to kill her son."

Matthew winces. "Sounds like a *National Enquirer* cover, doesn't it? But she has to know. I hope the hospital will let her go."

Marty snorts. "If you got a pulse they let you go."

At the third-floor nursing station Marty stops. "I'll wait for you here. Take your time."

In 315 Kate is perched on the edge of a chair like a bird ready to take flight at the first sign of a cat.

"Hi sweetheart," he says.

"Dad!" she says, slumping momentarily with relief. "I've never been so glad to see anyone in my life."

She feels fragile as a bird when they hug, like there's nothing to her in the thin hospital robe.

"I didn't expect you till tomorrow."

"I couldn't wait to see you." He steps back and looks at her. "You don't look too bad," he lies. "You just need some TLC, and your mother can't wait to give it to you."

"That will be wonderful." She smiles up at him. "I don't know if they'll let me go today. They think it was food poisoning but they're waiting for tests. You'll have to talk to Doctor Lee."

The doctor, who was on the next ward, arrives at the desk right away. Taking Matthew into a side room he says, "Your daughter has been ill for some time, I understand."

"Yes. It's been awhile."

The doctor frowns. "We have sent away a sample to a Vancouver lab. There's a toxicologist there." At Matthew's puzzled look he says, "Is your daughter careless about mushrooms, do you know? Would she know the poisonous ones?"

"I think so. But I suppose it's possible to make a mistake. If she's out of danger can we take her back to Victoria with us? Her mother's a nurse."

"Well, in that case..." The doctor starts shuffling things around on a small desk, and finding a notepad says, "Write down the phone number where I can call her with the lab results. She'll need lots of fluids and rest."

Matthew nods as he's writing.

"Tell her mother electrolytes, too. Depending on the lab results, she may need some tests for liver and kidney damage. She's pretty weak but the electrocardiogram showed no heart damage, so I'm hopeful."

When the doctor leaves Kate's room, Matthew finds her fully dressed and zipping up an overnight case. He helps her on with her jacket and zips it up. "It's chilly out there."

She looks up at him. "Dad. What did Emerald do to Sam?"

"Don't worry about that. He's fine. He'll tell you himself." He picks up her overnight bag. "So let's get you home. A friend drove me up in his car."

In a chair across from the nursing station Marty, who's been chatting to the nurse on duty, gets up and holds out his hand. "Hi, Kate. I'm Marty. Your old man's disreputable friend."

Kate smiles. "Does he have any other kind?"

The sun is shining as they pick their way through the puddles in the parking lot, Kate holding Matthew's arm. They're almost at Marty's car when Michael's truck splashes into the lot.

"Hey!" Brakes screech and Michael is out and running toward them. "Where do you think you're going?" He grabs Kate's arm but she jerks away.

"Don't, Michael," she says, and keeps walking. When he reaches for her again Marty steps between. "I believe she said 'don't,'" he says. They're at Marty's car now and the car locks thud up as if by magic. Kate slides into the front seat and locks the doors.

Michael glares at Marty. "That's my wife, and I want to know what the hell she thinks she's doing." He's getting loud. "And who the fuck are you? Get out of my fucking way," he yells. A couple going to their car stop and look.

"She's going with us," Matthew says. "For God's sake, Michael, don't make a scene."

"Shut up, you!" Michael yells. "I'll make a scene if I want to!"

Kate rolls the window down a few inches. "Stop it, Michael. I'm not going home and you can't make me." The window glides up, a soft, punctuated sound as it fits itself into the frame.

Marty, standing on the driver's side, raises his eyebrows at Matthew, and they're in and moving.

"Then don't come back," Michael screams, running alongside and smacking Kate's window hard with the side of his fist. "You'll be sorry!" And he keeps abreast, hitting the window again and again, yelling and swearing as Kate stares straight ahead, Marty unable to speed up because of a car ahead of them looking for a parking space. "Drop dead, Michael," is all Kate says. Michael stops when they come abreast of the truck, where Emerald, in the driver's seat, shoots a triumphant little smile at Kate as they pass.

Matthew reaches over and squeezes Kate's shoulder.

"I knew he'd make a scene," she says.

"It's all right, Katie. You're going to be all right. I thought he was going to break the window."

"Bulletproof glass," says Marty.

Kate reaches up and pats Matthew's hand. "I'm so glad you

were there, both of you. Emerald is welcome to him," she says. "But I'm sorry you had to hear that."

"Don't give it a thought," Marty says. "I've heard worse."

Kate mops at her face, suddenly covered with perspiration.

"Are you feeling sick?" Matthew asks, trying not to sound worried, though he's more than that, his gut in a painful knot since talking to the doctor.

"Just a bit. I'll be all right." And she puts her head back and closes her eyes.

After awhile Marty puts on an old Simon and Garfunkle tape, the song about talking to that old friend, Darkness, – what great songwriters those guys were, Matthew thinks – and Kate sits up and smiles at Marty. "That's one of my all-time favourites," she says. And as they talk music Matthew realizes with some surprise they're close to the same age, Marty only about five years older. His role as chief listener and adviser – make that bossy sponsor – makes Matthew forget how young he is.

"Bridge Over Troubled Waters" fills the cozy space with clear, rich, stereo sound. Kate laughs at something Marty said, and Matthew smiles. She still has a great laugh.

Kate turns toward him. "Dad, maybe we should stop and phone Mom?"

"Sure. I left a message at the hospital so she'll know you're coming. She was in the operating room."

Marty hands Kate his cellphone and she gets the hospital number and talks briefly to her mother. "Okay, Mom. I love you, too." She pushes the button and returns the phone to Marty. "Mom said she'd come to your place after work, Dad."

"That's fine," he says. Not really. He hasn't seen Delia since that day on Dallas Road, but he's got to sometime. Matthew leans back and closes his eyes. God, he's tired. He doesn't know when he's felt this tired.

Marty and Kate start talking again and to the low murmur of their voices from the front seat Matthew falls suddenly asleep.

B uddy barks when he puts his key in the door and his boisterous greeting almost knocks Kate over. Jesus, Matthew thinks, they've got to do something with the dog. He can't stay here.

Jim is sitting up smoking and drinking the leftover coffee and looking like he just woke up. Kate goes straight to the bedroom and comes back out. "Dead to the world. Buddy didn't even wake him," she says.

"Must be a teenager," Marty says.

Marty stays for coffee. Buddy takes an immediate shine to him, leaning against his leg and giving him chummy glances.

"Guess I'll have to take this guy home with me," he says, playing with Buddy's ears. "There's a fenced yard at my house. I'm usually home a couple of times a day."

"Do you mean it?" Kate says. "He might be —"

"That's an offer we can't refuse," Matthew interrupts before Marty can change his mind.

"Yah. Somebody knocked on the door and he barked like crazy," Jim offers. "I peeked out the spy hole and a big fat woman was out there shaking her fist and yelling something about dogs and cats and reporting you. Well," he adds, as if suddenly thinking he might have been rude, "maybe everybody looks fat through those things."

Matthew laughs. "No. That would be Tessie. Built like a four-suite apartment block."

Jim laughs, covering his mouth with his hand.

"Then we'd better blow the joint, eh Buddy? Before that scary lady catches you," Marty says.

Kate smiles. "Or Dad gets thrown out and has to go live with you, too."

"Perish the thought," says Marty. "Want to come over to my joint for pie and coffee, Jim?"

"Sure. I was just gonna go for a walk and get some smokes."

Matthew finds some twine to tie to Buddy's collar. An unnecessary precaution, since he wags out the door without a backward glance.

"Marty is very kind," Kate says when they're alone. "Isn't he?" she adds, as if perhaps she doesn't trust her judgement any more.

"Yah. He is, I guess, but usually he hides it better." She smiles but she's so white and his gut jabs him again. "I have to go up and beard the lion in her den, the fat complaining one. And I have go to the hardware store, and a couple of other places. You'd better lie down for awhile." Maybe she'll sleep.

She's already pulling off her shoes and he puts on a fresh pillowcase and brings a quilt his mother made from the linen cupboard. He opens the windows, suddenly aware of how smoky the place smells. As he unplugs the phone and lets himself out she looks already asleep, her dark hair accentuating her pallor.

He'll go have coffee with Marty. Gird himself for seeing Delia. And to let it all sink in.

An emotional hour after Delia arrives, she and Kate leave. Matthew sends Sam out to get Jim, who's been sitting and smoking on the bench out front. The man has good manners, Matthew thinks. But no doubt his presence there worried some older tenants. Strange-looking people make them fearful.

"Let's go find some supper," he says. "Then we'll talk to the police."

"I hope they believe me," Sam says. "But Jim saw Emerald chasing after me, didn't you Jim?"

Jim nods emphatically. "And the car when she came back. I saw that, too. And how mad she was. Brrrr!"

"If she doesn't get rid of the car," Matthew says, without much hope. And if Emerald insists Joey's with his father will they even investigate, he wonders, almost hoping not. Sometimes you just want things to be over. Then, remembering the sweet dark-eyed child, the small soft hand in his, the ugly bruise on his arm, "*I fell,*" he feels ashamed. Of course they have to know.

"I feel like a steak," he says, shrugging into his jacket. "How about you, Jim?"

Jim's eyes light up. "I could eat the hind end out of a skunk," he says.

"They only have skunk bum on Saturdays. Marguerita Monday and Skunk Bum Saturday."

Sam laughs. "You guys have the weirdest expressions."

"Teenagers don't, of course," Matthew says. Sam is wearing a clean T-shirt and sweatshirt of Matthew's with the sleeves turned up and he looks presentable, but Jim still looks like he just crawled out of a cave, and he doesn't want to embarrass the guy by offering him clothes, too. "We'll go to Bonanza," he decides.

H e has to hear it from Delia. She has to tell him if she's not coming back so he can try to accept it. Stop his momentary lapses into fantasy. They're all having Christmas at his mother's and he doesn't want to start feeling hopeful again, the way he can't help feeling when he sees her.

They meet for dinner at the Herald Street Café, famous for their steamed clams in tomato sauce with thick slices of bread for dipping. They loved going there when they first moved out. Delia is wearing a floral-patterned dress and in candlelight looks wonderful. He fleetingly wonders whether if he'd married a homely woman, it would be so hard. An unworthy thought, maybe, but an honest one.

Over dinner they keep the conversation neutral, though somewhat strained. Kate feeling and looking better already. How fortunate she is to be alive with no internal damage. The toxicologist told Kate's doctor that the mushrooms she'd ingested were borderline poisonous. However, he said, if she'd eaten any more she'd have had permanent liver damage. Or worse.

Sam is staying with Matthew and he's enjoying the company. Sam will start school after the Christmas break. Matthew has never seen a kid sleep so long; Kate isn't the only tired one. Matthew lets him sleep every day as long as he needs to. "I'm envious as hell," he tells Delia.

"Marty's talked to the director at the treatment centre and they could take Kate after Christmas."

"That's good, Matthew. Will you talk to her, or shall I?"

"I will."

Over coffee, the talk slows to a stop. Delia mentions the fabulous floral arrangement the café is noted for for the second time. He mentions the paintings again. And then they look at each other.

"Delia –"

"Matthew –"

"Let's start that one over," he says.

She's fiddling with her coffee spoon, looking like she knows what's coming. "Matthew, you're the one who asked for this meeting, but I also think we need to get things settled between us." She looks up. "That's what you want to talk about, isn't it?"

"Yes," he says, his heart accelerating. "But first I want you to know how desperately sorry I am for what I put you through with my drinking. I'm not just saying that because I want you back. And I think you must know I do. I'm only beginning to see what a self-centred jerk I was, and God knows you never deserved that."

He lights a cigarette. She puts the teaspoon down. "You're a wonderful, generous person, Delia, and I'll love you as long as I live." God, it's painful. He swallows around a lump in his throat. "Maybe not the way I do now. Maybe I'll have to find another way, but I'm –"

"Matthew." She reaches across the table and takes his hand. "Of course I forgive you. I know it was the booze, not you. And I'm sorry, too, you weren't the only one who was sick, you know. It couldn't have been fun to live with me a lot of times, all that self-righteous anger. But," and she looks away, "I'm not coming back, Matthew." She says it gently, her hand tightening on his and he hangs on like a drowning man. "I've started over now. I'm sorry."

He knew it. He did, really, he just hadn't been able to snuff out that little flame of hope. "Well," he says, "I just needed to know for sure. And I don't blame you. I've been *trying* to say goodbye but I'm not very good at it."

"I know," she says.

They're both quiet for awhile.

"I guess it wouldn't help to say I'm staying sober finally for myself. At first it was because I wanted you back, but I had a two-day slip and I know now for sure, I don't want that anymore."

"I'm glad, Matthew," she says, "I'm so glad for you." She gently lets go of his hand. He can't look at her, afraid he's going to burst into tears and disgrace himself. "Do you want a divorce?"

"Oh, no. There's no hurry for that. We've got enough to think about with the kids and everything."

He looks at her. "Good," he says. "Thank you, I appreciate that." And calls the waiter for the check.

He sits in his car for a long time after she pulls away in hers. Time does heal, Liz said. But a small voice inside him says, *Not always.*

It's time to start accepting life as it really is, not as he wants it to be. It's called reality, stupid.

Sighing, he finally starts the engine.

He looks at his watch. Five to eight. There's a meeting on Davies Street at eight. He can just make it.

Chapter Nineteen

To Matthew's surprise, the police were interested enough in Sam's story to call the Nanaimo RCMP, who said Emerald and Michael were under suspicion of vandalism at Sam's school. "I knew it was them," Sam said. They also have a complaint from the parents of an underage teenage girl who was planning to join the people moving out there after Christmas. The local police said the Nanaimo detachment will handle the investigation.

So it's an investigation.

A Sergeant Meyers called from Nanaimo to say they checked out the scene where the car chase ended and saw the damaged car, and after questioning Emerald about Joey's whereabouts they requested a search warrant. This morning they called to say they'd got it and wanted Sam to show them the spot in the woods.

Matthew pulls up across from a police car and a large white van parked outside the gate. GOD'S CHILDREN. NO TRES-

PASSING. Jesus, when did that go up? And that bit about gather together for safety and I will protect you. Who? God or Michael?

As soon as the car stops Sam is out and calling Felix. "Here, kitty kitty kitty!" climbing the gate, making Matthew nervous. They're supposed to stay on this side till someone comes for them. "Here boy! Here Felix!" Sam is straddling the fence now, his blue sweatshirt spotting with rain. Matthew shakes his head at him to get down.

Suddenly the large, bedraggled black cat is scrambling over the gate and onto Sam's shoulder. Sam buries his face a moment in the cat's wet fur and then, holding him carefully, he climbs back down. Inside the car Sam laughs as Felix butts his face again and again, purring like a tractor.

"I think he needs a new muffler," Matthew says. Frantically happy, Felix curls up on Sam's lap one moment, is climbing his chest the next, his purring punctuated with excited little meows. And scientists keep revisiting that same absurd question, do animals have emotions? Do scientists? You have to wonder. Finally Felix settles down and begins to lick the rain off his thick, black fur.

Two police officers come through the gate and proceed to take out large lights on stands from the side door of the van. It seems early for that but it's a dark day and will be darker in the woods, of course.

The bigger one comes over to the car and Matthew rolls down the window. Sergeant Meyers, a heavy-set, sandy-haired man with a crooked nose introduces himself. "And this is my partner, Constable Little." The tall, bald, mid-thirties man smiles and nods. "We're just waiting for Detective Sergeant

Murray. He's talking to the child's mother now."

A detective, Sam thinks, and can't help feeling excited. Of course there would be, in an investigation. It all feels so unreal. Like a dream. Like watching TV.

Then a good-looking, dark-haired man comes through the gate and over to the car and introduces himself. He looks professional in a dark raincoat and pants with shirt and tie, and Sam thinks of Fox Mulder.

"We need you now, Sam," he says, "to point out the spot where your dog was digging." He steps away from the door and Sam gets out. Matthew does,too. As they go through the gate, Sergeant Murray says, "If you can point it out from a little ways away, Sam. We'll be looking at the whole scene if we find anything."

"Sure," Sam says, and swallows, his heart beating faster. Constable Little is walking beside him and gives him a sympathetic glance as they pass through the yard. Emerald's car is gone, and Jim's spot empty, of course. With only Michael's truck there, the place looks deserted. Emerald's car must be at the police station, Sam hopes.

It's gloomy in the woods, rain falling harder now, plopping on the maple and aspen leaves, dripping from the fir branches down Matthew's collar. The path is muddy. From a few yards away, Sam points out the spot covered with pine branches, and the two officers set up the lights.

Sergeant Murray questions Sam about that day. What he was doing there. Where he sat to eat his lunch. When the tree was cut down. He asks questions and more questions, about the apple core, Buddy digging, what Emerald said, how Sam knew the ground under the branches was soft. And Sam tells him about the night he heard the hammering in Michael's shop and saw the light going back through the woods and stopping about here.

"What time was that, do you know?"

"After midnight. I wondered why Michael was working so late."

"And how long ago was that?"

"I dunno. Three weeks, maybe."

"And what made you think there might be a grave here?"

"I tried to make my dog stop digging and sort of fell into the soft ground. And Emerald followed us out there, and said we were snooping, and I wondered why she was upset. Yah. And how she'd never say where Joey went." He cracks his knuckles. What if he's wrong? If it was just the pot that made him think Joey was here? He puts his hands in his pockets so he won't seem so nervous.

Detective Murray has such penetrating dark eyes when he looks at him it's hard not to look guilty about the pot.

But of course he can't tell about that, seeing Joey with the bright leaves and pine needles falling on him in his *Lion King* shirt, he can't ever tell that, or about setting the barn on fire with the joint.

"And why did she try to run you down with her car?"

"Because I said I knew where Joey was. I guess —" he stops, "— she was afraid I'd tell."

It's around four and raining hard, and it's suddenly almost dark. The police have been adjusting the lights, and when Sergeant Murray tells them to turn them on it's kind of eerie in the woods. Nobody says anything for a few moments and they can hear the rain plip-plipping on the leaves, and the treetops rustling, like they're whispering and waiting. Some small creature hurries away through the leaves, maybe the one that gave a surprised squeak when the lights went on.

"Well, maybe she chased you because she was mad at you for suggesting that. D'you think?"

Sam shrugs. "I don't know. Maybe he's not there. But he just left one night without his favourite toys, and she said she sent them but I saw them after, and his clothes, too, at her place, and she wouldn't say where he was and got so mad when we asked." He says it all in a rush, then stops suddenly, thinking he's talking too much, and taking his hands out of his pockets, cracks his little-finger knuckles.

"We?"

"Yeah. My mom and me. We wanted to send him a present."

Sergeant Murray gets down on his haunches, looking at the ground, and the branches, examining the tree with the branches lopped off, looks at the surrounding trees and tells Sergeant Meyers to look at marks on a couple of trees. "Something straight-edged scraped by there," and the sergeant puts a yellow plastic strip around that tree and another one. Sam thinks about the yellow ribbons people tie around trees when somebody's missing, to welcome them back.

Sergeant Murray reaches under the branches, feels the soft ground, and finally he tells the policemen to uncover the spot.

"Watch it when you take those branches off," he says, and they start to carefully pick them up and lay them on a plastic groundsheet. Constable Little goes back to the van for shovels.

Sergeant Murray straightens up and walks back to Matthew and Sam. "Thanks, Sam. I may want to talk to you later. I'd like both of you to wait in your car for the time being."

Sam is grateful. He doesn't want to be there when they dig. As they pass through the clearing, a light is on in Emerald's house and they stop. Emerald is standing in the window with her arms crossed, looking grim but defiant. A tall, dark policeman moves into view, says something to her, and Sam lip-reads her response; a single hostile word. *No.* Like she's spitting tacks, Sam thinks. Michael, standing behind her, looks like he's looking for someplace to collapse. Or throw up. Like he looked when he said Joey was gone, Sam thinks. For a moment, he kind of feels sorry for Michael.

Against the dying light the big house looms large, its changed roofline now strange, unfamiliar, like a haunted house somewhere. Sam thinks of his room, of his fish swimming around, the neon tetras little flashes of blue in the dim light through his bedroom window. He's pretty sure Michael would feed them. He wonders when he'll be able to get his stuff, his books and comics and posters – especially Yoda made up of hundreds of tiny scenes from *Star Wars* movies – and his *Star Trek* cards, his Borg bank. And his old rock and shell collections. It's all he really wants.

Matthew starts his car and turns on the heat and they wait in the cozy space, listening to Felix purr and the rain pattering steadily on the roof. Settling in for the night again.

In about half an hour the gate clanks open and Sergeant Murray walks over and climbs into the back seat. "Hi Buddy," he says, reaching over to scratch Felix's neck.

"No, Buddy is the dog," Matthew says.

The detective leans forward between the front seats. "Someone's buried there all right."

Sam lets out a big breath he didn't know he was holding.

"We've sent for the coroner, and the crime scene unit. It looks like you're right, Sam," he says kindly.

"Yah. I was pretty sure," Sam says, his voice cracking. He doesn't want to cry in front of Detective Murray.

The signs on the gate are just visible in the dark. "God's children, eh?" the detective says.

"Yeah," Sam says, his voice steadier now. "A bunch of people are moving out here after Christmas."

"So we heard. It sounds like a another millennium cult in the making."

"They have a church in the barn," Matthew says.

"Oh? Looks like they had a fire there."

Sam's stomach shrivels. "Yeah. They did."

"You wouldn't happen to have a cigarette, would you?" the detective asks Matthew.

Matthew passes them back.

"Thanks. What about that other cute little place?" Sergeant Murray asks, rolling down his window to let out the smoke. "The one that looks like a playhouse?"

"It's full of food, mostly," Sam says. And..." he thinks again about the rolls of black plastic that spook him out, "I dunno. Stuff. A bunch of stuff."

"We'll have a look tomorrow," he says. "There's another lot we're keeping an eye on up by Campbell River. About twenty-five of them. Teachers up there are suspicious of child abuse."

"My mom wasn't one of them," Sam says. "Or me."

"Yes. I know. Must've been kind of weird around here for you."

"Yeah. Sort of," Sam says. Having somebody like Sergeant Murray say that feels really good.

"Will Emerald be arrested?" Matthew asks. He lights up, too, and rolls his window down partway. Sam shivers.

"That's certain now. Both of them, actually. Her car checked out against the damage to those trees, Sam. We found the spot right where you said it was."

Yesss! A deep, vengeful joy rushes through Sam. "I was afraid she'd get rid of the car," he said.

"No. It looks like she hit a brick wall."

"My God," Matthew says.

"Mine, too," Sam says, and they laugh. He's beginning to enjoy his role as the guy who got away.

"She strikes me as one of those people who think they'll never be caught," Sergeant Murray says.

"Yeah," Sam says. "Maybe."

Sam asks if a friend can come and get his fish.

"As soon as the investigation's over. We'll see they're fed." His cellphone rings and he puts someone on hold as he gets out of the car. "We'll be in touch, and thanks Sam. You've been great."

He steps out and, talking on the phone in the rain, motions Matthew out of the car. "Yes. Okay, I was just going to ask. I'll call you back." He folds the phone and puts it in his inside jacket pocket. "That was the coroner," he says. "He's on his way. The autopsy's day after tomorrow at eleven and we need an ID first. You've met the boy, right?"

Matthew nods.

"I don't want to ask Sam, and I understand your daughter's ill?"

"Yes. You want me to do it."

Sergeant Murray nods. "We'd appreciate it. It looks as if

your son-in-law's an accessory. For concealing the body, if nothing else."

"I doubt if he had anything to do with the boy's death. What time should I come?"

The lights of two vehicles appear, bobbing over the potholes as they turn in at the end of the road. Murray reaches into his car for a roll of yellow crime scene tape. "Come by the station at nine and I'll take you over."

"Sure. You know my daughter had nothing to do with any of this God's Children stuff? She's left him."

"Yes, we know. I'm glad she's out of here."

"She'll take the boy's death hard."

Murray shakes his head.

"What did he want you for?" Sam asks, when he's backing the car up to turn around.

"Oh, just to say they'd be in touch." He can be back home before Sam wakes up. When they turn onto the highway Matthew takes a deep breath, thinking how he never liked that place. How glad he is to see the end of it.

A short while later they meet a police car, another small car, presumably the coroner's, and a black van. At the sight of the van, Sam looks out the other window.

"Will they take Joey away tonight, Grandpa?" he asks, his voice small.

"I don't know, Sam. Maybe."

And Sam cries hard, bending over with his face in his hands and rocking as Matthew pulls over and awkwardly holds him, wishing he could cry himself.

"Poor Joey," Sam sobs. "Poor Joey. He was so —" and he can't talk for crying, "he was so little, wasn't he Grandpa?"

"Yes," Matthew says, patting Sam's back. "Yes. I'm glad you were his friend."

Sam finally blows his nose on Matthew's handkerchief and sits up. "Thanks, Grandpa. Thanks for coming out here and believing me and everything."

The ride is pretty much quiet, except for the radio and Sam sniffing and blowing his nose now and then. Matthew can't think of a damn thing to say to Sam that will make him feel any better.

"Detective Murray was cool, though, wasn't he, Grandpa?"

"Very cool."

"I thought he looked like Fox Mulder."

"Yeah?" Matthew says. "Now you mention it, he did. Too bad Scully couldn't come." And is glad to see Sam smile.

When they see the lights of Victoria, Sam asks if they can stop and pick up some cat litter.

"All right. But he can't stay at my place very long. And he's not sleeping in the damn dishes."

Sam laughs. Chad will want the fish, he's pretty sure. Maybe he'll get some more sometime, but he doesn't really care. He hated it when they got the ick and died, like maybe he hadn't looked after them right. Anyway, it isn't important.

They got away. Mom and him.

And Emerald's going to jail for what she did to Joey.

Chapter Twenty

hey're going to Christmas dinner at his mother's and Matthew is looking forward to it. His mother's turkey dinners are phenomenal, and his family will all be there. Delia, too, but he's had some time since they met, has been fiercely trying to live a day at a time and thinks he's prepared for it.

Jim declined the invitation – out of shyness, or a wish not to intrude, Matthew thinks, and they didn't press the issue. We'll bring you your dinner, they say, leaving him happily ensconced in front of the TV with Felix on his lap.

It's a beautiful, sunny day and he takes the scenic drive to his mother's, along Marine Drive around to Dallas Road so Sam can see the ocean. Baskets of flowers, harbingers of spring, already hang from house fronts, bright blossoms fluttering in the breeze; Christmas wreaths adorn jewel-coloured doors; sparks of red and orange lick the vines spilling over stone walls as they drive past the moneyed and mostly old, tasteful houses high up on their right. No one can deny this is a beautiful part of the world. Not even him. And this is a beautiful drive, on streets so smooth and clean you feel as if you're not really driving at all, just carried along an inch above the pavement by some invisible, benevolent force.

Beyond the wrinkled aquamarine sea down to their left, Washington's Olympic mountains, usually indistinguishable from low-lying clouds, rear up in all their distant, snowy splendour against a clear azure sky scribbled with swooping kites down on Dallas Road.

On the promenade, mostly older people and excited grandchildren clutching Christmas presents walk dogs, fly kites and toss bread to the hovering gulls. Supplying peace and quiet for parents preparing Christmas dinner, Matthew supposes. The day is a forerunner of spring that arrives so early he still isn't used to it. They'll be out for the annual flower count soon, people everywhere stooping over and writing numbers on lists. Sometimes he wonders about his nostalgic view of the prairies, where if they're out counting anything it would be potholes.

The towering holly trees on either side of his mother's building flaunt hundreds of clusters of vibrant red berries cupped in strong, shiny, scalloped green leaves. Nature's Christmas tree. The building faces south, and up against its foundation, long green spears and a few red tulip buds have already pushed through. It's a day to be grateful for. A day to be grateful, period.

Delia looks wonderful in a soft cream dress that shows off her admirable bosom and legs. She's brought his favourite holiday salad, a fruit and marshmallow concoction that nonetheless has a nice tartness to it, and she smiles at him as she places it on the table.

Kate looks coltish in a white T-shirt, short black skirt, black stockings and a velvety red, short, zippered sweater. She looks somewhat rested, the black shadows not quite so alarming. She's wearing makeup today, and red earrings sparkle against her cloud of hair. "Mom's Christmas presents," she says, when Matthew says how nice she looks. "Even the shoes. I only had what I came with."

A real Christmas tree decorated with ornaments from his childhood glows in the corner of the living room. The whole place offers up the incredibly nostalgic aroma only produced by a Christmas dinner in progress. His mother looks flushed and happy, all her chicks under her roof. Except for the prairie chickens, of course, who are heard from soon after they arrive.

Blair talks to his mother, then to Matthew, Blair's grandkids shrieking and laughing in the background. "Jan says Merry Christmas to her favourite brother-in-law, she's making gravy." Matthew loves his down-to-earth sister-in-law, who tempers Blair's tendency to pomposity.

His talk with Blair proves interesting. "I ran into your old buddy Bill Stevenson and he wants to talk to you, Matthew. They need a features writer at the *StarPhoenix* and wondered if you'd be interested." Matthew's old university roommate and serious drinking buddy, who packed it in long before Matthew, is assistant editor of the Saskatoon daily.

"Interesting. I'll call him tomorrow."

"Pretty bizarre situation out there, eh? Is Michael still in jail?"

"Bailed out yesterday by their church friends."

"Oh? For how much, do you know?"

"Fifty thousand, I heard. I'll talk to you about it later."

"Right. But keep me posted, will you?"

"For sure."

"How's it going for you, Matthew?"

"Okay. I'll be glad when the joyous season is over."

"I bet. Well, my hat's off to you."

"Thanks." They exchange Happy New Years and he hands the phone to Kate. Blair's unexpected pat on the back feels like a gift he's long been waiting for. Then everybody talks to everybody. When he hears Delia laughing on the phone with Blair and Jan, it's as if nothing has changed.

His mother asks him quietly if it will bother him if they have a drink and he says, no, go ahead, but soon after they're poured he walks out to the kitchen to top up his ginger ale and stays to peer in the oven, lift the lid on pots, look in the fridge. Then Sam comes out to get a Coke and they lean against the cupboard, talking. He wonders if he'll ever get comfortable with people drinking.

In the warmly lit dining room Matthew carves the turkey, one of the few domestic chores he excels at. His mother has them join hands around the table and says a heartfelt grace. To her delight an astonishing amount of food disappears into Sam's skinny body, as if he hasn't eaten for days.

It's difficult, being with Delia but not with her, and when they pour a glass of wine he excuses himself and goes out in the hallway to smoke. Apparently being *willing to go to any lengths to get it,* as it says in the preamble read at every meeting, can mean looking like an unmannerly oaf sometimes. He inhales, dragging the smoke as deep as he can, wanting some kind of buzz, however slight. Then, butting it in the ashtray by the elevator, goes back in. No one comments on his absence, but the wine bottle is gone from the table.

After dinner Delia pushes Kate into the bedroom for a nap, and she doesn't argue. On his way back from the bathroom he peeks in. Her eyes are open. "Want me to read you a story?" he asks.

"Hi Daddy," she says. "Sure." And she moves over on the bed.

Only when he's removed his shoes and lain down does he realize how exhausted he is. He can only imagine how Kate must feel.

"How are you doing, Katie?" he asks, propping up on his elbow to look at her.

"I'm worried, Dad. And feel so sad about Joey. I don't think she meant – for it to turn out that way. Surely she didn't."

"She probably didn't."

"And I feel guilty because Sam told me she hit Joey. I should have done something but I thought Sam was overreacting because we never spanked him. I never dreamed..."

"Of course you didn't."

"And I'm worried about what Sam and I are going to do now."

"Well, you know you can stay with your mother as long as you need to. And Sam and I will be roommates." He smiles. "That'll be awesome."

She laughs and pats his cheek. "All right. But just till I'm feeling better."

He says, as gently as he can, "Do you think you might need some help getting off those pills, Kate?" Delia told him she arrived with *The Valley of the Dolls* in her bag.

"I know I do," she says.

"What would you think about going to a treatment centre?"

"I'd go," she says, surprising him. "I wish I could go tomorrow. I'm tired of crying and feeling like a zombie. I need some help dealing with all the shit that happened there." She pushes the palms of her hands over her eyes. Puffs out a breath. "Oh, God."

He strokes her hair back from her forehead. "Good. That's the only decision you have to make for now." He lies back down and takes her cold hand, rubbing it to warm it. She always liked that. "Do my hand," she'd say to Delia or him, sticking out a small hand. She closes her eyes and takes a deep breath. Probably took a pill before lying down.

He lies there listening to the cheerful domestic sounds of dishes and voices and laughter. "What do you want done with this, Mom?" Delia asks. "In the top cupboard," she says. "Sam can put that up." Sam's voice, which is changing, blends with their voices, his two adoring grandmas. Delia's asked him about his friends and he's telling them a story, something about Jeff and a dream about *National Geographic*. "And the guy said they changed the name from *National Geographic* to *Pee On My Shoe.*" Delia laughs so hard. Matthew smiles. Sam will be fine, he's young and resilient. The wounded one is here beside him. Already asleep.

Still holding her hand, he thinks how comforting it is to drift off to sleep with the sounds of family in another room, the clinking of dishes, taps turned on and off, the happy domestic clatter and chatter of people cleaning up after a meal, and you listening with your stomach full of food so good you'd get up and eat some more if you had an iota of space left. It's like being a child again. *Backward, turn backward, oh Time in your flight, Make me a child again, just for tonight.* Such beautiful, sad words, he wishes he could remember the name of the woman who wrote them. As he's thinking all this, he falls asleep, too.

They wake to the sound of the doorbell and Marty's voice. He said he'd drop by if he could. He looks at his watch. Ten to seven, they didn't sleep long, but he feels refreshed.

"Is that Marty?" Kate sounds pleased. "I wonder how he's getting along with Buddy." She looks at her watch. "Oh, we've got to take Jim his dinner. He'll be hungry," she says, getting up and heading for the bathroom.

Marty came bearing frozen smoked salmon for Matthew's mother, Belgian Chocolates for everyone, and a small package for Matthew, obviously a book. "You can open it later," he says. Matthew chooses a horse head chocolate, and says "I wonder if they make horse's ass chocolates to send to people you don't like."

Marty laughs. He's looking very spiffy in a handsome, navy, V-neck sweater, white shirt and Spiderman tie – a gift from his daughter, he says. His black curly hair, still damp from the comb, shines under the kitchen light.

He smiles at Kate. "Buddy's in the car. Do you and Sam feel like going for a walk?"

"I do," Sam calls from the living room.

"I do, too," Kate says. "But we have to take Jim his dinner first."

"Sure. But maybe you should change into something warm. It's pretty cold by the water," Marty says.

As Kate changes into jeans and sneakers, Delia heaps a plate with Christmas dinner and a bowl with plum pudding and sauce, then covers them with foil while Matthew's mother finds a box to pack them in. And a hat and scarf for Kate.

"You don't want a chill."

Marty smiles as Kate pulls the hat down over her ears. She looks like an eleven-year-old. "You're looking a lot better," he says.

"Tell Jim to pop his dinner in the microwave," Delia says. "The pudding, too."

"I'll do it," Sam says. "I don't think he's ever used a microwave."

Matthew hands over the apartment keys and they're off, Marty carrying the box.

"Jim will think he's died and gone to heaven," Matthew says, as the door closes.

"That is one fine-looking man," his mother says, closing the door behind them. She's never lost her eye for the opposite sex.

"Yes, he is. I knew his wife in Al-Anon," Delia says. "He was so good to her, she said. She died of cancer a couple of years ago and he was devastated."

"Three," Matthew says.

"Oh, dear. So young." His mother looks thoughtfully at the door.

Then, armed with coffee and chocolates, they retire to the living room.

Matthew tells them about his talk with Kate. Marty's already talked to the director and they'll take her as soon as possible. Till then she'll stay here, and with Delia on her days off. They agree she shouldn't be alone anywhere for awhile.

"Kate checked her joint account with Michael. He cleared it out," Delia says.

"Jesus! Isn't there some law against doing that while you're out on bail for God knows what?"

"Never mind, Matthew. She's safe. They both are."

"Yeah. You're right."

"Things will work out."

"Yes," his mother says. "Let's just be grateful. When you think of what could have happened."

Sam might need some counselling, they agree.

He and Delia throw in fifty bucks each to give Jim till he can go to the welfare office after Christmas. Where he'll want to live is anybody's guess.

They wind up the discussion and Delia says she has to get back. Back to Nick, he assumes. She doesn't say.

"Thanks for the wonderful dinner, Mom. I'll talk to you tomorrow." She kisses his mother, gives Matthew a platonic hug. He feels her soft cheek, the spicy fragrance of Opium.

"Matthew," she says, stepping back and looking up at him, "I owe you an amend. You were right about Michael, and I was dead wrong. I'm sorry I thought you were overreacting."

"Well, I've been known to do that," he says. Then, remembering she'd taken their gifts up when they went, "Did you give that SOB an Irish sweater for Christmas?"

"You can't buy one for a hundred anymore."

"Don't tell me, I don't want to know. A bottle of Scotch?"

"You don't want to know."

He works at looking casually pleasant as he watches her get her things to go, a handsome black cloth coat setting off her hair. And then she's gone. He could kill for a drink.

And that's not all. He's taking double doses of Imodium to calm the mutant waters set off by all that's happened lately. He sees no reason to tell anyone except Marty about the trip to Nanaimo. The poor little boy in the *Lion King* sweatshirt with the huge bruise on his temple. Bruises elsewhere, they told him. That night, after Sam was asleep, the dam broke and he finally cried. For Joey. For himself. For the loss of Delia. And it felt like what he's needed to do forever. When you get right down to it, a lot of life is unutterably sad.

"Would you like a game of Scrabble?" his mother says when the door closes. "We've probably talked enough for now."

"If you don't mind, Ma, I think I'll catch a meeting. And you should put your feet up till they come home."

"All right, dear."

"It was great, Ma, and I love you for it."

"I enjoyed doing it. They're going to need all the help they can get," she says.

They're not the only ones, he thinks, driving through the Christmas-lit streets to the meeting, the rain that's held off all day drumming the car roof and blurring the coloured lights on houses and balconies to abstract watercolours. Kandinskis, maybe. He feels just as discomposed. He mustn't let being with Delia fan the dying embers of hope in the slightest. She did nothing to encourage that except to be there. Looking like she looks. Being who she is. The gift book from Marty is *The Language of Letting Go.* He'll need it.

Well, thank God Christmas is over. Maybe life can get back to normal.

Except what is normal, any more?

Boxing Day, he trundles out the Beast. He vacuumed before Christmas but the place needs doing again with all the extra traffic in and out. Outside two apartments, small, forlorn trees drop their needles in the hall. Amen to that, he thinks.

The alcothon meeting last night helped him unwind. And a lot of other people needed it, too, judging by the crowd at that meeting. Though many, sober for years, came purely out of gratitude. He feels some of that himself. They're running back-to-back meetings from Christmas Eve at six to midnight Boxing Day.

When he got home Jim told him he had a job with friends in Nanaimo and would be going to live with them. They own a motel and cabins and he's going to help them fix things up for the tourist season. "I hope you don't mind me phoning him long distance," he said. "But I've worked for him before and thought he might need somebody."

Matthew gave him the money. "It's just a thank you for what you did for Sam. And Kate, too."

"Thank you, and thank Sam's lovely grandmother, but I can't take it. I didn't want to stay there either, man, it was getting too crazy. That church burning was a sign."

Jim's friend, a fortyish, clean-cut, outdoorsy type picked him up next morning.

"We're expanding the place and he's just the guy we need. Jim can do anything."

"Say goodbye to Sam. Tell him I'll write," Jim said as the truck pulled away.

One problem solved. Would that they were all so easy. He underestimated Jim. He has a habit of doing that with people he doesn't know, still judging by appearances. Maybe Pudding Face is a scintillating bastard, what does he know?

What will happen in the new year, Matthew wonders, as he washes the laundry-room floor. He hasn't decided about the job in Saskatoon, not sure he's a feature writer. Marty said "Oh, you're just like all alcoholics. They think they can't do anything till they do it once and then they think nobody else can do it."

He thinks of Michael and Emerald, sheltered in the arms of their little congregation. Who probably will accept some logical explanation for Joey's death and find something noble and venerable in Emerald's desire to keep him close to her.

His New Year's resolutions are to try to live a day at a time – a still completely foreign concept – and to work on his resentments. Resentments are said to kill more alcoholics than anything else and he can believe it, and he'd like to make the rest of the journey – the last lap, so to speak – baggage free. He knows his resenting Michael and Emerald and Nick the Prick doesn't hurt them one iota, and he resents that, too.

Edna has asked him and Liz and Patrick for dinner tonight and he's pleased by the invitation, not even too worried about drinks – he can always leave early if he's too uncomfortable. But he'll be damned glad when the minefield that is Christmas is over. He'll try to catch an afternoon meeting for insurance.

He enjoys the dinner at Edna's more than he would have thought possible. No drinks are served, probably because of him, but no one seems to mind, they maybe had a couple before he got there. He'll have to find ways to cope with others drinking, or go live in a cave somewhere. He can't expect everyone to sign the pledge.

Edna's dinner is excellent, and talk flows freely. He enjoys Patrick's laid-back humour and they all like talking books, who's reading what – they all loved *Angela's Ashes* – and the ongoing soap opera that is BC politics.

"Was that your grandson I saw you with, Matthew?" Edna asks.

And so he tells them a little, not all, of what's transpired. It's not something he wants to talk about. "My grandson will be staying with me for awhile till they get sorted out. You'll be reading more about it in the papers, it's sure to get lots of ink."

After dinner they play bridge, something he hasn't done for ages, and Liz and Edna win, but not by much.

He and Patrick smoke on the balcony, and Joyce Fowler creeps down the street in her car and turns at the end of the building, coming home from some lonely Boxing Day dinner in whatever depressing restaurant is open, Matthew supposes.

"Her car's fixed, I see. That was pretty damn nervy, wasn't it? Somebody ramming her car and taking off," Patrick says.

"Yes. It would have to be her car. Apparently it was the car Tessie's been complaining about, always parking in her spot, she said. She sounded delighted about it."

"She would."

Mister Reilly goes by. Matthew tells Patrick about rumours of Mister R propositioning women in the elevator. Patrick laughs his odd, endearing laugh. "In the elevator? You'd have to be a man of few words, wouldn't you?"

Matthew walks back to his apartment around eleven thinking how good it feels to leave a social gathering with a clear head. Knowing you didn't do anything you'll have to apologize for tomorrow.

Back to work tomorrow. Liz sips coffee, her feet on the coffee table. She enjoyed the Christmas holiday. Doing Christmas dinner for her mother and a couple of friends from the library. Boxing Day at Edna's. She's spent the last few days very pleasantly. Lunch with a couple of friends. A movie. Caught up on some reading.

And it really is time to clean the apartment. Take down the tree. Do the laundry.

As she removes the decorations, she thinks about helping Matthew put up the tree. There's something about the man. A decent, funny man. What more could a woman ask? She sighs. He's grieving his marriage and she'll have to be satisfied to be his friend. Anyway, she doesn't trust men who jump from one woman to another like fleas between cats. So many do. Just the same, it would be nice if it developed into something more in time.

She puts away the tree ornaments, and goes into the bedroom to get some things from the closet. What's that dark pinstriped garment on the top shelf? Good God. Is that Maurice's pants? She pulls it out and holds it up. It is. They are. She's been wondering where they'd turn up. She drops them on the floor and goes to pour herself a drink.

She stands at the window, sipping. She definitely has a poltergeist. There's no other explanation. What she has done to attract this particular one she hasn't a clue. But actually, when you think about it, it's Maurice who's the attraction, isn't it, she's never lost anything that she didn't lose herself. Only Maurice's things disappear and reappear like the Cheshire cat's smile. A bit like Maurice himself, when you think about it. Since he's definitely not coming back, she's probably lost her strange, itinerant visitor.

She finishes the drink and, stuffing Maurice's pants into a large green garbage bag, goes out into the hall and throws them down the chute.

"There. Are you happy now? The Emperor has no clothes," she says out loud.

And she has a definite feeling that someone is.

Chapter Twenty-One

It's the middle of February, and Matthew has something new to worry about. Not Kate's health, though she'll be awhile recovering. It's Marty. Every time he visits Kate at the treatment centre she looks healthier and happier. Talking to Marty. Playing cards with Marty. Out walking with Marty. And if Marty's not there it's Marty this and Marty that with a light in her eyes that troubles him. Didn't Marty realize that in her vulnerable state she might misunderstand? Even fall for him. He has to talk to him.

At the restaurant Marty sits across from him wearing a blue denim shirt that looks very good on him. Matthew remembers his mother saying he was a good-looking man, and he can see how Kate might be attracted to him, even if he wasn't killing her with kindness.

"I want to talk to you about Kate, Marty."

Marty grins. "Kate is doing great, isn't she?"

"She seems to be. But she's only got a week left at the

Centre and then real life happens. I hope she can handle it." He lights a cigarette.

Marty waves away the smoke. "I'm going to offer her a job. She'll probably be teaching in the fall and this will help her out in the meantime."

"She's going to work for you? I'd like to know what the hell you think you're doing, Marty. Don't you realize how vulnerable Kate is right now? She might be reading more into all this than you intend."

Marty is looking at him with a little half smile he can't read, but it's starting to annoy him.

"What? I think I have a right to ask. You saw that idiot she's married to. She's likely to fall for the first guy who shows her some kindness. In a word – You."

Marty shakes his head, still smiling. "Matthew. Matthew, Matthew," he says.

"What? Matthew Matthew what?"

"Can't you tell?"

"Tell what?"

"I was beginning to think I'd never feel this way about a woman again."

Matthew is speechless. Though now he thinks about it he should have seen it coming.

And at the look on Matthew's face, Marty laughs his maniacal laugh, then gets up, leans across the table and kisses Matthew's cheek. "Hi, Dad," he says.

"Quit that, you damn fool. Cripes. You don't fool around, do you?"

"In case you haven't noticed, Matthew, I'm not eighteen years old. And neither is Kate."

Marty gets up to greet some regular customers. The man has friends everywhere. Matthew lights a cigarette while he waits. Well, well, life is full of interesting surprises, isn't it? "How do you think Kate feels about you?" he asks when Marty sits down again.

"I don't know. I'm just telling you how I feel. I know she's got a lot of stuff to get through. But she's going to be okay."

"And what about Sam? It would be a package deal, you know. *If* she feels the same about you. Which I doubt, though there's no accounting for some people's taste."

"Hey," Marty laughs. "Easy does it. Remember? And I love Sam, too. He's a great kid. I even love the damn dog."

"Good," Matthew says. "Then you can come and get Felix, too, and he can get up on your cupboard and lick the butter."

Marty laughs.

Matthew and Sam, with Buddy in the back, drive down to Dallas Road and park.

"You guys stay up here and play frisbee. I'm going down to the beach." Maybe he'll walk, or maybe he'll just sit and watch the world go by. Be by himself for a bit. It's almost the end of February, and he hasn't had much of that, though Sam stays with Delia sometimes.

He takes the spiral, cement steps down to the beach to squish along the wavy, shell-dotted shoreline for a bit. Then, spying a large, smooth, sun-warmed log, sits down with his back against it, and closes his eyes. Sun warm on his eyelids, he listens to the lapping water, the distant shouts and laughter of children, the excited barking of a dog. Soporific sounds.

He's been sober over four months and is starting to forgive himself for screwing up his life. Sobriety is getting easier, the dog that waited with teeth bared is slouching away, stopping to glare back at him less and less. But he knows just one drink would bring it snarling back, and he goes to two meetings a week because he wants to. Actually looks forward to going.

The soft, warm breeze flutters over his head, plays with what little hair he has, a tropical Hawaii type breeze. Spring does indeed come genteelly here, like the Victorian maiden in diaphanous gown and flowing tresses, tossing flowers from a basket, her slim bare feet silent on the grass.

Spring has yet to arrive on the prairie, but she'll soon be roaring into town in an eighteen-wheeler with a great clashing and gnashing of gears, her hair butch cut, a pack of Exports rolled up in her t-shirt sleeve over steely pecs. She'll tear through town, steel-toed boot to the floor, dirty snow flying in her wake, melting and drying and turning to dust, and faster than you can say I think it's spring, it's already summer and people are tanning on the riverbank.

He watches a family down the beach, throwing sticks for a small, black, nondescript dog which races into the water, paddling triumphantly back, proud little face with the stick held high, the kids rewarding it with praise and hugs. The look that passes between the parents as they watch. It's love. Just love.

Well, they say God is love, don't they, and maybe they're right. *God, as I understand him,* as it says in the big book, leaving room for skeptics like him. But his prayers feel a lot more natural now. He sometimes checks in several times a day, and he's comfortable with it. What he drank to be. Just comfortable.

Up above, on the bank, Sam plays frisbee with Buddy. Sort of. Buddy waits till it lands, then picks it up and tears off with it, amusing an old man sitting on a bench.

His mom and him are getting their own place next month, and Mom's started to work part-time at Marty's. He's a pretty funny guy, and their fries are great. Living with Grandpa is good, except he's kinda grumpy sometimes about little things like velcro stuck to his sweater, and the Beast, and why does everybody have to drive a great big son-of-a-bitching van. They've watched all the *Star Trek* and *Star Wars* movies again, and never miss *X Files* or *The Simpsons*.

He sees a cool-looking guy laying out a hang-glider on the grass, arranging it all just so, and sits down to watch. He's never seen anybody get ready to hang-glide, and he wonders if the bank is high enough here. Sam loves being close to the ocean, thinks maybe he'll be a marine biologist.

Several people have gathered to watch now. Asking questions. All waiting for the guy to take off, and it seems like he's never going to go, adjusting the equipment over and over, testing the wind, making sure everything's just right. Some people drift away, but Sam wants to see him go. He takes a Snickers bar from his pocket and drinks from his water bottle. It feels good to just sit for awhile.

When the guy finally straps himself in and makes his run, leaping off into space, Sam runs to the bank to watch, and after a rocky start, when the glider gets going okay, the guy looks back and waves. Probably at somebody else, but Sam waves back.

Life is sweet.

Matthew stands up and stretches. He won't be running a marathon any time soon but feels like a different person since he's sleeping an incredible six hours a night. Even the tremor is gone, and he's not quite "such a gloomy bastard," as Marty called him. He's trying to lighten up his reading, too, enjoying Frank O'Connor's stories again.

And he's finally making peace with where he is. All the people he loves most are here and he can't bring himself to leave them. For his sake, not theirs, but there'll be a trial and all that that entails and maybe he can help. Someday, when his mother is gone and he no longer feels the need to be near Delia, if only geographically, he might go back to the prairie. Or by then he'll be glad to be anywhere.

He gets up, brushes sand from his pants, and is heading for the steps when down the way a bit, a red hang-glider suddenly appears. It's just taken off and he stops to watch. It soars up, then wobbles a bit, even loses altitude, then catching a wind current, lifts and begins to soar against the clear blue sky. Looking back, the young guy laughs, waves at someone, then skims higher and farther out over the rippling water. Oh, to be young again, Matthew thinks, but not for long.

Crunching back toward the steps, he stoops to pick up an interesting stone, a smooth black oval with little starbursts of white all through it. He puts it in his pocket and climbs the stairs to the top of the bank.

Acknowledgements

Thank you to Edna Alford, a writer's dream of an editor, with a bloodhound nose for sentimentality.

Heartfelt gratitude to my friend Clinton Weese, whose generosity and patience with computer problems helped me write this book.

Thanks to Byrna Barclay and David Carpenter, for their valuable advice and for pushing me to get it done. And to Daniel Simmie, my teenage consultant and *Star Wars* aficionado.

At last, but not least, to Coteau Books, who first published me. It feels good to come home.

The writer wishes to acknowledge the support of the Saskatchewan Arts Board and the Canada Council for this project.

About the Author

Lois Simmie is a true veteran of the Canadian writing scene, a storyteller of the highest order who is known and acclaimed for both her children's literature and her adult work. She's the author of the Canadian classic novel *They Shouldn't Make You Promise That*, reissued by Coteau in the fall of 2002. *Betty Lee Bonner Lives There* is her latest book of short fiction, and *The Secret Lives of John Wilson* won the Arthur Ellis Award for non-fiction. Her seven children's books include three poetry collections, and the picture books *Mr. Got-to-Go* and *Mr. Got-to-Go and Arnie*. She lives in Saskatoon.

the return of a

Canadian Classic

"It made me laugh, it made me cry." – PETER GZOWSKI

Lois Simmie

They
Shouldn't Make You
Promise
That

THEY SHOULDN'T MAKE YOU PROMISE THAT
by Lois Simmie

"It made me laugh, it made me cry." – PETER GZOWSKI

ISBN: 1-55050-206-9

COTEAU BOOKS
WWW.COTEAUBOOKS.COM

Heroic Fantasy vs.

neon dreams

The Heroic Adventures of Donny Coyote

by Ken Mitchell

ISBN: 1-55050-263-8

A Superhero Story for Our Times

COTEAU BOOKS
WWW.COTEAUBOOKS.COM

Stories of heroic proportions are at Coteau Books